WITH PURPOSE & PROMISE

WITH PURPOSE & PROMISE

a novel

K. MELISSA BURTON

Tate Publishing & Enterprises

Published by Tate Publishing & Enterprises, LLC
127 E. Trade Center Terrace | Mustang, Oklahoma 73064 USA
1.888.361.9473 | www.tatepublishing.com

Tate Publishing is committed to excellence in the publishing industry. The company reflects the philosophy established by the founders, based on Psalm 68:11,
"The Lord gave the word and great was the company of those who published it."

Book design copyright © 2010 by Tate Publishing, LLC. All rights reserved.
Cover design by Kellie Southerland
Interior design by Chris Webb

Published in the United States of America

ISBN: 978-1-61663-434-6
1. Fiction / Christian / General   2. Fiction / Coming Of Age
10.05.28

Dedication

For my mother, who thought I could. And, especially for Brad, who gave me the chance to try.

Prologue

Fall, 1912

"Ouch!"

"Lilly Kate, stop wiggling and look straight ahead."

Another pin pricked my side as I turned my head and focused on a pink rosebud in the wallpaper. This time I swallowed my protest. Momma was making me a new skirt and blouse, and I didn't dare complain. After much discussion she had agreed to make me a new blouse, complete with satin scarf and pleated skirt in the fashion of the Gibson girl. She had agreed only on the condition that the skirt be made of sturdy material and a sensible navy color; the two pieces had to last all school year. She was also working on a matching jacket for cooler weather and would ship it to me later.

"We can't be making a new dress every time you see something in a magazine," Momma would tease. But I knew she enjoyed looking at the latest fashions as well. Dressmakers always enjoy looking at the handiwork of others, and Momma was the best dressmaker in town. I'd catch her at night studying the hemlines and collars of the models in *Harper's Bazaar* or *Ladies' Home Journal*. Often when the time came to make alterations on my old dresses, she would use an extra tuck or a few snips to give a well-worn dress a tad more style. I appreciated those little extras because they didn't make me look as plain as I sometimes felt.

"There. Now take a look in the mirror and tell me what you think."

I hopped off the well-worn oak stool and took three steps across the room to the full-length mirror. I smiled at what I saw before me. The blouse, although modest, showed off my long arms and neck, while the pleated skirt gave me a slim, sleek look. I twirled around to get a better look.

"Lilly Kate, I know you're my own daughter, but I must say you sure do look like a lady," Momma said with an obvious catch in her voice.

Momma's compliments had always been as rare and precious as jewels to me. I bowed my head and sighed. I knew she was thinking of Poppa.

Strange. Poppa had been gone for more than four years. I could carry on a conversation about him most any day of the week without becoming emotional. Each day I'd see a face or hear a voice that would trigger a gentle memory. Sometimes it might be the sweet smell of tobacco from a man's pipe. Other times it might be the large man behind me in church singing bass. Most often, these unexpected moments would be like a special gift from Poppa himself. But then, when I would least expect it, another wave of grief would sweep over me and cause me to catch my breath. It could be as simple as a phrase spoken by someone or as grand as a majestic sunset. Today, Momma and I both felt it as I stood in front of the mirror.

It wasn't the dress. It was stylish and adult, but this wasn't just about my appearance. It was the reason for making a new dress and what it meant to us that caused the two of us to feel such bitter sweetness in our souls. Some might call it irony. Others would call it providence. But however one looked at it, it was Poppa's death that had ignited the fuse that led to this moment. Every day for the rest of my life, I would miss Poppa like the desert misses the rain, but I would never see Poppa again this side of heaven, I chose to be grateful, oh so grateful, for the opportunity that was before me. I swallowed the sadness that threatened to overshadow the moment and looked in the mirror one more time, allowing myself to enjoy a morsel of pride and the sweetness of the occasion. I wouldn't cry. There was much to look forward to.

Chapter One

Most things don't turn out to be as fantastic, as glorious, or even one-half as enjoyable as you think they'll be. Take birthdays, for instance. Each year I'd look forward to turning another year older, certain the increase in age would somehow open new doors of opportunity before me. Yet, when the day arrived, I felt just exactly as I had the day before.

As it turns out, growing up isn't something you can usually detect. It's much more subtle and quiet, like the morning sun burning off the fog. You don't realize it's happening until it's nearly done. It's only in looking back that you can see how you've grown, how you've changed.

But every once in a while, perhaps only once or twice in a lifetime, something does happen that not only meets expectations, it exceeds them.

Since I was old enough to formulate a thought of my own, I had wanted to attend the one-room school in our tiny community of Fox Creek, Kentucky. Each time I heard the far-off school bell ring, calling students to their lessons, I'd stop my playing, tilt my head, and wish it could be me thundering up the oak steps with my book bag and lunch pail. Sometimes at family gatherings, I'd hear my older cousins talking about the teacher, practicing their reader, or figuring sums on their slate boards, and somehow I knew I wanted to be a part of that. Perhaps it was because I was an only child or because our farm secluded us from neighbors. Maybe it was a little of both. Regardless of why, school seemed to me a glorious place, exciting and serious all at the same time and full of children ready to play. On those rare occasions when Momma and I passed by when classes were in session, I'd hear a jumble of voices and desperately wanted to be a part of the excitement. Once, I begged Momma to let me stay, and when she refused, I threw a fit worthy of the record books. In return, I received a spanking that was in direct proportion to the size of my tantrum. Yet, with my heart set on school, Momma had begun to teach me reading at home, and I had even learned to write my name and numbers. Still, nothing would satisfy me until I became an official pupil at the one-room building known as Fox Creek School.

When my first day finally arrived, I awoke before Momma and Poppa while the night was still black as pitch and even the crickets slept quietly. I was dressed in my new blue and white gingham dress and sitting at the kitchen table holding my feed sack satchel Momma had made. I rubbed the apple-shaped appliqué Momma had lovingly stitched on the outside, then reached in to feel its contents yet again. Two pencils that Poppa had whittled sharp, a slate board, and my own tin cup were all that it contained, but Solomon's temple in all its splendor could not have been more precious to me.

At long last, I heard Momma and Poppa coming down the stairs and into the still, black kitchen. Poppa spotted me first. "I declare, Ruth! We don't got a daughter. What we got here is a rooster!" he said with a twinkle in his eyes. Momma just bent down, cupped my chin, and kissed me on the forehead.

That morning, I tried to eat breakfast, but it was no use. Even though Momma had added extra brown sugar and a dash of cinnamon atop my oatmeal, I could not be persuaded to eat. My stomach was already filled up with excitement and anticipation. "Don't make her eat, " Poppa chided after Momma had begged me to take a few more bites. "You don't want that oatmeal to end up on the front steps of the school." Momma gave a little laugh and conceded he was right.

My heart pounded like a freight train, and my skin was tingly all over. I could barely sit still while Momma plaited my hair. "Where is your patience?" Momma scolded in an exasperated tone as she struggled with my braids. With sudden fear I looked in my satchel that I'd continued to clutch and looked through its contents once more.

"Momma!" I cried with sincere panic. "You didn't pack me any patience!" To which Poppa responded by choking on his coffee.

After what seemed an eternity, Momma handed me a lunch pail filled with a couple of biscuits, an apple, and two of her fourteen-day pickles. It was time to go. I swung my satchel over my shoulder and tried to convince Momma she didn't need to walk me on my first day. I knew exactly where I was going. Poppa had helped build the new, white-framed schoolhouse two years prior, insisting that no child of his was going to be educated in some damp, dark, outdated cabin. I'd spent many afternoons up there admiring their progress. But Momma was firm. She put on her Sunday dress and walked with me right into the schoolroom.

The older kids were playing marbles, and a few groups of girls were chatting under trees while Miss Daphne worked inside and took down the names and information of the first-year students. The building was new, but my momma and poppa had both been pupils of Miss Daphne. To me, she seemed as old as Methuselah and more wrinkled than the walnuts that dropped from the tree in our backyard. But Miss Daphne's eyes still blazed a fierce blue, and you could tell by the way she walked with her ramrod-straight posture and quick gait that she was still a force to be reckoned with. Should anyone have had doubts, a rather sizable and well-worn paddle hung ominously on the far right end of the blackboard. The words *Education is its own reward* were carved into one side, so I certainly had no intentions of testing her resolve.

"State your full name," commanded Miss Daphne as my turn came. Momma nudged me forward, and I peered above the half-century old teacher's desk and could see Miss Daphne's hand firmly grasping a pen in anticipation of my response. Miss Daphne had known me since the day I was born, but as an experienced teacher, she must have also sensed how much the day meant to me and was committed to giving me the fullest experience.

"Lillian Katherine Overstreet."

"That's a mighty big name for such a little girl," Miss Daphne responded.

"My poppa says it's a name filled with purpose and promise!" I boomed without a second thought. Miss Daphne and Momma both suddenly suffered from a dry throat and put their heads down to cough. Modesty was a virtue I'd have to learn later.

But to my credit, I spoke the truth. I was named after two of my great-grandmothers, both of whom helped to clear this wild Kentucky land back when it was still a part of Virginia. According to family lore, either one was capable of planting five acres of tobacco, skinning a freshly killed buffalo, and making a cake from sawdust all in an afternoon. Even as a young child, I knew this to be an exaggeration. In a few months, our calendars would turn to 1900. The buffalo no longer roamed in herds, and the land was crisscrossed with train tracks and roadways; but even so, I was proud to be named after women so resourceful and revered. Momma had told me they were faith-filled women of strength. I wasn't sure exactly what that meant. I assumed it had something to do with hauling large pieces of wood for the fire or being able to carry a laundry pot without help. My understanding was clouded by childlike innocence. I only knew I wanted to measure up.

"Very well, Miss Overstreet. I'm sure you will not disappoint. We won't divide up the boys and girls until the bigger boys come back from working in the fields. You may take your things and sit on the first row next to Hezekiah Pruitt. We will begin in five minutes."

If there was one thing that could have dampened my spirits on this day, it was being forced to sit next to Hezekiah Pruitt. Known simply as "Dink" to everyone else, he came from an entire tribe of Pruitts too numerous to count. The fact he was at school and not at home working the farm wasn't so much a testament to his parents' love of learning as it was the number of people already available. He was the last of the line, and by all appearances, had received some hand-me-down genes. With no front teeth, a complete village of warts on his hands, a perpetual runny nose, and one eye that floated hither and yon, Dink gave most every other mother cause to reflect and be thankful for her own children.

Miss Daphne and Momma chatted while I carefully put my supplies away, trying desperately to ignore Dink and his sniffling. After a few moments, Momma came to my seat, kissed me on the forehead again, and quickly walked out the school door. As I watched out the window, I saw her stop beneath the old maple tree and dab her eyes with her handkerchief. A lump filled my throat, and my eyes began to sting.

"All right, everyone, let's begin with a prayer," announced Miss Daphne. I bowed my head, thankful for the chance to wipe my eyes.

School had begun.

Unlike birthdays and sometimes even Christmas, the anticipation of starting school was not better than the real thing. All my excitement, all my planning, all expectations were not misplaced. School was a living dream for me. From the moment Miss Daphne said "amen," I quickly fell into a routine, a steady cadence. Lesson. Practice. Lesson. Practice. Recess. Lesson. Recitation. Lunch. Lesson. Practice. Dismissal. The regimen suited me fine. Since Momma and Poppa had already taught me so much at home, I was quick to grasp what Miss Daphne was teaching. I enjoyed the predictability of each day and the presence of other children.

Soon, I became Miss Daphne's helper with my one and only pupil being none other than Dink Pruitt. Even though he sat on the boys' side and I on the girls,' Miss Daphne made a habit of putting us together. With time, I became accustomed to the warts, and the runny nose stopped after the first hard frost. Dink's front teeth even began to grow in after Thanksgiving, but no matter how long we worked together, I never could get used to his left eye swimming around.

"Pay attention, Dink," I'd scold when he seemed to be watching the upper grades instead of listening.

"I am!" he'd fuss back at me and point to his good eye. "I'm lookin' right atcha, Miss Highandmighty!"

But most of the time, Dink and I got along well. I discovered he'd picked up quite a few skills from all those older siblings. And, while I helped him learn to read from the *McGuffey Reader*, he taught me how to play marbles, steal third base, and increased my vocabulary by sharing some words he'd heard his older brothers use on occasion. "Just don't let your parents hear you say those," he advised conspiratorially. "My brother, Duke, told me only grown-ups can use those words when they're mad." All in all, it was a fair trade.

And so it went. School had lived up to all my expectations. And the books! Oh, the books. I poured through all the volumes Fox Creek had on its shelves. As I grew older, Miss Daphne had to borrow more from Gordon School and Rutherford. I'd spend my nights reading the latest mystery of Sherlock Holmes. I couldn't seem to get enough. "Daughter, I hope all that reading doesn't put crazy notions into your head," Momma would scold good-naturedly. Often I would find her reading something I'd just put down. We both knew I'd come by my love of literature honestly.

"I swanee! I believe I've walked into the wrong place. This must be one of them libraries I've heard so much about," Poppa joked once as he came in to eat and found Momma and me both absorbed in books. Momma was mortified that supper wasn't ready and scrambled to get it on the table, fussing at herself the whole time. Poppa was too good natured to complain, but that was the last time I saw Momma reading a book before the dishes were dried and put away.

There was always work on the farm—milking, churning, washing, or cooking for field hands. Each season brought with it its own set of chores and challenges. Winter was marked with the chopping wood and milking by lamplight. Spring brought with it the job of working the soil and planting. Summer, of course, brought the hot, lengthy days filled with mosquitoes and chigger bites. But the thick humidity also allowed for an occasional swim in the creek or the joy of churning a fresh batch of ice cream. Sunday church services were often followed by family potluck meals or picnics. I enjoyed those times immensely. Yet, in the fall, as the apples began to ripen and the kitchen started filling with summer's sweet and delicious bounty, my heart thumped with excitement as a new school year approached.

A week or so before school began, Poppa would hitch up Barney and Boaz and the three of us would make the twelve-mile drive into the county seat, Lawrenceburg. I loved the energy that the town offered. There was the ever-present *clop-clop* of horses' hooves, the stores, a restaurant, and—more recently—the occasional hum of a new automobile. Poppa hated the way the horseless machines rattled and smelled of oil and gas. "I jist don't see why everybody is in such a hurry. Seems to me they just should've left earlier." I disagreed. The speed and energy of everything never failed to excite me.

If we arrived in town early enough, we'd sometimes smell the mash being mixed at the bourbon distillery down by the river. The sickeningly sweet pungent smell always made my nose tickle, and Momma would sometimes cover her nose with a handkerchief.

When we finally parked the wagon, Momma and I would head to Hanks' Mercantile, and Poppa took care of Barney and Boaz. Together, we'd walk through the old weather-beaten screen door and see Mr. and Mrs. Hanks working in their matching muslin aprons. Momma was usually in need of some canning supplies and a few kitchen staples, but I was on a mission of my own. I'd march to the back corner and look over the few books in stock and see if there were any new titles. Often a few new penny novels would be on the shelf. But even if there weren't, I enjoyed perusing the handful of leather-bound books on display. Their deep, thick scent smelled similar to a horse's saddle but without the same depth of muskiness. There was a richness to it that always made me smile, much the same way Poppa grinned when he breathed in the air around a freshly cut field. I'd carefully open one volume and listen to the light crinkling sound the spine made, enjoy the book's weight and feel, and then waft the aroma of ink into my nose. Poppa once caught me observing my little ritual and laughed so loud I dropped the book. "Daughter," he proclaimed to all within earshot, "you're enjoying that book like some enjoy the distillery mash!" Momma was mortified, but I was undeterred.

Eventually, I'd pick out a new notebook, pencils, and any other item I needed for the school year. Momma would continue to chat with the Hankses, pay for our supplies, then take me to our local clothing store, simply known as The Fair, and purchase a new pair of shoes. For years I dreaded this obligatory tradition because Momma insisted on buying shoes that were too big for my feet. "You'll grow into them," she'd explain. For the first two or three months of wearing them I'd shuffle around with the grace of a drunken mule. But by Christmas, when the weather turned its coldest, my feet fit nicely, and I was grateful for well-fitted shoes. Once the shoes were purchased and after Momma got in a little neighborly talking, we'd meet Poppa at the restaurant for one of the few "bought meals" we'd ever get.

That was our routine for seven years. For seven years, I'd purchase my school supplies at Hanks' then buy my shoes at The Fair. For seven years, this tradition meant the fresh start to a new school term and the return of familiar routine. But as I was about to begin my eighth-grade year, a bit of anxiety crept into my soul. Eighth grade was as far as Fox Creek School went. I'd loved learning and the doors it seemed to open. Our little country school had been good to me, and Miss Daphne had been a tough taskmaster. For me, school seemed as natural as the change of the seasons, and deep in my heart, in a place where I did not dare let my thoughts venture, I longed for more. I'd learned just enough to be curious, just enough to wonder what more there was to experience. I wanted to continue my education. Yet, the nearest high school was Kavanaugh Academy, located in town. Had I been a boy with ambitions of attending Annapolis or West Point, Mrs. Kavanaugh would have taken me on as a board and tutored me herself, but only girls within walking distance went to her school. As much as I would have liked to attend high school, it was not a thought I nurtured. There was no point. My place was to be at home helping my family until the time came to start a family of my own. Who was I to dare imagine my life any different?

Chapter Two

In February my thirteenth birthday arrived, and along with it came the biggest ice storm in half a century. "Well, my little groundhog," Poppa announced that morning as I was washing my face, "it looks like you won't be going out to check for your shadow today." He was right of course. The sleet was still coming down, adding to the quarter inch that was already heavy upon the trees. Walking to school was out of the question; it would take all manner of skill and dexterity just to get to the barn, and sleet or no sleet, I still had to do my chores. Momma allowed me to put on a pair of Poppa's old britches while she stuffed a pair of his old boots with newspaper so I could wear them.

By the time I was ready to go outside, I felt a little like a swollen tick. My arms and legs were so padded that I had almost no control over them. I tried to follow Poppa's tracks he'd already made as I walked to the barn, but often his stride was too long. Walking in the ice-covered grass sounded more like walking on our gravel-covered road, and sleet pelted me in the face, making it difficult to see. I toyed with the idea of falling down and rolling down the hill like a timbered tree. With so many layers, I could hit a century-old oak without so much as a small bruise, and I'd likely get to the barn with less effort. I laughed at the thought but decided Momma might not appreciate my ingenuity.

Eventually, I reached the barn and opened the door. Poppa had his lantern lit and was already hard at work giving sweet-smelling fresh feed and hay to Barney and

Boaz. The shelter from the wind and prickly ice was a welcome relief, and the animals seemed content not to be outside. Our cow, Lady Jane, was standing placidly in her stall, munching on her breakfast. She nodded contentedly toward me as I pulled up my stool and got to work, but she quickly let out a disturbed grunt. "Sorry, girl. I know my hands are cold, but we'll both just have to make do."

Neither Poppa nor I said much that morning. Doing chores in the cold seemed to take all our concentration and energy. I finished up with Lady Jane and went into the hen house to gather eggs. There weren't many. The girls must have decided it was too cold to work, and the dark days of winter hadn't helped either. I pitied them despite the fact I knew their shelter was enough. Still, I tossed them an extra handful of feed to help keep them warm and prepared myself for the icy walk back to the house.

As I approached, I could see Momma in the kitchen window cooking breakfast. The soft light behind her silhouetted her figure. At thirty-three she was still youthful and vibrant, but to me she represented all that was true and wise. Even when she lost her third baby two years earlier, Momma had found a way to move forward. "Life is meant to be lived, daughter," she'd say from time to time. I knew there were days she still grieved, but through it all, she'd always been a tower of strength.

The smell of buckwheat pancakes and sausage links hit me as I lumbered through the back door. Momma had fixed my favorite for my birthday. My mouth watered and my heart quickened a bit just thinking how delicious they would taste this morning. Poppa came in a few moments later. Sleet pellets were stuck to his eyelashes, and a thin sheen of ice coated his coveralls. He breathed as though he'd run two miles instead of walked from the barn. "Ruth, I have never seen an ice storm this bad. I had to chip the barn door open just to get in," Poppa mused. "One good thing about it, the minner pond is froze over. I'll go out later and cut out blocks for the icehouse. Come summer, we might just be thankful for this here storm when we're drinkin' an icy glass of lemonade." Poppa was always looking on the bright side.

Finally, Momma called us to breakfast. Thin tendrils of steam floated upward from a large platter of pancakes surrounded by sizzling sausage links, more than we could possibly eat. Blackberry jam, molasses, and cinnamon apples were all set out as possible toppings, an act unusually decadent for Momma. "It's not every day someone goes from being a girl to a young lady." Momma smiled as she kissed me on the head. I'd not thought of my thirteenth birthday quite like that, but I appreciated Momma saying so. I was now a young lady. I liked the sound of that.

Poppa began to say the blessing. "Dear Lord, we thank thee for the bounty you have placed before us this day. May it go to the nourishment of our bodies. Thank you also for the one whose birthday we are celebrating today. May she grow to be a blessing to others as she has been to her mother and me. In thy son's name we pray, amen."

I fought back the sting of tears at Poppa's prayer as it unexpectedly pierced my emotions. In an effort to regain control, I quickly occupied myself with the breakfast fixed in my honor. Not wanting to play favorites, I decided to eat three pancakes, each with one of the different toppings. Poppa slathered his pancakes in deep, dark molasses and ate more than his usual share, having worked up an extra large appetite in the cold. Momma remained conservative, but I did notice her enjoying the jam a little more than usual.

Once the breakfast dishes were dried and put away, the three of us moved our things into the kitchen and sat near the old Union Crawford wood stove for warmth. Momma even brought in the sourdough starter and laid it behind the range lids, afraid it might get too cold on the counter. The wind was still howling, but we felt safe together. Momma's rocker made its usual gentle creaking noise as she sat and worked on another quilt, this one with a double wedding ring design made from some of my old dresses. Poppa lit the tobacco in his pipe and took the time to sharpen his knives while I sat on a stool darning socks. The tiny little pecks on the window continued to tap a steady rhythm, and it never occurred to me that this world of mine would ever change.

By midmorning the sleet and freezing rain had stopped. Everything outside looked like a crystal palace. Even the grass gave the appearance of thousands of tiny icicles carpeting the ground. But Momma's rose bushes drooped under the heavy weight of ice and our two new apple trees planted the year before bowed so low they looked as though they'd snap at any moment.

"Good thing they're young," Poppa mused. "The young can bend and not break."

Shortly before lunch Poppa announced he was going to the minnow pond to cut out ice for the icehouse. "I'd better get to it before the temperature warms up any more," he announced. Momma helped him layer on his work clothes and saw him out the door. She stood in the doorway for a moment and watched him walk down the hill toward the barn, a slight grin on her face. The love was still evident.

"We've got stew left over from last night," Momma finally said, turning quickly to me. "Lilly Kate, will you put it on the stove to warm and make a batch of drop biscuits? I've got this block almost finished, and I hate to stop now."

I happily did as I was told. Darning socks was not only

one of my least favorite jobs, I was also quite poor at it. It took every ounce of concentration I possessed to make my stitches small and even, and the fact that my efforts would never be seen by anyone but the owner of the sock seemed to make the chore all the more tedious and disagreeable. Cooking was a different story altogether. I enjoyed being able to go in and come out within an hour with a finished product—one that could be eaten, no less. Momma often said I was far ahead of where she had been at my age, but I doubted that to be totally true. She was almost as good in the kitchen as she was with a needle. Nonetheless, I did seem to do well with baking. I already knew which woods burned more slowly and which ones gave the highest heat. Sometimes, if the pantry was full and the hens had been generous with their eggs, Momma would let me experiment on a new recipe or a variation of an old one. Poppa loved to sample my experiments, especially my sweets. More than once he'd teased me about a cake or a pie, giving his own culinary advice. "Lilly Kate, that might be even better with a tad bit more brown sugar," or "That pie is mighty tasty, but what do you think it would be like with some nutmeg instead of just cinnamon?" We'd both laugh at his unsolicited advice, knowing full well that the only thing he could be counted on to make in the kitchen was a terrible mess.

Bam!

Momma dropped her quilt, and we stared at each other. It sounded like a shotgun out near the barn.

Bam! Bam!

We heard two more, this time nearer the house. My heart quickened. We ran to the window to see who or what was making the horrible noise. When we peered out, we quickly had our answer. There in the front yard were two large limbs that had fallen from an old elm tree a few yards back from the road. The fleshy white insides of the tree were exposed, and the tree's remaining limbs were clustered on one side. It looked as though their combined weight would snap the entire trunk in two. The storm had simply been too much.

"Well, that's going to be a mess to clean up," Momma mused. I could hear the relief in her voice. "I suppose that will be wood for the stove." If that was the case, I wished the tree had been a hickory.

I went back to my cooking. I'd made drop biscuits so many times, there was no need for measurements. Look and feel were my tests. The dough needed to be more tacky than rolled biscuits but thicker than muffins. Using a generous mound of lard, I coated an old blackened pan and, with a spoon, plopped down plentiful portions of the fluffy white dough into neat rows. Poppa always called them cat-head biscuits for their size or time-saver biscuits because you didn't need to keep reaching for more. Momma sometimes called them wasteful, but always with a grin. In a short time the bread went into the oven, and I quickly began gathering the dirty dishes. Cleaning up was definitely my least favorite part of kitchen work, but Momma would not tolerate a dirty bowl lying around to attract flies, mice, or who knew what else.

I reluctantly got back to darning socks and waited on the biscuits to bake. Poppa would surely be home at any moment, ready for a hot meal. By the time I'd finished another pair, the bread was done, but there was still no sign of Poppa. It was unusual. His stomach was as regular as a clock. I covered the food with a tea towel and got back to work. Within thirty minutes, Poppa had still not come back to the house, and there was a visible crease in Momma's forehead.

"Lilly Kate, get your coveralls on and go check on your daddy. The food is getting cold." I detected a slight edge to her voice. There wasn't any need for alarm. *Poppa just wants to finish the job before coming in,* I thought. *Why should I layer on all those clothes when I'll probably meet him coming up from the barn?*

But I knew better than to argue. I'd sassed Momma one time and gotten a firm hand across my face. Once was enough. I did as I was told.

I knew Poppa was working on harvesting ice for the icehouse, but I stopped by the barn first. All was as it had been that morning. Judging by the hay and feed, it didn't appear as though Poppa had even been in there.

I then went around back to the icehouse. Icehouse was a bit too generous a word. It was actually a natural hill that had been hollowed out, with a door placed in front of it. I often thought of it as my own personal cave, and during the blazing days of summer, it had been a welcome relief on more than one occasion. The icehouse did have a few pieces placed in it, but Poppa was not there.

Knowing he must be at the minnow pond, I headed in that direction. My stomach was telling me to hurry, but my heavy clothing made it difficult. My fingers and toes were already cold, but sweat began to trickle down my side.

As I neared the pond I saw what must have been the first crack Momma and I had heard earlier. A major branch had fallen from the century old Sycamore that stood majestically near the water. No telling the number of hours I'd logged up in that tree reading or daydreaming, but it was old and difficult to bend. Now a major portion of it had fallen, leaving another tree with a gaping wound in its trunk.

My mind didn't have much time to reminisce. Within seconds I realized more was wrong than simply the loss of a grand tree. For there, beneath the tangled mess of branches, I could make out the shape of Poppa's old work boots, still muddy and icy. They were perfectly still.

At that moment there came from within me a sound so primitive I would never have known it to be human. A sense of wildness raged within me as I raced to the tree and threw myself into the icy snarl of branches, trying desperately to free Poppa from his frozen cage.

Upon hearing my guttural scream for help, Momma had charged out of the house in a mad fury. In a moment of clarity that had to be a gift from God, Momma assessed the situation and rushed straight into the barn, coming out with two tobacco sticks. She lodged the sticks underneath the largest branch. Then, using a nearby rock as a fulcrum, she thrust her weight onto the opposite ends of the tobacco sticks, raising the branch about four inches.

"Pull him out! Pull him out!" she screamed.

I grabbed Poppa's boots and began pulling.

"Gently," Momma said, gasping. "We don't know how bad he's hurt."

Poppa was a tall man of considerable girth. He outweighed me by at least eighty pounds, but the ice beneath him had melted enough to create something of an icy slide. Pulling him out proved to be the easiest part of our task.

"Go get an empty feed sack," Momma ordered. I stood frozen and stunned as I looked at Poppa's face, cut and bruised with a tinge of blue around the lips. "Now!" Momma screamed again, bringing me back to my senses.

I sprinted into the barn, quickly ran to the feed box, and pushed up the cover. There, on top, was a half-used sack tied with a piece of twine. I hefted it out and dumped the extra feed on the floor of the milk room. This was no time to worry about waste or mess. My mind was racing and my heart thundering like team of galloping horses. *Oh, God! Oh, God! Help me! Help!* What was happening?

As soon as I handed Momma the sack I began to understand what she was trying to do. "Help me lay your daddy on top of the sack. I'll grab the corners and pull. You lift his legs and gently push." I did as Momma told me. It took both of us to get Poppa on the burlap material. Then Momma, with more strength than either of us knew she ever had, grabbed the corners and started pulling the sack and sliding Poppa toward the house. I lifted up his legs and tried to help push along. "We've got to get him inside. He's almost frozen." Poppa moaned in pain but never said a word. His cries reminded me of the time one of our cows got a hoof caught in a fox trap—low, mournful, and filled with anguish.

How long it took for Momma and me to drag Poppa to the house I'll never really know. In some ways, time was racing and events were moving faster than my mind could process them. In other ways, progress was so slow it was like a bad dream where you can't reach your destination, like trying to swim through honey or run while being tied down.

As we moved Poppa to shelter, I noticed his labored breathing. Each breath seemed to cause more pain. I could also see a strange angle in his upper right arm. It had to be broken. The bluish tinge around his lips had not improved—if anything, it was worse. *Oh, Father! Help us! I'm scared! Oh, God! What's happening?*

Momma and I eventually got Poppa into the house where Momma remained collected. "Lay him by the stove and put on a pot of water to boil. I'll take off his clothes." Once again I did as I was told, but every movement seemed somehow apart from me. I almost felt as though I was watching myself from across the room.

"Roooth," Poppa whispered as Momma was unbuttoning his coat. It was the first word he'd spoken since we'd found him. "Roooth," he whispered more faintly with a real hoarseness in his voice. Momma stopped what she was doing and put her hands under Poppa's chin.

"I'm here, James. I'm right here." Poppa's eyes seemed to wander around the room. "James, I'm right here," she said again. "Please, look at me. You're going to be all right. Do you hear me? You're going to be all right!" A panic had now crept into Momma's voice. "James, look at me!"

Poppa did look at her. At just that moment he tilted his head and looked Momma straight in the eyes. A gentle grin came across his face. It was the same grin I'd seen a million times when he had a funny story to tell or a tease he wanted to give. I thought he was about to speak, but instead, he took his left hand and placed it on Momma's shoulder, breathed in deeply, and was gone.

My daddy was dead.

All strength that had held Momma together came undone. "Noooooo!" she shrieked and beat on Poppa's shoulders. "Not yet! Oh, God! Oh, God! Not yet. James, we need you!" She put her head on Poppa's chest to listen and then began sobbing and moaning.

I'd like to say at that moment I was strong enough to go to my mother and hold her in her time of need. I was not. I stood there next to the stove, shocked. My feet felt like lead and my arms became numb and useless. I may have stayed that way for hours, except slowly, my stomach began to churn and a terribly odd but familiar sensation began to creep up through my body. I summoned my last ounce of strength, running out the back door. Though the ice was still covering the yard I made my way into the outhouse and furiously heaved out everything in my stomach. Sure nothing was left, I stood gasping for breath only to have my body jerk violently again. I kept gagging and choking, gasping for air. It was as though my body had been invaded by some disease and was going to every length to purge itself. At last, I sat down on the cold dirt floor. I was too weak to move and too stunned to care.

The next thing I remember, Momma was gently slapping my cheeks and calling my name. "Lilly Kate! Lilly Kate! Can you hear me?" I opened my eyes, and a look of relief came across Momma's tearstained face. "Oh, thank God. I thought I'd lost you too." She held me long and hard as I clung to her dress in a way I hadn't done since I was little.

"Momma…" My voice cracked, "I … I …"

"I know, sweetie. I know. Come in and let's clean up those cuts on your face." I had scratched my face on the branches when I had first jumped in to rescue Poppa and hadn't noticed until that moment. I put my hand up to my forehead and felt a line of dry, flaky blood that came down past my cheekbone. With the tips of my fingers, I followed it upward until I traced a gash in my skin above my right eye. Oddly, I felt no pain.

Momma and I held each other up as we walked the icy trail to the house. We reached the back door, and I hesitated. I didn't want to go in—didn't want to face what was past the door. If I could just stay outside, I could pretend it hadn't happened; I could pretend my poppa wasn't lying dead inside the house. Momma must have guessed what I was thinking. "He's in the bedroom. I wanted to move him there myself. It seemed only proper." How my little mother had managed to move Poppa into the bedroom and on the bed by herself is still a mystery to me.

Momma led me to the washbasin, and I looked at myself in the mirror. Some other small cuts and scratches were across my cheeks and nose, but the slash was evident above my eyebrow, sure to leave a scar. I didn't care. A few more inches downward and I may have lost an eye, but I didn't care about that either. "Let's use plenty of soap so it won't get infected," Momma said as she lathered up a clean wash rag. She then cupped my chin in her hands and began to wipe away the blood and clean up the cuts while I sat placidly. I marveled at her tender care for me at that moment. Most often she was a handle-it-yourself kind of mother, who was more likely to fuss at me for my carelessness than help clean me up. But I think helping me was something to do. That's what she needed: something to do, something that she could mend.

When we finished, Momma took me into their bedroom to see Poppa. He was stretched out on top of the bed with a blanket up over his chest. He looked almost peaceful, yet not quite himself. "I think his chest was crushed," Momma said with an obvious shake in her voice. "He held on just long enough to see us good-bye." I walked slowly to the bed. I wanted to hug him. I wanted to shake him and wake him up. Instead, I pulled back the covers and took his hand. They were typical farmer's hands, big and calloused with bits of black earth underneath the fingernails. I held up his fingers and looked intently at the thin brown rim on each of his fingertips. Was it there earlier today or was it from his struggle beneath the old, unbending tree? I slowly began to rub his hand with mine, over and over again. *They need to be warmed,* I kept thinking. *He's so cold. He needs to be warm.* But no matter how long or hard I tried, Poppa's hands remained cold. Dead cold.

It was then that I wept. I wept out of shock, anger, fear, and loss. I placed my head on Poppa's chest and begged him to come back. *Please come back.* Momma came and placed her hand on my shoulder. I could hear her crying too. I'd read in the Bible about people wailing and gnashing their teeth out of grief. That phrase had always seemed foreign, almost overly dramatic. But it was there in my momma and poppa's bedroom that I understood the drama was true and all too real. I felt I'd been ripped open and exposed.

Momma and I stood together holding each other for at least an hour. The sun outside had begun to wane. I was thinking we could just stay there together, the three of us, for the rest of the night. But Momma would have none of that. She suddenly straightened her back and looked me straight in the eye.

"Lilly Kate, we've got to get busy in order for your Poppa to have a proper funeral and burial. It's up to us. Go get Barney and ride to Mr. Hensley's house. Tell him what's happened. He'll know what to do."

I did just as I was told, this time without the slightest thought of complaint. The ice had melted enough to make the ride with Barney nasty and muddy, but not too slick. When I arrived at Mr. Hensley's, he opened the door with a wide grin and arms outstretched for a welcoming hug, but he could immediately tell by the look on my face and the cut above my eye that something was drastically wrong.

I don't remember telling him what happened. I don't even remember the ride home. I suppose both are just covered up in my memory. When I finally got back to the house, the sun had set and the air had grown much colder. The kitchen window was aglow with a kerosene lamp, and I could see Momma's shadow working near the stove. As I came in the back door, my body was overcome by a sense of heaviness. The weight of the day had begun to fall on me.

"Not much of a birthday," Momma said in an apologetic way.

"Not much of a day at all," was my reply.

"Lilly Kate, go on to bed. Tomorrow will be busy, and you'll need your strength. I'll sleep with you tonight."

Chapter Three

Sleep was slow in coming. Although my body was weary, my mind kept racing through the events of the day. Why was Poppa under the tree? Why couldn't he have moved five feet either way? Why did God let this happen? What are Momma and I going to do without him? Oh, why? Why?

No answers came, but deep and dark sleep eventually did. When I finally awoke there was the briefest instant when I had forgotten all events of yesterday, a time when life seemed as it was supposed to be. The faintest slit of sun was beginning to show through the lace curtains, and the fear that I'd overslept caused me to throw back the covers and bolt out of bed. But then, I remembered. The ice. The tree. The accident. Poppa was gone. The gravity of the event knocked me off my feet and back into bed. I touched the pillow next to me, only to find it wet. It was Momma's pillow, and my guess was that she hadn't slept much.

I walked downstairs and into the parlor, catching my breath at the sight before me. There was Poppa in his Sunday suit, lying atop our kitchen table. He was ready for viewing. I felt my stomach surge again, but Momma took me by the arm. "I'm so sorry, honey. I didn't hear you get up. I…I wanted to be with you. Mr. Hensley spread the word and some ladies from the church came by to…to get him ready. People will be coming by later."

Anger began to burn in me, and my breathing became labored. Why did people need to come see my poppa?

Why did they insist on seeing his lifeless body laid out? This was private. He was ours. He belonged to Momma and me. People didn't flock to the house when he was alive, so why should they come now? It didn't seem right. *Stay home!* I wanted to yell.

Momma must have sensed some of my confusion. "You know, I've never enjoyed going to a viewing. I always like to remember the person alive rather than lying on a table. It seems rather pointless to look at someone's shell when his soul is in heaven. But I go for the people, for the ones left behind. I grieve for them."

We walked up to Poppa. Oh, how he did look handsome! His shoulders still looked incredibly strong and his tall frame sturdy. The only hint that he wasn't just sleeping was the pale blue color still around his lips. Beneath his head was the quilt I knew Momma had made him as a wedding gift, giving him comfort in death as well as in life. I placed my hand on his shoulder, the same shoulder that I'd cried and laughed upon countless times. But no more. Now it was stiff, rigid. Momma and I stood there and cried together again. I could hear my heart beating in what felt like an empty chest.

By noon neighbors started coming in, each bringing a covered dish. They brought pecan pie, apple cake, and beaten biscuits with country ham. Mrs. Hensley was kind enough to remember how I loved baked cushaw with cinnamon and brown sugar. She brought two—one for everyone else and one just for me. By three o'clock our kitchen rivaled any potluck we'd ever had at church. The task of managing where to put the food and writing down who brought what was taken care of by the ladies in Momma's Sunday school class. I did manage to peek in once, and they seemed to rather enjoy the job because it apparently required a good deal of sampling.

Momma and I stood next to Poppa and greeted people politely as they came and tried to give us words of comfort. I'd never been certain what to say in those circumstances, but now I found myself unable to respond either. One part of me was grateful so many people loved my daddy and had so many kind things to say about him. The other part of me was angry. Angry he was dead. Angry their words seemed utterly hollow. Angry they had to come to our house at a time when I most wanted to be left alone. A low fury began to slowly burn in the pit of my stomach. I knew most of these people had tasted death before in their own family, but this was the nearest it had ever come to me, and I was finding the bitterness too hard to swallow. This was my daddy! *Just go,* I thought. *Go home!* Still, they meant well. I knew that. I knew that later I would be able to remember their words and find some tiny shred of solace in them. Right now, the wound was still too new. Telling me Poppa was in heaven didn't really make me feel better when what I wanted was for him to be with us, with me. Momma needed him. I needed him. It wasn't fair.

By four o'clock a wagon pulled up with a simple oak casket. Poppa's brothers, Uncle Chester and Uncle Pete, and some deacons from the church loaded up Poppa with his quilt and put him respectfully at the back of the wagon. I felt a chunk of my soul was in that casket too. Momma, me, and those who were still at the house followed behind. It would be a mile and a half march to the cemetery. The ground was a soppy mess from the melted ice, and I could hear the sound of suction and pulling of people's boots. I occupied my mind by watching the road ahead and mentally willing the horses to avoid the most muddy spots.

About half a mile from the cemetery, amid only the

sounds of horses' hooves and wagon wheels, we all heard Ethel Lewis give an excited, "Oh, my!" Everyone stopped and turned to see the commotion and found her desperately trying to balance on one leg while simultaneously reaching for her left boot, which was stuck squarely in the mud. This would have been awkward for anyone, but this was Mrs. Lewis, the self-appointed matriarch of all that was right and proper. She viewed impropriety as a scourge to be beaten and saw it as her God-given mission to do so. A few years prior, she complained that navy blue was too flashy for a preacher. "Every preacher should wear black to keep us mindful of the sin we all bear," she proclaimed in her high, clipped voice. After that, I noticed Poppa looking carefully through the Montgomery Ward catalog. A few weeks later, Brother Mac stood preaching in his usual somber black suit, but halfway through the sermon, beads of sweat began to form on his forehead. Suddenly, with a little more flourish than usual, he whipped out the brightest red handkerchief I'd ever seen and began wiping his brow—never missing a syllable. I looked out of the corner of my eye and saw Poppa grinning from ear to ear as though it was the best sermon he'd ever heard.

So there in the funeral procession stood Mrs. Lewis. Balancing on one leg, hips swaying like a heifer, hat bobbling, she was trying with every inch of her being to look dignified. Most of us stood there too shocked to move. A few others were simply enjoying the show. Finally, Mrs. Hensley stepped forward to help her out. Mrs. Lewis grabbed Mrs. Hensley as though her life depended on it, and Mrs. Lewis' boot was quickly replaced on its proper foot. The crusty old lady gathered all her remaining pride, grumbled a half-hearted word of thanks to everyone for our speedy help, and stood staring straight ahead ready to proceed. No one dared laugh aloud until Petey Monroe piped up, "Well, Ethel, I thought Baptists didn't dance, but I believe you done proved me wrong!"

With that, all dignity went out the window. Everyone stood there behind the wagon slapping each other on the back and holding their stomachs. It was a bright moment on the darkest of days. Tears once again came to my eyes, but this time they were tears of laughter. Poppa would have loved it. He always did enjoy a moment of levity. He enjoyed them even more when he could be the cause. It somehow seemed fitting to have laughter at his procession. It was in that moment I knew Momma and I would be okay. Hard times were ahead, and we'd barely begun to travel the long road of grief, but we were going to make it. We were young. We could bend.

The weeks that followed Poppa's funeral were as bleak as the weather. Momma and I went through the usual routines, but there was a senselessness about them. Even when the sun was shining, a murky gray veil appeared to cover everything. The most menial jobs seemed to take extra effort. No longer did I enjoy milking Lady Jane, and I hadn't baked a pie or a cake since the accident. Schoolwork got done, but there was no joy in it. I'd even stopped all reading for pleasure. Pleasure seemed foreign. Happiness was non-existent. As an only child, I felt alone in my emotions. It was the first time I'd wished for a brother or sister. In one sense, I wanted to protect my mother, to be her comfort. Yet I still had the need to be consoled myself.

I'd gone back to school within a few days of the funeral. Death was nothing new to any of the students—it was a part of rural life. Yet, everyone kept a respectful distance, even Dink. Each morning I would find all my pencils sharpened and neatly placed on my desk. Dink was also careful not to upset me with his usual ribbing, and he even let me win at marbles and gave me a few biscuits with sorghum. But after a couple of weeks, the novelty wore off. I grew tired of the soft treatment and let him know it.

"Dink, if you don't stop treating me like I'm some china doll, I'm gonna pop you square in the nose!"

Dink's good eye looked straight at me. A grin came over his face.

"Good to have you back, Lilly Kate."

Chapter Four

As April began, I started to have concerns about the farm. For the last eight weeks, Momma and I had been able to manage, but planting season was coming soon. If we were going to have tobacco to sell, feed for the cattle, and vegetables to eat, we were going to need to get busy. I was sure Momma was aware of this, but she never mentioned it. Lately, I'd often found her in the parlor with her Bible open and head bowed in prayer. Though my faith had been somewhat shaken, I'd been praying too, although I often felt my prayers only went as far as the ceiling. I knew in the deepest part of my soul that God would take care of us, but just how was unclear. Graduation was in a few months. Poppa was gone, and the farm needed more than Momma and I could provide. I wanted answers, but thus far, they weren't coming.

Two days later, as I was getting ready for school, Momma made an announcement. "I'll be going to town today. I may not be back when you get home, so don't worry, but do start supper."

I was shocked. Going to town in the middle of the week? By herself? Questions swirled in my head. I opened my mouth to speak but was quickly silenced. "We'll talk about this when I get home. For now, you just get yourself to school."

All day my mind raced. Why was she going, and why the secret?

"Lilly Kate. Lilly Kate? Lilly Kate!" Miss Daphne was

practically screaming. "Miss Overstreet, where is your head today?" she reprimanded.

"I … I'm sorry, ma'am. I've … I … well, I don't know."

"Well, I don't know either, but you need to find it, dust it off, and focus on your history. You only have six weeks until your graduation examination, and we haven't even gotten up to the War Between the States."

I could hear Dink muffle a laugh. He loved nothing more than to see me reprimanded.

"Hush up, Dink. You've got to take the exam too," I hissed. Dink just continued to snicker.

Momma got home just before dark. She seemed more enthusiastic than I'd seen her since Poppa's accident. I was itching to know what was going on, but I didn't dare ask. I knew she'd tell me; it was only a matter of time.

We sat down together for a supper of ham and biscuits. I anticipated the asparagus would come on soon, but the larder was looking low and I was beginning to get a little worried. If Momma was concerned, she surely didn't show it. There'd been no mention of our vegetable garden or our tobacco crop. I'd started some seedlings out in the barn, but without question, we were going to need some help.

"Daughter, you've got graduation coming up soon. What is it now, eight weeks?"

"Yes, ma'am. But I still have to pass my examination. That's just about six weeks away," I responded.

"Oh, I'm sure that will be no problem. You've always made very good marks, and Miss Daphne knows how to prepare her students for the exam. You'll be fine."

I appreciated her encouragement. While not a mother prone to bragging, she did hold my schooling in high regard. I'd heard her say on more than one occasion she wished she'd had the chance to go further herself.

"Have you given any thought to what you'll do after graduation?" Momma asked.

The question was odd. What was I to do? Fox Creek School only went to eighth grade. I certainly wasn't getting married any time soon. What did she *think* I was going to do?

"Well, I thought I'd just stay here with you and manage the farm. You know, we need to get going. We're a little behind on the vegetable garden, but I've started some seedlings, and …"

"We won't need it," Momma interrupted.

I stopped chewing and sat stunned. What did she mean? I'd noticed her appetite had waned since Poppa's death, but I had no intention of starving. I was still growing. I personally found food to be a very good thing.

"We're moving," Momma announced in a tone as casual as if she was asking me to pass the butter. "We're selling the farm, and we're moving. I went to town today to arrange everything. I've rented a little house on Posey Street, not much, but enough for the two of us. I plan on taking in sewing for the ladies in town. And you, young lady, are going to high school at Kavanaugh."

I dropped my fork mid-air, and a loud clang filled the kitchen.

"I took your grades up to Mrs. Kavanaugh herself, along with a letter from Miss Daphne. She said she'd be more than happy to take you on."

My mouth dropped open, and I stared at Momma in disbelief. She sat there grinning as though her plan was coming together perfectly.

"Now, Lilly Kate," Momma said with a smile, "I've told you not to sit around with your mouth open."

I jumped out of my chair and put my arms around

Momma. Despite all that I'd ever thought, despite all the odds, I was going to high school. I was going to Kavanaugh!

The next six weeks were a blur of activity. Dink and I constituted the entire graduating class and, therefore, studied for our graduation exam together. Without question, I was stronger in grammar, literature, and history. However, Dink had proven to be quite the mathematician and was able to give me some much needed help—especially with fractions and geometry. Dink had seemed genuinely happy for me when I told him I'd be going to high school. While he had no desire to be stuck in a classroom one more moment than necessary, he knew I did. Throughout the years, he'd become the closest thing I had to a brother, and he knew my deepest thoughts. That also meant he was perfectly capable of teasing me at any given moment.

"Well, Miss Highandmighty. Since your going to Kavanaugh, you think you'll be going to Annapolis too? Maybe West Point?"

I was not to be outdone. "As a matter of fact, I thought I might just do that. I'll cut my hair, put on a uniform, and sneak on in. I'm sure if I could just learn to spit far enough, nobody would notice the difference."

Dink looked at me a moment, and a blush of color came to his cheeks. "No, Lilly Kate, I'm sure they would notice the difference."

The exams came and went, and no surprise to anyone, Dink and I both passed easily. Miss Daphne had never had a student fail the eighth-grade exam, and based on the level of practice she'd given us, she had no intentions of ruining her record. By the time I got the exam in my hands, I was almost relieved to see it.

Two weeks later, the entire school and the families of both Dink and I gathered for our graduation. Momma had somehow found the time to make me a new dress for the occasion. I was almost sinfully proud of its cream-colored fitted bodice, high, lacy neck, and long, fitted sleeves. No longer did I have to wear those old pinafores that made me feel like a little girl. Momma called it a tea dress and said it would be useful once we moved to town. For his part, Dink didn't wear his usual overalls. He somehow managed to find a pair of trousers with a shirt and tie. Although he'd never admit to it, I also caught a whiff of pomade in his hair.

"Who's high and mighty now?" I teased. Dink responded by poking me in the ribs with his elbow then looked at me with mock seriousness.

"Every once in a while, it's important to show just a little bit of class," he chided.

Miss Daphne began the ceremony and made a speech about how proud she was of us and how she was sure we'd go on to be exemplary citizens and leaders in the community. In truth, it was the same speech she gave every year at graduation. I could have predicted the entire thing. But at the end, she surprised me as she added something special.

"And this year, I am pleased to announce that one of our own will be attending Kavanaugh High School in the fall. There, she will receive the most rigorous instruction, and be held to the highest of standards. I expect her to do well, and I'm sure we will be hearing about many good things from her in the future. To help her on her way, the children and I collected some money and purchased a gift, which we hope she will find useful."

Miss Daphne reached beneath the lectern and pulled

out a book that seemed large enough to flatten a small child.

"Lillian Katherine Overstreet, will you please accept this as a gift of our good wishes and many successes in the future."

Startled, I went forward to accept the gift. Everyone was clapping and none more enthusiastically than Momma and Dink. I could tell by the grins on their faces they were both in on the surprise. When I took hold of the book, I realized it was an unabridged collegiate dictionary. It had come from the Hanks' Mercantile. Miss Daphne must have felt I would need it in my studies. I knew this was no small gift. Work had gone into its purchase. Inside was the name of every child in the school, from the little primers on up to Dink. Miss Daphne had even written a little note:

> Lilly Kate, I've known from the beginning you had a keen mind and curious spirit. You have a gift for learning. You'll do well no matter what challenges you may encounter. Remember, no matter what obstacles you face, the cream always rises to the top.

Chapter Five

The next day Momma and I moved in earnest. Poppa's brothers, Chester and Pete, had bought the farm, and although they claimed to purchase it as a way to help us out, even I noticed they got it for a rock bottom price. Poppa would never have let it go so low, but Momma said a widow in need couldn't be too picky. Besides that, Poppa had purchased some equipment that was to be paid from that year's tobacco crop, and Momma needed to pay the note. Resentment would have swelled in me at any other time, but there was too much newness and excitement to allow anger to grow. I was also enjoying watching my uncles strain as they moved the heavy furniture. I'd even hidden my new dictionary in one of the drawers for good measure.

I'd thought I might feel a tinge of sorrow in leaving the only home I'd ever known, the place that held so many memories of my Poppa, but miraculously I did not. Perhaps it was my youth and exuberance or maybe even a little naiveté, but I think it was Momma. She took control of the entire move like a little general and never looked back. She'd always seemed happy on the farm, taking care of Poppa and me, but there was a sense of freshness about her, an energy I'd never seen before. I knew at night she was often still racked by grief because of the wet pillow I'd find in the morning. But by day, she displayed the uncanny ability to push forward, to move on. Although too young to articulate it, I was proud of her.

Once we loaded up the wagon, Momma and I crowded on the front seat with Uncle Chester and drove to town. After we got unloaded, Barney, Boaz, and the wagon would be his, but Momma had arranged for his help as part of the deal. As we neared Lawrenceburg, my heart began to beat a little faster. Never had I spent the night in town, let alone lived there with all its stores and people. By anyone's standards, Lawrenceburg was just a small country town. But it would still be the most cosmopolitan place I'd ever lived. I'd been to Louisville once when I was ten to see the state fair. That particular day still stood out as a highlight with its colorful merry-go-round and delicious peanuts and pretzels. Still, even in a small town, our lives would be different, but just how different I couldn't tell. Momma sat next to me with her back straight and her chin tilted slightly upward. She looked as cool as a glass of lemonade. I had to sit on my hands just to keep from fidgeting.

When we arrived at Posey Street and saw the house, I sat stunned in my seat. Posey Street was little more than an alley off Main Street. The house was a simple rectangular box with a dilapidated front door and a window on both sides. Apparently the builder had tried to give the appearance of symmetry but was off by a good half foot. There was no porch, only a bare patch of ground in front of the door, and the stark yard was void of any flowers, with the exception of several healthy dandelions.

"It's enough to keep us dry and warm. It's also close to everything," Momma noted.

She was right on that point. Kavanaugh School was less than a half-mile walk east, and the post office was on the same block. The mercantile store was the next block over, as was the bank and Ballard's Drug Store. But perhaps most significant in my mind was the First Baptist

Church not one hundred yards from our front door. I'd seen the impressive brick exterior with its large stained-glass windows and tried to imagine something equally as impressive on the inside. However, nothing I pictured in my head seemed grand enough to match the outside. I knew that where two or more were gathered in His name, the Holy Spirit would be there, but I also knew that our country church looked like a chicken coop by comparison. Some thoughts were best left unsaid, though.

"Will we be attending First Baptist?" I asked, pointing to the church.

"Certainly. We'll go tomorrow. I've already spoken with Mrs. Bond, the wife of the man who's renting us this place. She's assured me there's an active training union with other girls your age. I'm sure you'll make lots of friends."

Friends at church weren't really my greatest concern at the moment, but if the thought of me talking with other girls my age made Momma feel better, so be it.

"Are you two just going to sit here and gab the whole time, or are you gonna git workin'? I got things to be doin,'" Uncle Chester interrupted. I stared a hole right through him. If I'd been an animal, I would have growled. There were times I couldn't believe a man so rude and slovenly was a blood relative of my gentlemanly daddy. More than once I'd asked Poppa if he was sure they were really brothers, and he had assured me it was so. You can imagine my relief when I later discovered they were only half brothers, my two uncles having a different mother. Being reared on a farm, I was well versed on the laws of procreation, and I was thrilled to know Uncle Chester's nasty traits and personality quirks stood less chance of being passed to my own children than those honorable characteristics of Poppa's. If I could've, I would have lifted him up and dropped him like a sack of feed.

Momma and I began unloading, and for the first time I saw the interior of the house. It looked only slightly more promising than the exterior. The front door led into what might be called, on a good day, the parlor. There had been an attempt to hang some paper at one time, but now it was dingy and peeling. However, it did have a small fireplace at the far end that I found charming because of its diminutive nature. The mantle, although aged and in need of work, had some beautiful detail work that seemed out of character with the rest of the house. At the other end of the room was a doorway.

"This will be our bedroom," Momma announced as she led me into the space. "We'll use the parlor for our guests, and we'll share this one."

A month earlier I had not understood Momma's desire to sell or give away so much of our furniture, but now it was making sense. There simply would not be room. Although nothing fancy, our farmhouse had always been plenty spacious, especially for just three of us. On holidays or reunions, we were easily able to accommodate our guests. Our new house was miniature by comparison.

Along the back of the house was the kitchen. Up to this point, I'd seen little to impress me, but it was in the kitchen that I found the house's saving grace: running water. Since the time I could walk, one of my chores had been to haul water from the well. Momma had begged Poppa to put in running water, but this was the one area where Poppa had remained firm. "Now, Ruth, there's no sense in spending all that money when we got water just ten steps outside the door. On a cold day, that's what I call runnin' water!"

To be honest, I'd often thought if Poppa had been the one hauling all the water, he may have conceded, but he never did. There were times it seemed the barn had more modern advancements than our kitchen. But now, in what seemed to be the most unlikely of places, we had a real indoor pump spout.

"Lilly Kate, come take a look at this," Momma said, smiling.

My heart did a little flip. There were few things in the entire world of modern conveniences that could top running water to the kitchen. Certainly advancements had already been made in mechanics—we'd read about Henry Ford assembling cars by the hundreds up in Michigan, and we'd even heard about some new flying machines— but those wonderful feats of engineering had little to do with me. No, there was only one thing that could make me happier than water in our kitchen—an indoor toilet. And there it was. At the far end of the kitchen was a tiny room that had obviously been added on after the original house had been built. If I put my hands on my hips, my elbows would touch the walls, but no matter, it was a bona fide toilet with a pull chain for flushing.

"Well, now," I said, grinning at Momma from ear to ear, "shall I test the plumbing?"

———————————————

That first night, Momma and I both had trouble falling asleep. So many changes had left us exhausted but wide awake at the same time. Since Poppa had died, our lives had been one big change after another. I was grateful to Momma for risking so much to allow me this chance to go to high school, but I was beginning to feel a little guilty. Maybe this wasn't really what Momma wanted. Maybe she was doing it all for me. And then there was school. I had no idea if I could keep up. What if it was too hard? What if I couldn't make it through? Then our move would have been for nothing.

"Momma, I just want you to know how much I appreciate this move so I could go to high school. I know it's been hard and will probably continue to be hard, but I promise to do my best. I know you're doing this for me, and I don't want to let you down." There was a long silence, and I could almost hear the tears coming down her cheeks. "I'm sorry. I didn't mean to upset you. I just … I just want you to know that I'll work really hard, that's all."

"Honey, listen to me." Momma sat up in bed and held my hand. "I miss your father every minute of every day. I loved him with every ounce of my being, but the world is bigger than Fox Creek. There were times that I felt the isolation was pressing in on me so much I could hardly breathe. I know you're my own flesh and blood, and I may be a bit biased, but your daddy and I had decided long ago that you deserved a chance to go further in school than we did. We'd already determined we'd somehow pay boarding for you so you could go to high school, although heaven only knows how we would have afforded it. I feel guilty about it now, but when we discussed sending you to town for your schooling, I was a little jealous—jealous because I wanted more schooling myself, jealous because I wanted to see more and do more than farm life allowed. I prayed God would take the desire from me, but it just wouldn't go away. Then, when your poppa died, well … I just knew that God may have closed a door, but He had opened a window, one that allowed both of us to crawl through. Do you understand what I'm trying to tell you?"

I lay there silent for a moment, trying to process what she was telling me. Momma had always been a good mother, one who would talk to me about events and not talk down to me. But at that moment, she seemed more vulnerable than ever before. I wasn't sure what to make of it.

"What I'm trying to say is this move wasn't all about you. Sure, I wanted you to go to school, but it's a chance for me to spread my wings too. God has already confirmed to me this was the right move for us. Therefore, my happiness here is not dependent on your school record."

"Momma, I had no idea you were unhappy."

"No, honey, not unhappy, just curious. And, as I look back now, it may have been the good Lord's way of preparing me a little, of making me ready for this move. *All things work together for the good of those who love the Lord.* That's been my favorite verse for years, but now I'm beginning to see it being worked out in our lives."

My mind was swirling, and my emotions were so tangled I was having trouble identifying one from the other. Yet once again one emotion seemed to come to fight its way through stronger than all the others. I was proud of my mother.

"You know, Momma, we're going to be okay, aren't we?"

"Yes, Lilly Kate. We most definitely will be."

Chapter Six

For the next two weeks, Momma and I worked on fixing up our new little home. Mr. Bond was more than happy to have renters willing to make improvements, and once again Momma rose to the challenge. Having seen the house earlier, she was somewhat prepared. From the farm she'd carefully bundled some daylilies and cuttings from her rose bushes. She even had a small basket of iris and daffodil bulbs that held the promise of color for the next spring. We tore down the wallpaper that clung stubbornly to the wall and replaced it with a pattern that had a decidedly feminine flair with its dainty pink roses and trellises. I spent an entire day sanding the mantle and found all those details to be excruciatingly difficult to buff. But once it was painted, it gleamed like a piece of artwork and was a definite focal point for the entire room.

Momma had been careful about the furniture we'd kept. The solid cherry wood pie safe Poppa had made for her as a wedding gift stood proudly at one end of the kitchen. We'd also kept the iron bed frame and oak dresser, but Momma had taken the liberty to make a few new purchases as well. In the parlor there were two new wicker rockers along with a rolling teacart. I had to admit they fit the room perfectly, small and feminine. We hung the few family photos we had and proudly displayed our collection of books on the mantle. Overall, the effect was quite nice.

At the end of our second week, we were almost finished painting the front door when men whom I'd never met pulled up in a wagon carrying a large crate. "Oh, it's here!" I had no idea what *it* was, but anything so large took all of my attention. Momma was already at the wagon looking it over before I could even put down my brush.

"Now, gentlemen, please be very careful," Momma pleaded as the men started to unload the crate. "I can't have anything happen to this. Let's just put the crate on the ground, and then we'll be able to unpack it and take it into the house. I think it will be easier that way."

I was still in the dark but soon figured out what was going on. The crate was clearly marked as having come from Elizabeth, New Jersey. As the daughter of an expert seamstress, I knew that town to be the North Pole of the sewing world. I'd seen the advertisements in women's magazines and newspapers hailing the product as a woman's must-have for the new century. Momma had gotten herself a new Singer sewing machine.

The men did as they were told and opened the box right there on our front lawn. Once all the packing material was pulled away, I saw a shiny new treadle machine with an oak box. It really was beautiful. Momma was beaming as though it was a diamond, and in some ways, I could understand. She'd been battling for years with her old hand-me-down machine that often jammed in the middle of a seam. Recently, I'd heard an increase in her groans of frustration as the machine itself seemed determined to make any job more difficult.

"The description said it contained an oscillating shuttle to form a lock stitch," Momma explained with pride. I wasn't quite sure what that meant, but based on her expression, I was sure it was good, so I smiled broadly and nodded my head in return.

After the men gently pulled it out of the crate, Momma showed them where she wanted them to place it in the house. I should have known. There was an empty wall opposite the fireplace. The machine fit there perfectly.

"I'm going to take in sewing," Momma reasoned. "I need a dependable machine. I took some of the money from the sale to purchase it." But there was no reason to justify herself. Momma had been due a new machine years ago. It made me happy just to see her joy.

Early the next week, Momma took out an ad in the local newspaper and hung out a sign advertising her new business: Seams to Me Dressmaking and Alterations. Her play on words turned out not only to be witty, but also effective. By mid-week she was getting a few customers and quickly asked me to make one of my pecan pies before they came. I took this as her attempt to be hospitable and certainly didn't mind. I'd rediscovered my joy for baking. However, for the next three weeks, every time she scheduled a client, she'd ask me to bake a dessert. I was beginning to think Momma had a devious streak in her and was trying to force her clients to come back for alterations. But in the fourth week of her business, during the hottest part of summer, I discovered the root of her plan.

Mrs. Othello Riddle had been by for another fitting. She was the wife of J.T. Riddle, co-owner of the Riddle Brothers' Distillery. As such, she had more money than she knew what to do with and could have purchased her clothes from any store in the eastern U.S. Nonetheless, she wanted her wardrobe to be "one of a kind" and had all her pieces handmade but with imported material, of course. Material from the mercantile store just wouldn't do. She'd also found Momma to be more discreet about her measurements than a few other local dressmakers, and given her ample waist, I could understand her concern.

"Mrs. Overstreet, I've noticed your young daughter seems to have a gift for baking. We're hosting a party next week for some of Mr. Riddle's employees, and I do hate to heat up the house with baking. Do you think she could supply some desserts for the occasion?"

There it was. Momma wasn't trying to fatten her clients; she was trying to find me work. Oh, how clever!

By the time Mrs. Riddle left, we'd determined what I was to bring and the price. At first she'd wanted cream pies, but I mentally calculated the price of eggs and white sugar and decided that wasn't a good proposition. With a little persuading, I convinced Mrs. Riddle that a blackberry cobbler would be perfect since the berries were in season. I didn't tell her that blackberries happened to be the only produce growing in our backyard at the moment. Along with that, I'd bake two pecan pies and a batch of molasses cookies. Both of those items had main ingredients readily available.

"Well done, daughter," Momma commented after Mrs. Riddle left. "I do believe you have a sense for business."

"I got it from you!" I retorted.

Once Mrs. Riddle was pleased with my work, other orders began to come in. By the end of the summer, Momma and I were happily busy—not too much, not too little. We weren't wealthy, but we weren't starving. We weren't used to purchasing so many food items at the store and originally hadn't budgeted enough, but with time, we became accustomed. We even grew to like some of the pre-canned foods just hitting the shelves, especially those by Campbell's. But Momma had already designated a plot in our backyard for a garden the next year where we'd be growing tomatoes, green beans, and butternut squash. It would be tiny in comparison to our one on the farm, but it would give us something fresh of our own. I was surprised by how much I missed it.

And Momma was right about another thing. I did make friends at church. Well, one good friend at least. Jimalee Jenkins was the same age as me but about a head shorter and three times as brazen. The first time I met her she was wrangling two of her younger brothers while simultaneously trying to carry on a conversation. She then continued to destroy all mannerly protocol by asking a series of personal questions.

"Where do you live? Do you have any brothers or sisters? Luke, stop biting John! Did you make that dress yourself? It's real purty. I like it. Luke, what did I tell you?"

And with that, we became fast friends.

I quickly learned Jimalee got her name from her father, James, who was so afraid he would never have sons that he decided to bestow his name on his firstborn, regardless of gender. The second half of her name came from the great Robert E. Lee himself. Jimalee said her grandfather once met him during what her family referred to as "The War of Northern Aggression" and to this day speaks of General Lee as though he was a close friend of the family. However, Jim Jenkins and his wife Mayme did go on to have sons, four to be exact. In an effort to be orderly and simultaneously biblical, Mr. and Mrs. Jenkins decided to name their children after the Gospels: Matthew, Mark, Luke, and John.

Jimalee adored Sunday school, but not for spiritual growth. She said it gave her a welcomed break from her brothers. She'd just finished eighth grade but had no intention of going to high school for a couple of reasons. First, she hated being confined indoors. She claimed sitting still for so long made her skin practically crawl, and reading books was pure torture. "To tell you the truth, I'd rather wash clothes, bale hay, and slaughter a hog in the same day than read a book!" To which, after seeing the shock on my face she responded, "Well, you can eat on a good hog all year long, can't ya?" Secondly, her parents needed her help on their farm that was just a mile outside of town. Apparently, while her siblings seemed to have more than their fair share of energy, it had not yet translated into productive work. In fact, Jimalee claimed they were so rowdy they almost scared the milk cow dry the summer before.

However, Jimalee wasn't opposed to school entirely. In fact, she was counting down the days until it began. Even little John would be attending this year, and Jimalee was practically giddy with anticipation.

"Just think," she confessed to me one Sunday before worship, "I'll be able to use the outhouse without worryin' about one of them tryin' to play a trick on me." She then went on to assure me that her backside once had a ring of black for two weeks thanks to Matthew, Mark, and an old bucket of paint. I didn't hear a word of the sermon after that.

By late August the days had grown considerably shorter, although the air remained heavy and moist. The katydids were singing, giving yet another sign of the end of summer. Soon I would be starting back to school, high school to be exact. My initial excitement had turned to apprehension as the starting day drew nearer. Momma and I had passed Kavanaugh numerous times on our evening walks. With the exception of the sign out front, no one would have known it was a school. It did not, in fact, start out as such.

Mrs. Rhoda Kavanaugh was married to a local doctor who made a good living. He'd purchased the massive Georgian style home for his growing family. However, Mrs. Kavanaugh soon had other ideas.

Always one to be a bit unconventional, Mrs. Kavanaugh decided to start her school as a way to educate her own daughters. Having been well educated herself, she saw no reason to deny her daughters a solid academic education despite what critics might think. Mrs. K, as she was fondly known, didn't believe too much reading interfered with a girl's feminine nature, more specifically, her ability to have children. Instead, she agreed with former First Lady Adams: well-educated mothers make for well-educated sons.

Her rigorous teaching methods soon grew a reputation, and mothers and fathers who had sons with military dreams began to ask for her help. She then began to tutor students for their entrance exams into Annapolis or West Point. Some even came from far away and boarded in the rooms upstairs. These fellows were known as "house boys" and were held to standards even more rigorous than the average student—including Saturday morning classes and mandatory church service followed by a theological discussion of the sermon.

Some of these details I already knew, but others I discovered in the summer prior to my first year. None did anything to settle my nerves.

For two weeks prior to the start of school, Momma began to worry about my clothing. "Farm clothes are fine for the farm, but they don't seem appropriate for high school. You need something more suitable." She gave a sigh of resignation. "I suppose we'll just make do for now."

I'd saved my baking money to purchase school supplies. I knew money was tight by the way Momma always counted the coins in the change jar, and I didn't want to add another burden. Yet, I realized there was little more to purchase in the way of supplies than any other year. I'd be buying my books from a sophomore, and I had no clue as to anything special I might need. I'd have to make purchases as the need arose. Instead, I turned my attention to the fabric. *Anyone grown up enough to earn the money is certainly grown up enough to decide on material for a new dress,* I reasoned.

Making my way into the mercantile, I began to run my hand over the fabric bolts the way I'd seen Momma do a thousand times before, testing for quality. My head knew I needed something sturdy, but in my heart, I also wanted something a little more daring. I decided on some simple muslin for some new foundation garments. Mine had grown increasingly tight and uncomfortable. Thank goodness a corset could wait. It seemed ridiculous to me that some women insisted upon their stomachs practically touching their backbones before being seen in public. On more than one occasion I'd seen women gasping in tiny breaths just from walking down the aisle in church. I continued to touch and survey the bolts, hoping the Hanks' couldn't see my uncertainty. And finally, after several minutes, I made a decision and was proud I had money left over.

Yet, on the way home, an idea popped into my head. I had a notion to do something slightly daring, something almost frivolous. I wasn't sure Momma would approve, but then again, she might. For a moment, my thoughts swung back and forth trying to decide what to do, grappling with the pros and cons of my choice. In the end, I decided to make one more stop before heading home. *It won't hurt to look*, I told myself.

When I finally got back to Posey Street, I was so anxious to show Momma my purchases that I had her stop in the middle of her work and take a good look at my bundles. After holding the fabrics, Momma nodded approvingly.

"Well, I'm glad to see I've brought up a sensible girl," she boasted. "I just don't see any sense in some of those gaudy colors they have these days. And such good, sturdy fabric too! Those frilly fabrics are pretty, but they just don't last as long." Momma fingered all the material and eyed me proudly. I swelled from approval. Yet, I had one more item to show her. I'd saved the best for last.

For as long as I could remember, I'd wanted a hat, not the silly little straw hats with oversized bows that girls sometimes wore to church. Oh, no. I wanted a woman's hat! If there was anything I ever coveted, it was another person's hat. I loved the colors and the way they made you look as you walked down the street, completely tall and proud. I'd often thought if I had a hat, a real ladies' hat, I'd feel like the Queen of England.

Now, with such practical choices of fabric, I'd decided to splurge on headgear and make a visit to Miss Cunningham's millinery. Initially it was just to look, but in the end I couldn't resist. I began to pull out my most prized purchase. My heart was beating like Christmas morning. I asked Momma to close her eyes and wait just to build up the anticipation. I knew she'd love it as much as I did.

"Open your eyes!" I cried as I placed the hat on my head. "What do you think?" Momma stared at me blankly for a moment. She must have been stunned. The beauty of it was just too much to take in at one time. How could anyone not love purple and red ostrich feathers placed on what the advertisement called a "distinctive velvet crown and brim?"

Momma's eyes bulged as she covered her mouth with her hand and took a deep breath. "That certainly is unique. I've never seen anything like it," she finally said. I beamed with satisfaction. "It's quite extraordinary," she stated. "In fact, I just don't know of anyplace around here you could wear such an extraordinary hat."

"But don't you think it's beautiful?"

"Why, it's … it's … unbelievable!" I understood her inability to find just the right word for it. I felt exactly the same way. Putting it on, I walked to the mirror to take another look. Miss Cunningham at the store had already told me no one else in town had even touched the hat yet. I felt special to have something so new, so fashionable. I kept tilting my head from side to side to examine my appearance. The hat was still a bit loose, but I was certain it would still work. Certain. "I'm just not convinced Lawrenceburg has an event worthy of such a hat," Momma explained. "I know you're proud, but I'm afraid you wouldn't get much use out of it."

She was right. Not even the most well dressed ladies at church wore hats like mine. I began to ponder about my predicament. "Maybe something will come up soon. I'll save it for just the right event."

"Yes, sweetie, I think that's best."

With my head held high, I put my hat back in the box and walked into the bedroom to find a place worthy of its storage. When the event came for such a hat, I was ready.

Chapter Seven

Everyone knew school began promptly at eight a.m. With nervous energy fueling my body, I arrived about twenty minutes early on the first day. I was not alone. Others had already begun to congregate on the front porch. Judging by the conversation and causal stances, some of the students were already familiar with the routine as hellos and hugs were exchanged. I recognized a few others as being Ruby Likens and Eunice Bond, the daughter of Mr. Bond, our landlord. We went to church together but were not close. She often gave Jimalee a look of disgust and then turned her attention elsewhere. Jimalee either never noticed or truly didn't care. Eunice and Ruby were wearing their new dresses that Momma had made. I'd even helped with the buttons and hem. Standing with them was Beatrice Riddle, Mrs. Riddle's only daughter. She had a full head of beautiful blonde hair and a creamy pale complexion to match. Her figure was also at least two years ahead of the rest of us, and judging by the way she was standing, she knew it. Her mother had been quick to tell Momma that Beatrice's new dress was coming from New York, a fact I found both fascinating and outrageous.

I'd seen Beatrice a few times when I went to the Riddle's house with my baked goods. She'd always seemed preoccupied with something or someone else, often with two or three young gentlemen around her. It never occurred to me to mind her lack of friendliness. But now that we were at school, I decided to be cordial and speak to the other girls. "Hello," I began. "You all look so nice in your new clothes."

Beatrice turned to me with a steady gaze and slowly looked me up and down. "Oh, look. It's the dressmaker's daughter. Lucy, is it?" She grinned.

"Actually, it's Lilly Kate," I corrected.

"Whatever," Beatrice said with a shrug. "Aren't you one of our cooks?" she asked in a voice loud enough for all to hear. "I didn't know cooks came to this school." Ruby and Eunice started giggling. I stood there stunned, feeling as though I'd been punched. I wanted to reply but could think of nothing to say. I was dumbfounded. She was correct, but her tone had an acidity to it that burned through my fragile confidence. Walking away, I fought the stinging feeling in my eyes and a hard knot forming in my chest, and I silently vowed to keep my distance.

At precisely eight o'clock, the door opened, and everyone was ushered in. I knew the school was originally a home, but until now, I had been unable to imagine the interior. Everything at Fox Creek was simple, practical, and sturdy. A blackboard, benches, desks, coat hooks, a few shelves, and a teacher's desk were its humble furnishings. And now, the polar opposite was before me. Upon entry into Kavanaugh, we walked into a grand foyer lined with rich, wood paneling that practically radiated from polishing. The floors were made of wide, smooth oak slats with beautiful graining. And rugs of various colors and designs were placed in common areas. I felt as though I'd walked into a picture I had seen once of a house in Europe.

There were no rooms large enough to hold all the students at one time. However, by opening the doors to each room on both sides of the foyer, there was space enough for everyone. Chairs were lined up in neat rows and people made their way to a seat. Still feeling bruised and unsure,

I cautiously made my way to a middle row and sat near the end. Wanting something to do, I began organizing my tablet and pencils, only to look up and see a lanky, redheaded boy walking past my row, looking up and down the seats. He looked as nervous as I felt. "Hello, I'm Huey Hughes," he said as he stopped next to my chair. He stuck out his right hand as he took the seat next to me. I swallowed a laugh, unsure if he was serious or making a joke.

"Lilly Kate Overstreet," I responded. "I'm a freshman this year."

"Well, golly, so am I! To tell the truth, I didn't sleep a wink last night. I've heard all about Mrs. K, and I'm so scared I think I've developed a hundred more freckles." He smiled a toothy smile, and I was immediately at ease.

"I know what you mean. I'm the first in my family to attend high school. I have no idea what to expect."

I wanted to continue, but the ringing of a bell quickly cut me off. Everyone promptly took a seat. I'd never seen a group get so quiet so fast, not even in church. We all faced forward, where a lectern had been placed, and beside it stood an American flag. Then Mrs. Kavanaugh stood up to address the student body. The first time I laid eyes on her, I thought perhaps I'd made a horrible mistake. She wasn't especially tall and certainly not rotund, but her solemn presence filled the entire room. Often dressed entirely in black, she commanded attention from even the most rowdy boys and talkative girls. As she rose to address the students, no one dared to whisper. I'm not even sure I breathed.

"Ladies and gentlemen, the faculty and I would like to welcome you to another school year here at Kavanaugh High," Mrs. Kavanaugh began, her eyes methodically working up and down each row. "I trust you are ready to begin. I expect nothing but absolute excellence, and that will mean hard work. The only way to a solid education is the hard way, and seeing that as the only way, it is also the easy way. Let me remind you that school begins promptly at eight a.m. Tardiness is unacceptable. However, school ends when you have mastered your lessons for the day. For some, that will be later than others."

I couldn't be sure, but I thought I detected the slightest little smile cross Mrs. Kavanaugh's lips. "At this time, I would like to extend a special welcome to our freshmen class, the largest class yet with fifteen. I trust you will find your years here at Kavanaugh to be both productive and enlightening." She paused for a moment and glanced around the room at the new faces. "I assure you it will mean work." I could see the Adam's apple in Huey's neck bounce up and down as he gulped. "Now," she finally began again with a lighter tone, "Allow me to introduce the rest of the faculty." And with that, I started high school.

———————

Mrs. Kavanaugh was correct. School was often quite difficult. I spent hours pouring over my books, writing reports, and studying for tests. I never dreamed it could be so demanding. Countless were the times I would be studying late into the night with the *whirr-whirr* of Momma's machine in the background. Miss Daphne had been thorough and rigorous, but Mrs. Kavanaugh and the rest of the faculty were relentless. Some students stayed well past supper before she was satisfied the lesson had been learned. Others were asked to come early for special tutoring. There were a few times I almost thought about quitting... almost. Those moments were few and far between. Deep down, I knew I didn't dare. I was not a quitter. And, in truth, I was doing very well. My grades were among the highest in the class. Even though I still struggled some in mathematics, I had a powerful ally in Huey Hughes. Without realizing it at the time, Huey had become the brotherly figure that Dink Pruitt had been at Fox Creek. And, also like Dink, what Huey lacked in looks, he made up for in brains and congenial whit. He also had the wonderful ability to make complex ideas seem simple. Together, with my knack for literature and history, we became a formidable pair with one of us often scoring the highest on a test. We developed a friendly rivalry that pushed me to study a little longer and a littler harder than I'm sure I would have done on my own.

In November after school started, an event took place that was worthy of front-page coverage in the local paper. It seemed the ladies of a local civic group called the Pierian Club had felt Lawrenceburg was still in the Dark Ages "literarily speaking, of course," and had begun collecting books for a library two years earlier. I knew this because Mrs. Bond and Mrs. Riddle were members of the Pierian Club and the lending library board. They shared a good deal about their efforts during fittings at our home. It also didn't hurt that their club's meeting place was just a matter of yards from our front door, and I would often hear the women talking together after a meeting. Secretly, I wanted to peruse their collection and bring some choice books home to read, but I didn't dare ask.

I'd heard of Andrew Carnegie of course. Everyone knew him as the steel tycoon and one of the "Captains of Industry." His philanthropy the last few years had made him even more famous than his business dealings. Apparently, the ladies of the Pierian Club decided Lawrenceburg should benefit from his generosity as well as anyplace else. They took a chance and asked him to make a donation to the building of a library. Mr. Carnegie obliged with a whopping five thousand dollars! That money was quickly used to build Lawrenceburg's first official public library.

School had let out early the day of the grand opening, and Momma, Huey, Jimalee, and I stood among the crowd in the cold, blustery wind to watch the ribbon cutting. Members of the Pierian Club stood behind Mayor Varney like a row of proud soldiers as he made his speech, most of which no one heard because of wind and restless children. If I stretched, I could even make out Beatrice Riddle standing in the front row. She'd told everyone at school that morning exactly how the ceremony would go and how Mr. Carnegie's letter was addressed to her mother, not the club. I'd tried to listen politely, but Huey stood behind her making faces and mocking her every word.

Nonetheless, it was a proud day for everyone, and none more so than Mrs. Riddle, president of the club. After a few moments of speaking, Mayor Varney made a dramatic movement of his arms and ceremoniously handed the scissors to Mrs. Riddle. She too must have felt the need to make a speech, but all we could see were her moving lips. Huey took the opportunity to "read her lips" and whisper her speech in my ear.

"Ladies and gentlemen," he began in a mock high-pitched voice. "I want you all to look at the new hat I have purchased for this occasion. I had it shipped from Paris."

Jimalee and I began laughing, and Momma poked me in the ribs to shush me. She might as well have fanned a fire. We began to laugh harder, which further encouraged Huey as he continued to mock Mrs. Riddle, "Mr. Carnegie asked me to remind everyone to please wipe your filthy feet before entering, and whatever you do, wash your hands before handling these books that I—I mean *we* have collected." By the time those in the front began clapping at the end of Mrs. Riddle's speech, my side was aching from suppressed laughter, and Jimalee was convinced she was about to wet herself. Momma had even walked away in mock disgust, pretending she didn't know us.

Once the ribbon was cut, the wave of people began to drift forward and get the first glimpse at the town's new library. Despite Huey's teasing, we were both actually anxious to see it. Jimalee claimed she was only there to get away from her brothers, but I did notice a sparkle of curiosity in her eyes. When we finally entered, we were not disappointed. The stately brick exterior perfectly set the tone for the interior. With ornate woodwork on the walls and shelving, it immediately gave a prestigious feeling. The large windows accompanied by the new electric lights made everything much brighter than I was accustomed to. There were even columns and a fireplace in the entry. But, of course, my favorite part was the books. While others were admiring the architecture, I quickly wove my way through the crowd to the rows and rows of books. I'd never seen so many in one place. *Where will I begin?* I thought to myself. I ran my fingers over the spines and read some of the gold embossed letters. I spotted *Jane Eyre* and *Wuthering Heights,* each by a lady named Brontë but with different first names. I'd heard of *Alice in Wonderland* by Lewis Carroll, but hadn't yet had a chance to read it, and of course there were numerous books by Charles Dickens. I even found a section of poetry and spotted a few familiar names like Barrett, Bradstreet, and Shakespeare, and my favorite, Edgar Allan Poe.

Eventually, the others caught up with me. "Isn't it wonderful?" I asked, not really listening for an answer.

Jimalee was not as impressed. "I still say I'd rather be butcherin' a hog!"

Despite the fun I had at her expense, I really was grateful to Mrs. Riddle and the other club members for the work they had done on the library. I spent countless hours there researching or studying. I sometimes got inspired to write a little story of my own while sitting among all those great writers, but no matter how hard I tried, my tales seemed to come out sounding trite and amateur. The only bad part about the library was tolerating Beatrice's constant presence. She must have felt a sense of ownership in the building and, as such, spent a good deal of time doing . . . well, I don't know what. I never actually saw her reading. In fact, she regularly made it a point to pick up the books on my table and quickly drop them in disgust. "Oh, I don't need that. I have that one at home," she'd say in a voice much too loud for a library. It was just one of her many jabs that I had to swallow.

Not only did I use the library on a regular basis, Momma was also enjoying its choice of books and magazines. It seemed to satisfy a deep-seated desire she had to learn and grow. Often, she'd ask me about my studies at school and pepper me with questions. Initially, I thought she was trying to make sure I was keeping up or at least helping me retain my lessons. But soon I came to the realization that Momma was more inquisitive than concerned and was soaking up the information like a thirsty flower, feeding her intellectual curiosity. It was a revelation that I found both comforting and sad.

Momma was also finding tremendous fulfillment in her church involvement. While always active at Fox Creek, the distance and demands of farm life predicated how much service she could offer. Yet, almost as soon as we started attending First Baptist, Momma joined the Women's Aid Society and began helping collect supplies for the Indian reservation schools out west. The idea of assisting people in a place so unlike her own ignited a new passion in her. It was as though a new window had been opened and she was seeing through it for the first time. She'd even grown fascinated by the efforts of Lottie Moon, a missionary in China. Momma listened with rapt attention as someone would read an account of Miss Moon's trials and victories in China, and I could see in her the same fervor I often felt about a subject. "We can't all be missionaries out west or overseas," Momma once proclaimed after a Women's Aid Society meeting, "but we can all do our part." And we were doing just that. Between the two of us, our lives had changed dramatically in the past year, but we were adjusting. We were bending.

Chapter Eight

Gradually, our lives had settled into a routine. Momma and I filled our days with work and study. Her business was good, and I had been able to sell my baked goods from time to time to make my own spending money. Beatrice's remarks still stung, though I never told Momma about the incident. I didn't want to hurt her feelings or give her cause to worry. I'd been careful to avoid Beatrice's sharp tongue, although I still sensed her disapproving looks and saw her whispering. I made a concerted effort to avoid her—a task not always possible in close quarters. The last time I made desserts for one of the Riddle's numerous parties, Beatrice caught me on the front porch leaving school and made a rather loud point for all to hear. "Momma said to tell you to please bring the food to the back—that's the servants' entrance." If I'd known the exact piece of cake that was to cross Beatrice's lips, I'd have put a stone in it.

Momma and I even adopted an old tomcat; or rather, he adopted *us* by showing up at our back door with the gift of a dead mouse. The orange tabby was almost as round as he was long, and when it became apparent that we were his new family, I started calling him Taft, after our country's new president, whom he seemed to resemble.

Our lives swam along like this for the first year. Work. Study. Work. Worship. Play. Work some more. Momma's business continued to grow steadily and so did her activities at church. For my part, I continued to study diligently, and although sometimes painful, I could sense a little more growth in myself. I still felt out of place among some of the other, more sophisticated, townies at school. I was always afraid of seeming like a hillbilly, and while I hated feeling self-conscious, the nagging in my brain never seemed to go away.

Often at night I would sit on our bed with Taft at my feet and try to write a small poem or short story. Words seemed to jumble in my head, and I was never able to find the perfect way to articulate my thoughts or feelings. I marveled at the way Twain and Dickens found the perfect words to paint a picture in my brain and the ease with which all of the Brontë sisters seemed to evoke emotions. By contrast, my words seemed flat, stilted, and lifeless. They even bored me. More often than not, I simply kept a journal of the day's events and school's many triumphs and disappointments. Yet even this simple bit of writing became something of a refuge for me. When penning my words, my tangled emotions seemed to loosen and straighten out. On days when anger or frustration burned, the mere act of writing in my journal seemed to douse the blaze. My journal became my tonic. More and more frequently, I found myself spending my baking money on writing supplies.

At the beginning for my sophomore year, I began working for *Tiger Beat*, our school's monthly newspaper. I had been asked to be a proofreader simply because word leaked out I had a dictionary at home. No less than once a week I'd bring home a pile of stories, ads, and announcements with the sole purpose of finding mistakes. Occasionally, Jimalee would come over under the guise of helping me; but, in most cases, very little proofing actually got done. Still, I welcomed her company.

"Why do you let her treat you that way?" Jimalee asked one evening when I lamented about Beatrice's latest jabs.

"I don't *let* her. I just choose not to respond."

"She's nothing more than a spoiled rich girl. She's a bully!" Jimalee was never one to mince words.

"I know that! But . . . it's complicated."

"Just because her mother is a customer for both you and your Momma is no reason to put up with her."

"It's not that," I defended. "All Beatrice Riddle wants is to get my gizzard. Well, I'm not going to let her. Everybody else stumbles all over themselves to do what she says just to avoid her wrath. Well, that's not going to be me, but I'm not going to be rude either. Momma says to kill people with kindness, and that's just what I plan to do."

"I'm sure I could come up with something quicker than kindness to teach her a lesson."

"Yes, I'm sure you could."

It was in one of these proofreading sessions that Jimalee and I stumbled upon an interesting little detail about Beatrice's name. "Who would name their kid Beat Rice?" Jimalee exclaimed. I quickly grabbed the story out of her hand to see what she was talking about. Soon, I spotted it. Someone had inadvertently left an extra space in Beatrice's name making it appear like Beat Rice. I'd never noticed that before.

Jimalee and I held our bellies in laughter for the next twenty minutes as we pictured Beatrice Riddle in her fancy store-bought clothes trying to cook pounds of rice in her kitchen, only to end up whacking it with a rolling pin.

"Does she even know where the kitchen is in her home?" Jimalee asked through tears of laughter.

"Do pigs fly?" I responded and set us off on another wave of hilarity.

By the time Jimalee left that night we were both tired from all the hysterics, but a tiny plan began to simmer in my mind. It bubbled and brewed along with my courage.

It was a plan that I knew would bring Beatrice off her pedestal. I just wasn't sure if I had the nerve to pull it off.

———————————

Two days later, *Tiger Beat* came out with its usual excitement and fanfare. I watched as copies were quickly passed around the classroom and everyone clamored for a look. For me, the moment normally was anticlimactic since I'd already read each piece three or four times. Today, however, my interest was piqued for different reasons. I didn't have to wait long before getting the response I was hoping for.

"Hey, I didn't know we had someone named Beat Rice in our class," a student jibed.

Another called out, "Hey, Beat Rice! Are you good friends with Whipping Wheat or Thrashing Oats?"

Beatrice stormed over and snatched a copy out of Robert Searcy's hand and quickly scanned the paper. I could tell the moment she spotted the error in her name by the way her neck began turning red and a little vein popped out on her forehead. Steam was practically coming out of her ears. The entire room erupted in laughter as Beatrice yelled, "I don't see one thing funny about this!" She then proceeded to throw a little tirade by hurling the paper and then huffing out of the room, slamming the door behind her. The students erupted with applause over the show we'd just witnessed, and I felt more than a little pleased with myself.

Apparently, an evening at home did nothing to diminish anyone's sense of humor or Beatrice's sensitivity. When she arrived at her desk the next morning she was greeted by a bowl of rice and a rather large hammer. As Beatrice's neck once again grew red and her jaw became locked in fury, the cackling started again, this time with even greater fervor. Even Miss Campton seemed a bit tickled by the prank, but our laughter was soon interrupted with Beatrice's rage.

"Just be quiet!" Beatrice screamed. "Everybody just shut up!" The room fell silent as Beatrice stood shaking next to her desk, eyes blazing with lightning-hot fury. With her jaw clenched in anger, Beatrice looked over the room. Her eyes eventually locked on mine.

"*You!*" she yelled pointing straight at me. "*You!* This is your fault! You're supposed to catch the mistakes, but I guess you're just too stupid." We all sat in stunned silence as her tirade continued. "You're nothing more than a low-class hick. You shouldn't even be here. This school is for serious students. Why don't you just go back to that creek you came from? You shouldn't even be here!"

No one knew quite what to do. Even the unflappable Huey stood motionless and quiet. My heart was hammering in my ears, but I simply couldn't speak. I could feel the glare of dozens of eyes focused on me waiting for a reaction. My mouth went dry, and I sat paralyzed by shock. The anger that was hurled at me was like a bullet searing through my chest. I had no words. Thankfully, Miss Campton stepped in with a cooler head.

"Beatrice, why don't you excuse yourself and get cleaned up. When you return, I can assure you this will not be a topic of conversation." After Beatrice walked out, Miss Campton looked at me. "Are you okay?" she quietly asked. I shook my head in affirmation because I didn't trust my voice at that moment. I turned in my seat and hurriedly found something to do. Huey gently put his hand on my shoulder, but I couldn't even turn my head to acknowledge him. Had anyone else said anything to me, I'm certain I would have been the one who needed to be excused.

Within a day or two, most everyone seemed to have forgotten the entire incident. Lectures continued to be given, notes were taken, and homework was turned in. However, the scene still continued to loom over me like a bad dream I couldn't shake. It clung to me for a couple of reasons. First, I felt slightly guilty about it. Certainly Beatrice deserved it. She actually deserved a lot more. No one deserved to be knocked off her pedestal more than Beatrice Riddle. But I had stooped to her level. I had purposely done something that I knew would inflict pain. That, I knew, was wrong. I felt ashamed and asked God for forgiveness, but I still didn't dare tell Momma. Her record on forgiveness wasn't quite as perfect as the Almighty's, and I didn't want her forcing me to give a face-to-face apology. After the verbal beating I'd taken, I thought Beatrice and I were pretty even. That being the case, I decided I'd rather feel a little guilty, thank you very much.

Secondly, a tiny piece of me couldn't help but wonder if Beatrice wasn't at least partially right. Was I really just a hick from Fox Creek? Did I have any business at Kavanaugh? I'd been in high school for more than a year now, but there were still countless times I felt woefully plain and out of place. Everyone else seemed much more confident and sophisticated. Algebra still gave me fits, and I had to work hard on everything else. Nothing seemed easy. Often, I would second-guess myself over the silliest things, such as where to sit at lunch or how to fix my hair. Even my clothes were homely compared to everyone else's. Had it not been for a tragic twist of fate, I wouldn't be at Kavanaugh at all. I tried to walk with my chin held high and behave, as Momma said, "As though you've got some sense." But I still suffered inwardly. What good was all this going to do me? I wasn't attending college or military school or looking for a well-to-do husband. What was my purpose?

Thus far, I'd been able to hide my insecurities under a pile of busy activity, but Beatrice's remarks only brought my concerns to the front of my mind. For days after the rice incident, an argument raged in my head like a violent thunder storm. One moment I'd convinced myself Beatrice was wrong; I did belong at school. Another moment, doubt would creep back in like water under a door.

It wasn't until the following Sunday when Reverend Searcy was preaching from Psalm 139 that I realized I was exactly where God had intended me to be. In this particular psalm, David was singing out of joy and gratitude. If anyone knew about being unfairly treated, it was David. Chosen as the king when he was a boy, hunted by the man he was to replace, on the brink of capture and certain death many times, David knew suffering. He knew what it was like to feel alone and out of place. Even so, he was grateful and felt the safety of God's arms. He sang that he was "fearfully and wonderfully made," and then, "in thy book all my members were written … when as yet there was none of them."

David knew he was where God wanted him to be. God had ordained David's days even before he was born. And, if he did it with David, then he did it for me too. God knew I'd be here in Lawrenceburg, and he meant for it to happen. My being at Kavanaugh wasn't an accident. Certainly, Poppa's death would have never been my chosen pathway. Still, God had used it for good. Beatrice was wrong. Yes, I was a country girl from Fox Creek, but my God had put me in school for a reason. The reason was yet unclear, but I had a purpose for being here … and a promise.

It would be quite convenient for me to say that within a week of my Psalm 139 revelation I became a bold, confident woman—one who spoke out for what was just and gave help to those in need. That would be convenient, but completely untrue. I still struggled. At times I would feel a sense of pride and self-assurance about a job well done or a compliment given. It was moments like these I felt blessed to be alive, like every nerve ending in my body was heightened, and I was almost invincible. But just as the wind can change direction without notice, so could my sense of confidence. Whether it came as a snub from Beatrice and her friends or the sting of a less than desirable grade on a test, self-doubt would always creep in.

Shortly before Thanksgiving during my sophomore year, I reluctantly agreed to travel with Momma to deliver food and aide baskets to some families living near the river. Mr. Gash from church had agreed to drive us, so one Saturday Momma got up early and started gathering the supplies. I had wanted to spend the day reading a new novel I'd checked out from the library, but when I mentioned my plans to Momma, she gave me one of her looks that clearly indicated her disapproval. I'd have rather had an anvil dropped on my foot than suffer the disappointment of Momma, so off we went together as a pair—one happy to help, the other with her tail tucked between her legs.

Momma and I didn't say a great deal on our ride. I was still a little miffed about having my arm twisted and was making a mental checklist of all the things I'd rather be doing. I'd even placed darning socks somewhere on my imaginary roster, such was my disgust regarding our errands.

As my list reached about its tenth item, our wagon

pulled up to the first house. My head snapped to attention when I saw it. Although larger than our Posey Street home, the wood frame house looked as though it would blow over in a strong wind. The weather-beaten wood was a sad shade of gray, and the roof was sagging like the back of an old mule. The windows, what was left of them, were covered in grime. Where there wasn't any glass, someone had made a vain attempt to patch the openings with newspaper.

As we approached the house, my nose tingled from the mixture of foul odors. Shoddy fencing had allowed animals to roam freely in the front yard, leaving their feces anywhere they chose. Momma and I had to side-step a few cow patties as we made our way to the sagging front porch.

Momma knocked boldly as though she was paying a social visit to a dear friend. When the door opened, it revealed a thin, sallow-cheeked girl younger than me, holding a baby on one hip.

"Good morning," Momma spoke in a cheerful voice. "I'm Ruth Overstreet, and this is my daughter Lilly Kate. We're from the First Baptist Women's Aid Society, and we've created a gift basket for you for this holiday season." Momma held up the basket for the girl to see some of the items inside. It was a first glance for me too, and I could make out several cans of soup, some evaporated milk, corn meal, and baking soda.

The girl still didn't say a word but looked into the basket. I saw her lick her lips and swallow as she scanned the goods. "Daddy says we ain't supposed to take charity," she announced flatly and without conviction.

"Oh, well, I wouldn't consider this charity." Momma stumbled a bit and then quickly regained her composure. "This is a gift, and it would be rude to turn down a gift. Don't you agree?"

The girl's eyes sparkled a bit. "Yes, I suppose you're right," she conceded. She opened the door enough to allow us in. "Don't pay no attention to our mess," she meekly apologized. "The twins is like two tornadoes runnin' through the house all day long. I'm sorry. I forgot my manners." The girl haphazardly wiped her right hand on her apron and stuck it out in front of us. "My name is Elora, Elora Hicks."

"Elora. That's a beautiful name. I've never heard that before." They were some of the few words I'd uttered since we'd left town, and I was a bit surprised to hear them myself.

"Thank you kindly. It's an Irish name. My momma and her people came from there. She always wanted me to keep a bit of it with me, I reckon." Elora was now grinning slightly after the compliment.

"Where is your momma?" I asked innocently enough. Momma shot me a dagger-sharp look, and the smile on Elora's face quickly faded.

"She passed shortly after this one was born," she replied, gesturing to the baby sitting on her hip.

Never in my life had I wanted so much for a hole to open in the floor and swallow me. How many times had Momma warned me about thinking before I speak? Had I simply kept my mouth shut a few moments longer and looked around, I would have been able to see there was no mother in this house. The interior had faired somewhat better than the outside, thanks, I presumed, to the efforts of Elora. Although everything had the look of heavy wear, there had been at least an effort to keep things clean and neat. Across the room was the kitchen, small and cramped, but no more so than our own. A rocking chair sat next to the fireplace with a quilt neatly folded and hanging on the back. Yet, beside the chair stood a row of whisky bottles, some empty, some still partially full, and I quickly surmised Mr. Hicks was using them to dull some of the pain from the family's loss.

The dining table was perhaps the piece that most broke my heart. Its heavy wooden legs and thick table-top looked as though it had fed many generations of the Hicks family, its scratches and dents telling the tales of many meals gone by. But in the center was a cracked vase filled with cut greenery and red berries gathered from outside. Someone had tried to bring a bit of beauty into an otherwise dreary environment. The effect wasn't so much an improvement, but a reminder of what could be or maybe ought to be.

"Where shall I place the basket?" Momma asked in an effort to break the tension.

"Just set it on the table. I'll put things away before Daddy gets home. He might be sorely upset to know we had some visitors." Elora dropped her eyes to the floor in a bit of shame and protectively rubbed the baby's back.

Momma walked over to the table and continued the conversation as though there was no awkwardness at all. "Well, you have a mighty fine basket here, if I do say so myself. There's enough in here for at least three good meals, maybe more. Someone even took the time to knit some stockings for the little one. That will be handy as the weather grows colder."

I recognized a slight little lift to Momma's voice, as sometimes happened in an effort to be cheerful when the reality was far from it. She quickly turned and walked to Elora, placing her hand on her shoulder. "Miss Hicks, we know you're carrying a great burden since your mother died, and you're doing a marvelous job. I know your daddy is still taking it hard. However, it would be a blessing to us if you would let us help you sometime."

Momma's words hung in the air like smoke. Elora's jaw grew stiff and her eyes began to get a little misty. She quickly looked down at the floor. "Daddy don't like charity," she said again unconvincingly. There was an uncomfortable pause, and Elora's head shot up. "But I'm a hard worker. In fact, I'm mighty good at ironing clothes. Somehow, it gives me comfort to see all them wrinkles pressed out and the fabric become all crisp and clean."

Momma gave a slight nod, then squeezed Elora's shoulder a little tighter. "Certainly. We will keep that in mind. It's quite possible there are ladies in our church who need some ironing done and would love to pay someone to help."

Elora gave a sigh, allowing herself the luxury of a full smile, and Momma straightened her coat. "Lilly Kate, we need to get going. This young lady has work to do, as do we."

Momma and I said our farewells and made our way back to the wagon where Mr. Gash was waiting. "How'd it go?" he asked.

"We have much for which to be thankful, don't we Lilly Kate?" Momma was looking at me, but my eyes were glued to the Hicks' door where I could still see Elora looking out and holding the baby.

"We most certainly do," I replied more to myself than to Momma. "We most certainly do."

Chapter Nine

After our visit to the Hicks' home and others like it, I understood why Momma insisted I go with her to deliver baskets. It was then that I began to see my life for the blessing it was. Certainly Momma and I experienced our share of hardships, and we weren't anywhere near wealthy, at least not when compared to the Riddles and Bonds of the world, but we had plenty. I had clothes to wear, even if they weren't the fanciest, and shoes that fit and kept my feet warm. I was also blessed with a Momma who loved me and worked hard. Mostly through her efforts and thrift we were able to sit down each evening to a filling, hot meal. Our home, although tiny, was also clean, neat, dry, and warm. But, most importantly, it was filled with understanding, encouragement, and love. I was a very blessed girl indeed. And it was at that moment that I determined to live like it.

Fall, 1911

The beginning of senior year was filled with excitement and anticipation. I was going to be the editor of *Tiger Beat*. During the last eighteen months I'd slowly proven to be more than a copy editor. I began to write simple stories about school events, such as the fall carnival and the spring fling. With time I was gradually given the job of covering more heady topics, such as the latest entrance requirements for Annapolis and West Point. I had grown to like seeing my name under the headline. I knew it wasn't the same as having it printed elegantly on the spine of a book, but I enjoyed taking down all the information and organizing it in a way people not only could understand but maybe even enjoy.

As the editor, it was to be my job to write the editorials. In the past, the editors had occasionally handled a hot topic ranging from political races to the need for a universal secondary education. But more often than not, the editorial page contained opinions on less than pressing issues, such as school dress codes and moving picture reviews. While I was not one intentionally to stir up trouble, I'd grown to have some definite opinions on a few matters. Yet, I wasn't sure if I yet had the nerve to share them.

As I walked to school at the start of my senior year, I vividly remembered my first day at Kavanaugh. I felt awkward, insecure, and uncertain of what to expect. Much had changed since then. Not only was I three inches taller, I had the confidence that came with experience. High school had been good for me, and within nine months, I would be graduating with a diploma, the first in my family to do so. Some of the others, like Huey Hughes and Richard Davenport, were making college plans. They'd already been pouring over applications and sending off for handbooks. I knew that was out of the question for me. I'd been blessed to get this far.

As usual, everyone gathered on the front porch before the door was opened. I immediately recognized the freshmen by the way they looked around for someone they knew. I quickly spotted Huey's red hair and went to greet him. He too had changed during the last three years. He was no longer just a matchstick with knees and elbows. He'd filled out and turned into a handsome young man. Although Huey and I had never been more than friends,

I wasn't oblivious to this fact and noticed him receiving a few admiring glances when I walked up. Huey, however, had other things on his mind when I approached him.

"Hey, Lilly Kate. Look. I finally got some information from Georgetown College. Doesn't it look great?"

I had to admit I'd heard of Georgetown College. It was a Baptist college about forty miles away, but it may as well have been another world as far as I was concerned. Huey always thought my lack of interest in his college information was just apathy. In reality, I was a bit jealous, and it was hard to get excited for Huey when I knew college could never happen for me. Still, I looked at the information to appease him.

"It says here that girls have started taking classes with the guys!" Huey exclaimed with apparent interest. "Now that's what I call progress!"

I was already aware of Georgetown's decision to allow girls to take classes with the boys. That's how I'd heard about the college in the first place. It started on a trial basis two years prior, and there were those in our church who were ardently against it. "It's next to fornication as far as I'm concerned," touted Duce Crawford. "I don't see any good that can come from this. Those girls don't need to be taught Latin. They need to be taught to be ladies. Why they would want to go to college in the first place is beyond me."

Truthfully, there was quite a bit that was beyond Duce Crawford. He was a stout, burly man who huffed and puffed his way into church every Sunday and sat six rows back on the left side. I quickly observed that any effort at progress that did not originate in his mind was, by his definition, a terrible idea. He was the one individual who could be counted on to raise what Poppa called "a bona fide stink" on any topic. I could never quite figure out why everyone seemed to grant him such levity, but all did seem to take his brusque comments with a grain of salt. Even so, no one was certain he still didn't hold to the notion the earth was flat just because he didn't come up with the idea.

Still, even with all the good-natured souls in our church willing to overlook Mr. Crawford's comments, they'd struck a nerve with Louella Shelton. The eldest in our church by at least ten years and the wealthy widow of a businessman, when she spoke, everyone listened, including Duce Crawford.

"Oh, Ducey Boy, quit your bellyachin'!" she spoke up after Duce's comments regarding women in Georgetown College. "You think a woman is only good for lookin' pretty, changin' diapers, and fixin' biscuits. Pshaw! I recall it was your momma who taught you to read in the first place. Seems to me, the more schoolin' a woman gits, the better off her children will be." Mr. Crawford sat bug-eyed with his mouth slightly open. Mrs. Shelton continued, "What's more, I for one wish them well. This is the twentieth century, after all. Times are a changin',' and this is one change I think is overdue."

I could have clapped. Mrs. Shelton quickly became a woman after my own heart. She not only spoke what I felt, but she did it with incredible confidence! I could tell by the way Momma pursed her lips that she was a little uncomfortable with Mrs. Shelton's public tirade, but my heart truly rejoiced.

Yes indeed, I was aware that women were taking classes at Georgetown.

———————

At promptly eight o'clock the door opened and everyone went in. Huey and I sat together through opening assembly once again, and I couldn't help but be a bit grateful. The past three years had been filled with hard work and the rewards it often brings, but there were also trials and a few disappointments. I was thankful to be facing this year, my final year, with promise and the confidence that comes from experience.

Mrs. Kavanaugh stepped forward to give her opening speech. It was the same speech as the three years prior and delivered with the same solemnity. And it received the same response because everyone knew she meant every word of it. While we all respected her, we also held a healthy dose of fear. She'd recently grown accustomed to carrying around a large, black umbrella. No one understood why. Even on a clear day, she would keep it by her side. Then, when Willy McDugal fell asleep in class, the piercing *thwack* it made as she slammed it on his desk gave us all our answer. Mrs. Kavanaugh now used the umbrella as something of a fifth limb—and no one wanted to be on the receiving end of whatever it had to give.

The enrollment had grown in my three years, and consequently, so had the faculty. While Mrs. Kavanaugh was still clearly in charge, the faculty had grown to six with the latest additions being an elocution teacher named Miss Davenport and a recently married new physical education teacher named Mrs. Rutherford. I could see the entire male population of the school become dreamy-eyed as Mrs. Rutherford walked up to the podium to welcome us. She was tall and lean with coal black hair and light green eyes that showed up beautifully against her pale, creamy complexion.

"I'd like to say how honored I am to be a part of this wonderful institution, Kavanaugh High School," Mrs. Rutherford began with a smile that showed her pearly white teeth and deep dimples. "This year, I hope to teach the ladies about kinesiology and wellness. In doing so, I have many ideas that I think you will find both exciting and challenging, including some games I have learned about while attending Hamilton College. In particular, I'm looking forward to teaching you a new game some of you may have heard of called basketball."

Quite frankly, she could have talked about painting our faces green and making us walk on our hands. No one cared. By the time she was finished, every boy was practically in love with her, and every girl wanted to be just like her. I could almost see Huey drooling, such was his happiness. Although all the teachers received a respectful round of applause at the end of his or her welcoming speech, Mrs. Rutherford's was undoubtedly more robust. We'd all found our new favorite teacher.

As first period was about to begin, Huey whispered excitedly in my ear.

"Hey, did you hear the news?'

"No, what are you talking about?"

"Beatrice Riddle is out for the semester."

My mind went into overdrive trying to process this information. I knew the Riddle family had gone on a European vacation over the summer. We all knew. The topic had never been far from Beatrice's lips for her entire junior year. After their departure, Mrs. Riddle had sent frequent letters to Mrs. Bond, each piece of correspondence giving vibrant descriptions of the family's experiences. Mrs. Bond in turn shared with everyone willing to listen. A few even made it into *The Anderson News*. My personal favorite was the one that went into great detail describing a vicious stomach flu contracted by Beatrice.

"Did she stay at a school somewhere in Europe?" I asked.

"No, they say she's sick and won't be back until after Christmas.

"What's wrong with her?"

"No one seems to know, not even Eunice and Ruby. Maybe some strange disease she picked up on the trip."

I couldn't question Huey any further. Class was beginning, but I was having trouble focusing. Certainly Beatrice was not my favorite person, but I wouldn't call us enemies either. Since the incident with the newspaper, she'd kept her distance, and I'd tried my best not to rouse her. Of course, with a school our size, she couldn't ignore me completely. There were a few times we were required to be on the same team or study in the same group. We were both cool but civil. And, to her credit, Beatrice always pulled her fair share of the load. She was spoiled and pretentious, but I'd learned she was definitely not stupid. Whatever was keeping her out of school had to be serious.

During lunch, Beatrice's illness was all the talk.

"I heard she's got typhoid," said a new freshman I didn't recognize.

"Typhoid? Nah, I heard it's TB," said another.

TB. Tuberculosis. There was not a person in the school who did not know someone who had been affected by the terrible disease. The bacteria would settle in a person's lungs and fill them up. A person with TB usually suffered for several months from a dry cough, fever, and lethargy. Often a TB patient had to spend months in a special ward of a hospital with other TB sufferers confined to their beds. However, Beatrice's parents may have chosen for her to stay at home. They certainly had the room and the means to treat her there. Even so, if Beatrice had contracted TB, having her back after Christmas seemed optimistic.

As the day drew to an end, my head felt like it was stuffed with information. The teachers had all carefully told us about their expectations and given us an overview of the reports, projects, and tests we could expect. It was all a bit overwhelming, and even Huey seemed a tad unnerved.

"Golly, they must spend their entire summer dreaming up ways to make us work," Huey bemoaned as we gathered our books to go home. I had to agree. There was no letting up just because we were seniors. In fact, it was quite the opposite. The faculty seemed bent on the idea that this was its last chance to educate us, and therefore they needed to cram as much information in as possible. Even on the first day, my arms were already aching from the books I needed to carry home.

"Miss Overstreet!" I heard a familiar voice call me as I made my way to the door, and my heart nearly stopped. "Miss Overstreet, will you please meet me in my office?" It was Mrs. Kavanaugh, and it was more a command than question. Huey and I looked at each other with our eyes round with surprise. Being called into Mrs. Kavanaugh's office was serious business. Even big strapping boys heading for military school came out looking like whipped dogs. Two years ago Edgar Combs went into her office and was unable to speak for a day and a half. He claimed he'd been scared mute but wouldn't give any further details.

I tried to look calm as I followed Mrs. Kavanugh. At least a dozen pairs of eyes were boring into me as we passed through the hall, all wondering what I'd done to warrant a visit to her office. I started flipping through my memory like papers in a file cabinet trying to find some sin for which I was now about to seek repentance. All the while I could feel the juices in my stomach start to bubble and my pulse throb in my neck. I just knew I was going to be ill.

As soon as we walked in, Mrs. Kavanaugh shut the door behind me. "Have a seat, Miss Overstreet. I need to discuss something quite serious with you." I took the chair across from her large mahogany desk, thankful to sit since my legs had turned to jelly. No woman had the ability to intimidate like the one in front of me. Mrs. Kavanaugh walked behind her desk and straightened a few papers before sitting down. I glanced around and noticed her black umbrella hanging on a coat rack near the door. *At least it's not within arm's reach,* I thought as Mrs. Kavanaugh adjusted her chair.

"Relax, Miss Overstreet. You're not in here for any punishment," she said, seeing the confusion and fear on my face, or perhaps she'd noticed its total lack of color. "You're actually in here because I need to ask a favor of you." Immediately I heard a sigh escape from within me. The corners of Mrs. Kavanaugh's lips curled up just a bit, and my heart felt as though it was attempting to get back into a normal rhythm.

"Lilly Kate, we have a rather unusual situation presented before us. As I'm sure you are already aware, Beatrice Riddle will be out for the entire semester."

"Yes, ma'am. I know. I thought maybe it was TB."

"No, she's nothing contagious. I can promise you that. However, she would still like to graduate with her class in the spring and is, therefore, in need of a tutor. Do you understand what I am trying to say?"

My mind was buzzing. "Are you asking me to tutor Beatrice until she comes back?"

"Yes, that's precisely what I'm doing. However, it is a bit more complicated. For reasons I do not feel at liberty to discuss, your discretion regarding her condition will be paramount."

"I ... I'm not sure I understand."

"You will. Your job will involve keeping Beatrice up to date with all of her subjects. She'll turn her reports in to you, and you will bring them to me. You'll even take her exams to her house and administer them to her and bring them back to school for grading. I'm sure you see the importance of honesty in this."

"Yes, ma'am. I do, but ... but I'm not sure I'm the right person for this. She has friends who would be more than happy to help. We're not close ..."

"I'm aware of that. However, you are a strong student capable of keeping up with the job. Besides, while Beatrice may need the company of a friend, she is in desperate need of a tutor." Mrs. Kavanaugh paused. I sat looking down at my hands clasped in my lap trying to think it through. I didn't need this. Tutoring Beatrice Riddle was not how I'd planned to spend my senior year. "Lilly Kate, I cannot force you to do this. I will not hold something over your head and make you take on this task. Nonetheless, I would like for you to go and at least visit Beatrice. Talk with her a bit. Then come back and tell me of your decision."

Walking home, my mind whirled. There was not an ounce within me that wanted to tutor Beatrice Riddle, not a fiber in my being. I developed a solid rationale for turning down the job. She had other friends. She had a family that could find someone else. I was already overloaded with school and work. *Get someone else to do it*, my mind said over and over. *She wouldn't want me anyway*. A battle was raging in my heart and mind. I was trying to find an excuse, any excuse that Mrs. Kavanaugh would find plausible. Half a dozen perfectly good reasons popped into mind. Given another hour, I was sure to come up with half a dozen more.

But then, like a lightning bolt in my brain, I remembered something Reverend Searcy had read the previous Sunday from the book of Matthew, "And whosoever shall give to drink unto one of these little ones a cup of cold water only in the name of a disciple, verily I say unto you, he shall in no wise lose his reward." I'd learned as a child that when the Scripture said *verily*, it meant to listen up! Well, I was listening, and I didn't like what I had to hear, but I knew what I should do. I'd been thinking about it from the opposite direction. I'd been thinking about doing a favor for Beatrice, or perhaps it was a favor for Mrs. Kavanaugh. But that was wrong. It wasn't really about either one of them. I should think about it as doing something for Jesus, something that would honor Him. *Why, Lord?* I thought. *Why Beatrice of all people? She hates me, and I'm not too fond of her either. Isn't there someone better suited for this, someone she actually likes?* Uncertainty gripped my chest as my feet moved slowly like heavy blocks. *Why me?*

Then I reached the intersection of Woodford Street and Main. To turn right would lead me home. Home to a quiet place to read and study. Home to a mother who gave words that would uplift and not tear down. Home to all that was comfortable.

I paused, took a deep breath, and took a left. *This is going to be difficult,* I consoled myself as I headed to the Riddle's. *Verily difficult.*

Even after having seen it hundreds of times, the grandeur of the Riddle Mansion was still impressive. The red brick Queen Anne-style home stood back from the road just enough to admire it, but not so much as to take away from its remarkable details. With its combination of clear and stained glass windows, detailed woodwork, and impressive front porch, everything about the home sent a message of prestige and wealth. It was no doubt beautiful. That could not be denied.

I walked through the front gate, unsure of where to go. Whenever I'd delivered baked goods, I'd always gone to the back kitchen door. I decided that was still best since my visit wasn't entirely social. I passed the family's carriage house along the way. Our tiny home on Posey Street was not as big as the building that once held the family's carriage and buggy and now held one of Mr. Ford's Model A automobiles.

When I knocked on the back door, Miz Tessie, the home's chief cook, warmly greeted me. "Chil o' mine! How are you? Come give Miz Tessie a hug." Miz Tessie then proceeded to give me one of her infamous bear hugs that emptied the lungs of all air. "You got some goodies that I didn't know nothin' about?" I shook my head and tried to catch my breath.

"No, ma'am. I'm actually here to see Beatrice." Miz Tessie stepped back, tilted her head, and gave me a quizzical look.

"Miss Beatrice is feelin' poorly," she responded a little more defensively than I would have expected. "What you wantin' to see her for? I don't recall you two bein' the best of friends."

"Mrs. Kavanaugh sent me," I stuttered. "To be her tutor—so she could still graduate with the class." With her bottom lip stuck out, her eyebrows furrowed, and a hand on her hip, Miz Tessie slowly nodded her head.

"I see," she said very seriously. "Let me go get Mrs. Riddle. She tell you what to do." Miz Tessie left the room, and I stood there in the kitchen feeling out of place. I didn't understand her defensiveness, which made the entire situation even more awkward. Whatever disease Beatrice had contracted had evidently put the entire household on edge. It seemed my presence was only stirring the pot.

Mrs. Riddle walked briskly into the kitchen. "Oh, Lilly Kate. I'm glad it's you." She shook my hand more warmly than usual. "Follow me. We'll talk as I take you to Beatrice's room." Mrs. Riddle then led me through a hallway and into the foyer. I found it difficult to listen to her. Instead, I wanted to take in the lavish surroundings. I'd thought the Kavanaugh's house had been impressive, but this was truly a mansion by anyone's standards. Ornate woodwork, lush carpet, and intricate wallpaper were everywhere. A giant grandfather clock stood majestically in the foyer, ticking methodically and echoing throughout the house. I looked down at my dress. What had seemed sensible and appropriate this morning now felt plain and out of place. I fought back the feeling of self-consciousness that threatened to rear its ugly head. This visit wasn't about me.

As we approached the landing at the top of the staircase, I could see a window at the far end that faced Main Street. Beneath it sat a window seat covered in plump, floral covered pillows. *Perfect for reading*, I thought. On both sides of the hall were three doors. Each was closed, but we walked to the last door on the right. Before we entered, Mrs. Riddle paused.

"...so I'm sure you understand the need for discretion," she finished. She'd been speaking the entire time, but I had not truly heard her. I nodded respectfully as though I'd been listening and waited for Mrs. Riddle to open the door. She knocked quietly two times before entering with me following close behind.

As soon as we entered, I spotted Beatrice standing near her window with her back to us, staring outside. She was wearing a long, white cotton gown trimmed with satin ribbons and delicate lace. Her golden hair was down below her shoulders, shiny, clean, and apparently brushed, but not fixed in any way. "Beatrice," her mother announced in a rather stern voice. "Lilly Kate is here. She's going to be your tutor."

Beatrice slowly turned around. Her faced held a blank expression, one very near to sadness I'd never seen on her before, and her eyes reminded me of a fawn I once saw whose mother had just been killed. For the first time ever, a tiny twinge of sympathy for Beatrice pricked my conscience. She looked at me, then glancing down, placed her hands on her bulging belly and looked away. "Try not to stand so near the window, dear," her mother scolded. "Now, I'll leave you two to get to work."

Beatrice and I stood silent for a moment, the space between us filled with awkwardness. I had a hundred questions going through my mind. When? Where? Who? But I had no right to ask any of them. Only one seemed appropriate, "How are you feeling?" I stammered, a hint of embarrassment in my voice.

Beatrice let out a short, scoffing sound. "Well at least *you* didn't ask me how something like this could happen."

"No one told me anything. I promise. They just said you weren't contagious."

"Ha. I'm sure that would make my mother happy to know," Beatrice nearly spat. Anger was now written all over her face. Yes, anger, but there was also loneliness. For the first time, I began to wonder how long it had been since she'd gone outside or talked to her friends. Her ashen skin and circles under her eyes seemed to indicate it had been a good while. I struggled to make conversation.

"We've got a new physical education teacher at school," I offered, trying to fill up the silence. "Her name is Mrs. Rutherford. She's a newlywed and right out of college. She says she's going to teach us some new games. Everybody is already in love with her."

"Why would I care about that?"

"Because you'll be with us again after Christmas. You'll meet her then, and you'll graduate with the rest of us in the spring." I paused and swallowed. "I'm here to help make sure that happens."

Beatrice looked at me and carefully measured her words. "I know why you're here, and I knew you'd be the one to come."

Flustered, I asked, "How did you know?"

For the first time, Beatrice looked me straight in the eyes. "Because you're the one I requested."

———

At home, Momma was fast at work on the sewing machine, her foot pumping in a steady rhythm matched by the work of her slender fingers. Pins were stuck between her lips, and a look of determination crossed her face. I sometimes hated to see how hard she worked, all hunched over the machine with only the light of the oil lamp to see. Yet, she never once complained. Of course she'd worked hard on the farm doing everything from working the fields to managing the books. But those jobs were varied. Sewing was so sedentary and confining. A part of me wanted to be able to free her from the confines of the sewing room, and I held out a thread of hope that someday I'd be able to do just that.

"I'm sorry, Momma!" I gasped as I burst through the door. "I had to help a friend with some studying. I didn't know I would be this late. From now on I'll try to…" I was rushing to the kitchen to start supper.

"Lilly Kate, slow down. It's all right. Mrs. Kavanaugh came and spoke to me after school today. She said you'd be helping Beatrice while she was recuperating. I'm certainly glad to see you two getting along. I didn't know you'd become friends."

Momma spoke lightly and gave no hint of knowing about Beatrice's condition. Mrs. Kavanaugh must have told her what she'd told me, nothing more. I decided not to tell Momma either. It just didn't seem to be my news to share.

"I think I'm going to need to spend at least three afternoons a week there. Will that be okay, or should I ask Mrs. Kavanaugh to find someone else?"

Momma stopped her sewing. With the deftness that comes from experience, she finished a final stitch and snipped the thread. "Do you know what I'm making here?" she asked. Momma then raised her arms and held up one simple, muslin, pullover shirt. It was much too small for me. I looked at her with a puzzled expression. "These are shirts for those children who are in the reservation schools out west. The Women's Aid Society at church is shipping a trunk one week from today. In it there will be all sorts of items those children need, including these shirts." Momma rose from her chair and started folding a pile of other muslin pieces. "I'm doing this as a ministry for those in need. As odd as it may sound, it seems to me Beatrice is a girl in need. Tutoring her is now your ministry. Far be it for me to keep you from it."

For reasons I couldn't understand, I felt a wave of gratitude. I ran to Momma and flung my arms around her. "I love you!"

Momma laughed in surprise. "I...I love you too. What's the meaning of this?" My sudden burst of emotion came as a genuine surprise to us both. I was just grateful—grateful for a happy home and a loving mother. I looked into her eyes and smiled. "I just thought you should know."

Chapter Ten

By the end of the first week of school, I'd visited Beatrice two more times and was itching to see Jimalee. I knew she'd have plenty to say about my tutoring arrangement with Beatrice. The two were polar opposites. Not only did their personalities not attract, they repelled. Jimalee and I met in town to do our weekly Saturday shopping, but before I could utter a single syllable, Jimalee marched up to me and put her hand on my forehead.

"What are you doing?" I demanded.

"I heard about how you're helping that little Miss Priss, and I was just checking your temperature. I know you can't be well." Jimalee was not smiling. Her lips were pressed together while her chin jutted out slightly. Her eyes held the desperate look of someone who had just been betrayed. Her nostrils were even flaring.

"Wait. Listen. It wasn't my idea. Mrs. K asked me…"

"After all that she's done to you!" Jimalee's voice was well above the town noise. "For the last three years she's been nothing but rude. She's called you a hick. She's given you the cold shoulder every chance she's had, and now you're going to spend every spare minute helping her!"

The harsh tone of Jimalee's words stung. In the time we'd known each other I'd never once heard her speak to me with such hostility. She had a temper, that much was certain. Yet, it had never been hurled in my direction, loyalty being one of her most endearing traits. But there was more. I saw in her eyes a bit of jealousy and perhaps even fear. Jimalee had said on more than one occasion how she enjoyed the solitude of my home after the raucousness of her own. Of all people, she also knew how busy I'd become with my responsibilities at school. She wasn't just angry I'd be working with Beatrice; she was scared it would affect our friendship.

"Listen, Jims. This wasn't my idea," I pleaded. "Mrs. K asked me to do it as a special favor. I didn't think I could say no."

"But *why*? What about Eunice and Ruby? You know her little friends would be more than happy to help. Of all people, you know that."

I struggled to explain myself. I wanted desperately to tell Jimalee everything—the baby and Beatrice's request. Yet, I'd been sworn to secrecy. I'd given my word.

"Well," I shrugged. "Maybe she knew her friends would be more interested in talking than working. Maybe she needed someone who actually studied. Did you think of that?" My voice was beginning to rise. I could feel my face begin to heat up. "I'm just trying to do the right thing, and I'm not sure I appreciate your...."

"Is that you, Miss Highandmighty?" I was interrupted. Jimalee and I both turned to see a dusty coverall-clothed boy crossing the street. From the looks of his clothes he'd already been working a few hours, but the dirt didn't hide his broad shoulders or the well-formed muscles. Based on the low whistle that escaped from her lips, Jimalee must have noticed too. The boy was wearing a black work hat, making it difficult to see his face, but within seconds of hearing his voice and seeing his gait as he crossed the street, I knew exactly who it was.

"Why, it's Dink Pruitt!" A smile spread across my face. "I almost didn't recognize you!" Dink spread out his arms and gave me a hug. "What have you been up to?"

"I swanee, Lilly Kate, you sure do look like a lady. You must've been a city girl after all."

"Don't you dare accuse me of such things!" I punched Dink on the shoulder. "I think I still have some Fox Creek dirt under my nails."

"Maybe you do at that," Dink continued. "I'm just in town workin' with a construction crew. I convinced my 'ole man he could do without me till it came time to house tobbacah, so he let me come."

Jimalee cleared her throat.

"Oh, I'm sorry. Dink, this is my friend, Jimalee Jenkins. Jimalee, this is my friend, Dink Pruitt. We went to school together."

My two dear friends quickly locked eyes on each other. Dink stuck out his hand to give a polite shake, but Jimalee seemed a little dumbstruck. When she finally reciprocated, I could have sworn she also curtsied.

"Pleased to meet you, Mr. Pruitt."

Mr. Pruitt? My eyes grew as big as saucers in astonishment. Jimalee's idea of formality usually only went as far as pulling up her bloomers before wading in the creek. She was fond of reminding me that an ounce of pretension was worth a pound of manure. Clearly, she was finding Dink to her liking. For his part, Dink's lazy eye seemed to be twitching, so I could only surmise the feeling was mutual. An idea began to shoot off in my brain. Jimalee wouldn't miss my company so much if there were someone else to take my place. I decided to help foster this friendship.

"Um, excuse me, Dink," I interrupted. "Jimalee lives on a farm just outside of town. Her family raises cows, hogs, tobacco...."

"Anything we can eat or sell," Jimalee finished.

Dink's good eye was still fixed on Jimalee, as was his crooked grin. I may as well have fallen into a crack in the sidewalk. "Well, Miss Jenkins, has your tobaccah turned yella yet?"

In truth, it was one of the least poetic lines ever spoken in the English language, but never could there have been a more fitting recipient. Jimalee's face practically glowed from Dink's attention. I just stood back and watched the show. "As yeller as the sun," she responded. "We'll be cuttin' soon, and I'll have to help my ma feed the field hands."

"Is that right? So, you like to cook too?"

"Oh, nothing fancy." Apparently Jimalee was uncharacteristically overcome with modesty as well as a dose of formality. "Just plain 'ole country cookin.' You know … ham, biscuits, sawmill gravy."

Their conversation continued in this vein while I watched in disbelief. In all the time I'd known both of these people, it had never occurred to me they were so much alike. Jimalee was practically the female version of Dink. That might have explained why we became such good friends so quickly. Never had I thought of pairing the two, but a bit of providence had done the job for me. I realized quickly that my time with Beatrice was not going to be a concern for Jimalee anymore. She now had other, more pressing matters to think about.

———————

At church I was peppered with questions from every direction. Jimalee was giddy over meeting Dink and couldn't get enough information. "How many brothers and sisters does he have? That many? What was he like in school? Was he the type that teased all the girls, or was he a teacher's pet? Was he born with that lazy eye, or did he get kicked by a mule?" On and on the questions went. By the time worship service began I'd recalled even the most mundane facts about Dink and his family, all for the benefit of Jimalee's curiosity. The love bug had not only bitten Jimalee, but it had seemingly sunk its teeth in a little deeper than usual.

After the service was no better. The questions continued, but this time from a number of women in the church. Apparently word had gotten around about my tutoring Beatrice, and questions abounded.

"How is she feeling, dear?" Mrs. Crawford asked with high interest. "Her mother doesn't seem to be able to make it to any of our meetings. Does Beatrice ... does she have a fever?"

"What about her color? Is she pale?" Mrs. Bond interjected. Her daughter Eunice was not twenty feet away, casting frequent glances in our direction. I knew exactly where this was going, and I was feeling more than a little uncomfortable. Anything I said was going to be reported to the ladies of the town within twenty minutes. I was beginning to feel a little like an animal cornered before the kill. I'd heard these women turn gossip into gospel fact on more than one occasion, and now they were trying to use me to get more information for their rumor mill. The fact that they were coming to me was not only unusual, it was a testament to the Riddles and how quiet they'd kept the entire matter. As far as I could tell, everyone still believed Beatrice to be suffering from some rare European disease contracted on her family's trip overseas. Apparently, these two ladies were still skeptical. I didn't want to lie, but speaking at all risked giving too much information.

Mrs. Crawford must have seen the concern on my face and quickly made an attempt to rid herself of any hint of impropriety. "Relax, child, we're just wanting to know so that we can be more specific in our prayers."

"Yes, we want to petition the Lord on Beatrice's behalf," Mrs. Bond added with a sugary smile. At that very moment I was doing some petitioning of my own.

Sweat had started to roll down my back, my leg started twitching, and my knuckles had grown white clenching my Bible. My heart sped up from both anger and nervousness. *How dare they?* I thought. *No wonder the Riddles want no one to know.*

"Hello, ladies." Momma stepped in. *Thank you, Lord!* "Wasn't that a lovely service today?"

"Well, yes. Hello, Ruth. Mrs. Bond and I were just inquiring about Beatrice Riddle. It's so tragic that she can't get out for the next few months, you know. But we hear Lilly Kate is … making visits to … to keep Beatrice up on her studies."

"Yes, I'm quite proud of my daughter for all her hard work."

Mrs. Bond could be held back no more. "I'm sure you are, but we were just wondering, for the sake of prayer of course, how Beatrice was doing physically."

I sent up another little silent prayer and began to respond. I'd planned on saying something vague like, "Oh, she's on the mend," or "She's coming right along." But there was no need. Before I could utter the first syllable, we were interrupted by a rather large flock of geese flying southward. The leader and his followers were honking directions when one of them made a rather generous delivery that landed squarely atop Mrs. Crawford's hat. I'll never know what the little fellow had eaten, but by the looks of Mrs. Crawford's head, he was feeling much better now.

Mrs. Bond was momentarily struck dumb in disbelief, while Mrs. Crawford gasped and *eeked* in utter disgust. She quickly removed her hat, only to find that some of the poor goose's gift had also gone through the weaving of the material, leaving her even more outraged.

"This is … oh, for heaven's sake! Well, I never in all my life! Duce! Duce! Where is that husband of mine? Duce!"

Her face was past red and was beginning to turn plum colored. A group of young boys who had been throwing rocks in the distance had witnessed the entire scene. A few of them were now rolling on the ground holding their stomachs while the others were hooting and pointing. All were clearly enjoying themselves.

Mrs. Bond eventually regained her senses and quickly ushered her friend back inside the church, away from the glaring eyes and pointing fingers. Momma swiftly grabbed my elbow, giving me the signal to start walking away. The two of us held our composure as we crossed the road, but no sooner had we walked through the door than Momma and I bent over in laughter. For the next fifteen minutes, had anyone looked into our little window, they would have seen two women rolling on the floor and holding their sides, tears coming from their eyes.

Chapter Eleven

During the next three weeks, Beatrice and I continued to meet. What I thought would be a distraction to my studies was turning out to be an advantage. I discovered what every teacher before me already knew—when you must teach someone, you learn it better yourself. Because of the reviews I had to give to Beatrice, I was not falling behind in my work. In fact, I was keeping up nicely. Even math was becoming a little easier because I had to explain it to Beatrice. For her part, Beatrice was a fast learner. Never once did I hear her complain about the work, even as report deadlines and testing dates began to draw near. When I made reference to her good attitude about her mounting studies, she quipped, "What else am I suppose to do to pass the time?"

Beatrice never mentioned the baby. I could see her belly slowly swelling, and my head filled with questions, but I didn't dare ask. The Riddles had allowed me to look into a small window of their lives. That was more than I'd ever expected. Asking Beatrice to open the front door was out of the question.

At school everyone seemed to have fallen into a routine. While Beatrice's absence had created a buzz at first, she'd quickly become something of an afterthought. No one seemed to miss her haughty looks or snide remarks. Not even Ruby and Eunice seemed overly concerned. This lack of concern began to make me feel even sorrier for Beatrice. Not only was she going through her own little nightmare, but the entire school seemed to have lost interest. In a turn of events that no one could have ever predicted, I was growing more and more sympathetic toward Beatrice Riddle.

It was sometime near the end of the first month of our tutoring sessions when Beatrice slammed down her books and shouted, "I think I'm going to go crazy in this room!"

To which I glibly added, "Nope. Too late. You've already *gone* crazy."

"Oh, come on, Lilly Kate. It's not funny. You get to walk all around town and see people every day while I'm stuck in here like … like some prisoner or some caged animal. The only time I get out of this house is at night when I can take a walk out back. And you're no help at all!"

"Me? What have I done?"

"Nothing. Absolutely nothing. And that's just the problem. You come in here and teach me my lessons just like you're Mrs. K herself, but you never talk about anybody else or what's going on at school. Of course, I knew you wouldn't gossip. That's why I asked for you, but you could talk to me, at least a little!"

Once again my heart softened for Beatrice, and I grew perturbed with myself. While I'd been busy trying to help with her homework, I'd ignored her greatest need—friendship. "Okay," I said closing my books and laying them aside. "What would you like to know?"

"Anything. Everything. I don't care. Just tell me what's going on in school. I feel as though I'm starving."

"Well, Mrs. Rutherford has taught the girls a new game. It's called basketball. Sometimes there are six or seven players, but we play with five each. I could show you how it's done."

"Please do. Anything sounds interesting to me."

I stood up and started bouncing an imaginary ball. "This is called dribbling. Any time you move with the ball, you have to be dribbling. Mrs. Rutherford said that the girls' rules say you're only suppose to dribble three times before passing, but since she learned the game from a man, she's teaching us the boys' rules.

"There's a difference?" Beatrice asked with indignation.

"Apparently, some people don't want the girls to be too aggressive." Beatrice rolled her eyes and a nodded in sympathetic agreement. "Anyway," I continued, "I was terrible at first, but then it got much easier. You dribble the ball down the court, and you throw it to a girl near a basket, or goal. She's supposed to put it in for two points. Our goal is eight feet high. Mrs. Rutherford said it's supposed to be ten, but she lowered it because we're learning. When the ball goes into the basket, you score."

"That sounds easy. What's so exciting about that?"

"Oh, it isn't easy at all. You see, while I'm dribbling, all five of the other team members are wanting to stop me from scoring, either by taking away the ball or by guarding me."

"Guarding you?"

"Here, stand up and let me show you."

For the next fifteen minutes Beatrice and I played an imaginary game of round ball in her room. I showed her how to guard and informed her that, as girls, we were supposed to keep our hands straight up and not break the vertical plane. But again, thanks to Mrs. Rutherford's generosity and lack of knowledge of all the girls' rules, we were granted a little levity. Beatrice practiced dribbling with one hand as she moved. Even with a protruding belly, I couldn't help but notice she seemed to have an athletic bent about her.

"Hey, what do you do when the ball goes in the basket?"

"Mrs. Rutherford told us when the game was first invented that people had to climb up a ladder and go get the ball. Now, people just cut a hole in the basket."

"Why didn't they do that to begin with?"

"Beats me. Maybe the fellow who invented the game liked climbing up on ladders."

———————————

Before the next time I went to visit Beatrice, I asked Mrs. Rutherford if I could borrow a ball for practice. She seemed thrilled at the idea that some of her teaching was taking hold and generously gave me an extra peach basket as well. I knew if I was seen walking down Main Street toward the Riddles' with a peach basket and a ball more than a few eyebrows would be raised. In an effort to avoid uncomfortable questions, I covered the basket with cloth napkins and worked at looking nonchalant. As I made my way down Main Street, shoppers and businessmen alike grinned and nodded politely.

"Got something good in there, young lady?" asked Mr. Wells as he stood outside his barbershop puffing on his pipe.

"I certainly hope so," I replied as I walked passed quickly, in hopes he would not want a peek.

But no sooner had I passed Mr. Wells than out from the newspaper office stepped Mrs. Crawford and Mrs. Bond. "Well, helloooo, Miss Overstreet. My, you must be taking something down to the Riddles' house. I'm sure it's delicious. What is it this time? Cookies? One of your scrumptious chocolate cakes?"

"Oh, just a little something I threw together."

Mrs. Bond didn't seem to be taking my hint. "Don't be modest. What is it dear?"

It's a ball that I'm going to bounce upside your head, you nosey twit, I raged in my head. But no. That wouldn't do. I decided to take a more graceful route. "To tell you the truth, it's something new. It may not amount to anything, but if it does, I'll let you know." With that, I walked on.

Beatrice and I finished two history lessons, a geography assignment, and no fewer than ten algebraic equations before I had a chance to surprise her with the basketball, but her expression was worth the wait.

"Wow! How'd you get it here without everyone seeing?"

"I put it in this and covered it with napkins," I said holding up the peach basket. "Everyone in town thinks this is your dinner."

Beatrice laughed. "I'm beginning to look as though I did eat that ball for dinner."

Her candor surprised me, but not totally. Slowly, I was seeing a side of Beatrice I'd never known existed. And to be honest, I liked what I saw. No longer was she just the rich girl with store-bought clothes and a haughty air. As odd as the thought would have been three months ago, Beatrice was now a friend.

"Okay, what do you say we hang up the basket on the door frame? You practice dribbling, and I'll try guarding you." I was starting to sound like Mrs. Rutherford.

Beatrice began dribbling before I could even take a defensive stance. Considering this was the first time with a real ball, she was doing remarkably well. I was thankful her room was so spacious. I was struggling to keep up with her. However, her first shot was completely off. Not only did she hit the door facing, but she knocked a gold-framed picture off the wall as well. Both of us were standing in the middle of the room laughing when Mrs. Riddle burst through the door. "What is going on in here?"

I sobered up immediately, but Beatrice seemed undaunted. "Oh, Mother. We were just playing a game Mrs. Rutherford has been teaching the girls at school.

Apparently, I'm not any good at it yet, as you can tell from the picture in the floor."

The glass in the picture frame was broken loose, but not shattered. I was still fearful of being thrown out of the house never to return again, but Beatrice behaved as though this sort of thing happened every day. "We're finished with all the other work," Beatrice said, her eyes pleading. "I want to be able to do this when I return."

The hard lines in Mrs. Riddle's forehead began to soften, and the edges of her mouth started to turn slightly upward. For the first time I began to think about how hard this ordeal was for her too. Her baby was having a baby, and she was trying to protect Beatrice in the only way she knew how. By taking away her life for a few months, she was trying to save her life for the future, for her return. She'd made some tough decisions recently and put her own life on hold, but at that moment, what she saw in the middle of the room was her daughter, smiling and happy.

"Why don't you two take that ball to the basement and practice down there? It may be dark, but you won't be knocking any pictures off the wall or tripping over any furniture."

I'd never been in a basement before, but I'd seen my fair share of cellars, and the two seemed remarkably similar. Both were damp, dark, and gave me the creeps. A part of me would have rather gone back upstairs and done more homework, but Beatrice would have none of that. She was determined.

"Let's take down that rope and hang the basket on the nail," she suggested. The job naturally fell to me, so I climbed up on some boxes and made the switch. "We should've cut a hole in the basket so it will fall through when we score," she continued.

"Aren't you being a little optimistic for someone who's never played this game?" I teased.

"Nope. I'm just that good," she retorted. And after just thirty minutes of play, I had to agree with her.

Chapter Twelve

By mid-November Jimalee and Dink were officially courting. Once the tobacco was housed, they began meeting every Saturday. At first I'd go with them, but after a few weeks, I knew I was out of place and stayed out of the way thereafter. Jimalee's salty wit seemed a perfect balance for Dink's good 'ole boy nature, and I couldn't help but believe my two friends were going to be seeing a great deal of one another for a long time to come. The only thing left to do was to watch and wait.

And it was the waiting that was killing me. Sometime during the week, Jimalee would usually come over for a visit under the pretense of helping me edit stories for the *Tiger Beat*. Editing, of course, was not her priority. As soon as Momma was busy working and the whir of the sewing machine could drown out our voices, Jimalee began to give me the latest edition of all news pertaining to Dink Pruitt.

"...and then he said to me, 'Jimalee, you've got eyes the same color green as Old Man Lewis's pond.' Now ain't that romantic? It sounds like somethin' right out of Song of Solomon!"

I'd always smile and say, "That Dink always did have a way with words."

"I'll say! When he's talkin' to me I feel just like a little girl on Christmas mornin.' My stomach starts to flutter, my spine starts to tingle, and...and...I hate to admit this, but...well, I sometimes start to sweat just like an old workhorse!"

"Golly, Jims! Have you started to snort when he comes around too?" I teased.

"Oh, stop. You know what I mean," Jimalee retorted. Then she paused and looked at me thoughtfully. "Or do you?"

"Or do I what?"

"You've never been sweet on anybody, have you?" It was an honest enough assessment, but one I wasn't expecting. For reasons I couldn't quite pinpoint, it made me feel slightly irritated.

"Why? Does it matter?"

"You bet it matters! You're fixin' to graduate high school. Aren't you worried about finding yourself a husband?"

"It's never crossed my mind," I said emphatically. "In case you haven't noticed, I've been a little busy." There was a defensive tone in my voice I couldn't quite explain. The topic of marriage was making me uncomfortable.

"Oh, forgive me," Jimalee mocked. "Yes, you've been incredibly busy … with your nose stuck in a book! You better raise your head up and start thinking about what you're going to do after graduation. This town is small, and your choices are sorely limited. I seriously doubt you'll wanna be stuck baking cakes and pies for the rest of your life."

She was right, of course. What was I going to do after graduation? Up to this point, a high school diploma was my ultimate goal. My life and ambitions had revolved around Posey Street and Kavanaugh High. After that, what?

Jimalee's pointed question rattled around in my head so much it started to hurt. Huey wasn't helping my predicament either. Lately he'd seemed more quiet and withdrawn, as though he was carrying some invisible burden.

I wanted desperately to talk with him; he'd always been able to shed light on a situation, but what with the school newspaper, homework, and tutoring Beatrice, I never had the chance. I tried to put it to the back of my mind, to think later, much later.

Beatrice and I continued to practice basketball in the basement until she became so large she would simply stand and shoot while I rebounded. She was apparently spending time in the basement without me because I noticed she was getting quite good.

"You'd better stop that or everyone will know you've been getting secret lessons," I joked. Beatrice seemed in low spirits. *She's uncomfortable,* I thought. *Probably needs to rest.*

"Oh, of course," Beatrice responded, words dripping with sarcasm. "I'm supposed to be weak and frail. We can't have anyone knowing I had enough energy to play a game."

"I'm so sorry! I didn't mean... I was joking... That's not what..."

Beatrice looked at me seriously. "You've never once asked." It was a statement of fact, not a question. "You've never asked me anything about how all this happened. Why not? Most people would."

"I guess I didn't think it was any of my business."

"Well, of course, it isn't. But that doesn't seem to stop most people in this town from asking all kinds of questions about any number of things!"

I stood silent. Beatrice waddled over to the steps and slowly guided herself down and sat on a wooden tread. She stretched her legs outward, and I noticed her bare, swollen ankles. Unsure of what to do, I walked over and sat next to her.

"It's a boy," Beatrice offered.

"What?" I asked, perplexed.

"It's a boy. I can't say how I know, I just do. It *feels* like a boy."

Not ever having had children, I didn't understand how a woman could know this about her unborn child, but Beatrice said it with certainty and conviction. She seemed to want me to know. She was opening that door of her life I'd refused to knock upon. Before I could ask anything else, Beatrice continued to pour herself out to me.

"You're probably wondering how this all happened," she said with a touch of hurt in her voice. "I can tell you I never, *ever* intended for something like this to happen to me. I'm not promiscuous. Honest, I'm not!"

"Beatrice, you don't have to explain yourself to me. What's done is done. I don't need to know details."

"No, but I want you to know! I want you to hear the truth," Beatrice implored. I sat, stunned, but listening. "It all started a little more than two years ago. My father was hosting another one of his parties for employees. There was nothing unusual about that, of course, until he introduced us to one of his new employees he'd brought in from Lynchburg, Tennessee, Tom Hanley. As soon as I saw him I felt a jolt go through me. He had dark hair, deep black eyes, and a square jaw. Tom later told me his grandmother was a full-blooded Cherokee, and even now I believe him. When he looked at me, I thought I'd melt into a puddle right there.

"Father grew to love Tom. He'd always hoped my brother Paul would go into business with him, but when Paul made it clear he intended to stay in Louisville and practice law, Father was crushed. Tom became like an adopted son. Father said he had a mind and nose for the business, which is no small compliment coming from J.T. Riddle! Father began to have him over for supper about once a week. For the first year or so that I knew him, we would sit at the table and have small talk like everyone else, but that lightning-bolt feeling remained. With a little investigation, I discovered he was fourteen years older than me, twenty-nine. I'm sure he knew my age too, but it seemed insignificant at the time.

"Eventually, Tom and I began to take walks together after dinner. My heart would race the entire time, but he was very courteous, always walking on the outside of the sidewalk, never so much as a hint of impropriety. But by the time my junior year began, Tom had begun to tell me he thought I was beautiful. He'd sometimes put his hand on my back when no one was looking or hold my hand under the table."

Beatrice paused and stared coldly at the basement ceiling. Her jaw was becoming tight, and I could see the rim of her eyes growing red. When she continued her voice was pained but determined.

"We began to steal away to have some privacy. It's not difficult when you're home is surrounded by a wooded area. I think Mother and Father suspected something but were either afraid to admit it, or perhaps they even liked it a bit. After all, they both adored Tom and treated him as a member of the family.

"But one day last March, things got out of control. It was unusually warm, and Tom came by after school. He was supposedly on an errand for my father. Mother was at one of her club meetings, and Tessie had the day off. I invited him in, even though I knew I shouldn't. Oh, how I wish I hadn't. But I did! If only I hadn't … if only I'd just talked with him on the front porch." Beatrice's voice cracked, but she resolved to continue.

"Tom came right in. With little more than a hello, he began to kiss me. It wasn't our first kiss, but Tom seemed almost … almost hungry, ravenous even. I'd be lying if I said I didn't like it. I did. It felt wonderful to be so wanted. But then his hands began to touch me in places he'd never touched me before. I was startled, but I didn't want to stop…not really, not yet anyway. But, within a few minutes, I knew things were going too far." Beatrice started choking on her tears. "I begged him to stop, but he just kept saying, 'You know very well what I'm doing. You've been asking for this for a long time.' I tried pushing away, really I did, but he was just too strong!"

Beatrice laid her head in my lap, sobbing. "There's no need to go further," I told her. "No need to rehash the details."

"I told him no. I told him to stop, but he wouldn't!" Beatrice wailed. I patted her hair. I was angry enough to spit nails but unsure of what to do. "I tried to yell for help, but he smothered my mouth with his hand and threatened to hit me if I did it again."

"Didn't you tell someone, Beatrice? Did you not tell your mother and father?" I implored.

"I was too ashamed! I felt like it was my fault. Tom kept saying I'd asked for it, and I thought maybe he was right. Maybe I'd led him to believe it was okay."

"No! It wasn't! You told him to stop!"

"I know. I know that now. But…I wasn't thinking. I just wanted to feel clean. When my parents came home, I was in the bathtub. I told them I didn't feel well, and they left me alone. The next morning, I decided I just wanted to forget it ever happened. I wasn't sure anyone would even believe me after the way I'd been running off with him. I realize it doesn't make sense, but I couldn't think clearly. I just wanted to wipe it all away. I just wanted to pretend it never happened."

The two of us sat there in silence. I was humbled by Beatrice's confidence and ashamed of my previous assumptions. Oh, how unfair! Not only was Beatrice's innocence stolen from her, but she was also suffering the consequences.

"During the next few weeks I just tried to behave as though nothing happened. It was always there, of course, nagging at me like a pain in the chest, but I kept thinking it would go away. Time is supposed to heal all wounds, right? I still hadn't told anyone. Then after a month, I knew something was wrong. 'You're just late,' I told myself. I was in complete denial. Aside from that, we were getting ready to sail to Europe and everyone was so ... so happy and excited. Who was I to ruin everyone's trip?"

"On the boat, I became very sick. Mother, of course, assumed I had seasickness. I'd hoped she was right. But when I continued being sick after we arrived in London, she began to suspect something more and started asking questions."

I was beginning to feel like a snoop. I didn't need to hear all of this. "Beatrice, really, you don't have to tell me. It's okay."

"No! I must tell you. Despite what I may look like right now, I need to tell someone. I need to get it out, and since you're my closest friend, it should be you." Beatrice sniffled. "Once Mother found out, she was livid. She accused me of being a tramp and of disgracing the family. You've never seen such anger. Father was no better, but he didn't yell. Instead, he just went into the study and didn't come out for two days. The only thing we heard out of him was a few glasses crashing against the wall.

"I tried to tell them what happened, but they didn't seem to believe me, not at first. Eventually, Father wrote to some people he knew in Lynchburg and found out more about Tom. As it turns out, he's been married before. All anybody knows is that one day she was at home and the next day she had packed her things and left without so much as a note." Beatrice smiled a twisted, sardonic smile. "I think I know what happened, don't you?"

My heart was pounding and my stomach felt queasy.

I reached out and put my arms around Beatrice and held her. "I'm so sorry. So, so sorry." It was all I could say, all I knew to say. It was all that could be said.

"At first, Momma was going to have me shipped off somewhere, but I didn't want that. I wanted to finish school, so after it became clear what had happened, they felt sorry enough for me to stay here and be tutored because I do want to graduate."

Beatrice laid her head in my lap. She was emotionally spent. I stroked her hair as a mother does a child and fought back the tears of my own. "I promise, Beatrice. I promise to do everything I can to see you graduate on time. We won't let Tom Hanley steal that away from you too."

Chapter Thirteen

"Lilly Kate! Lilly Kate! Look! It finally arrived!" Huey was running up the school sidewalk to catch up with me before school began. He was waving an envelope in the air as though it was a flag on the Fourth of July.

"Silly, what is it?" I asked with a smile, happy to see my friend once again showing some enthusiasm.

"It's my acceptance letter to Georgetown College! See?" Huey tore open the letter again for what looked to be no less than the hundredth time to show me. "It says right there I've been accepted into next year's freshman class."

Huey's face was nearly as bright as the morning sun. There was no mistaking the joy. "What are you planning to study, Huey? I don't think they give out degrees for class clown," I teased.

"That's just what I've been wanting to discuss with you, but you've been so busy that I haven't had the chance."

"We're a little early. Tell me now," I said with a vague remembrance of having brushed Huey off a few weeks earlier. "I'm all ears."

Huey began. "Well, you know how I've been a little...distracted lately? It's because I've had a lot on my mind. I was wrestling with some things, and I finally made a decision." Huey paused and looked at me seriously while fingering the spine of his book. "This may come as a shock to you, but I'm going to be a minister!"

My mouth dropped open so far that if there had been flies around, one would have surely made its way inside.

I stood shaking my head, and Huey continued to look at me with a goofy grin and hopeful eyes.

"Huey Hughes, I had no idea! That's wonderful! It's fantastic!" I dropped my books and gave him a hug. "When did all this happen?"

"I started to feel the call back during last summer's tent revival out at Sand Springs. I went with my cousin Carl, hoping to see some pretty girls and maybe eat some good watermelon, but I guess God had other plans." Huey was still smiling from ear to ear and looking a little pink in the cheeks, as though he'd just been caught in the middle of another one of his infamous pranks.

"This is wonderful!" I practically yelled. "You're going to be minister, a *college-trained* minister at that!

"Hey, that's something else I wanted to tell you." Huey grew excited again. "Why don't you try going to college? Your grades are even better than mine."

"Oh, Huey, I'd love to, but you know we don't have the money. I was fortunate to even be able to come this far." We started walking into the school just before the bell rang.

"Yeah," Huey continued, "but you can apply for one of their scholarships, like me. You might be able to get your costs paid. Come on, Lilly Kate. You might as well give it a try."

I felt a little pitter-patter in my chest. "Do you really think I could get a scholarship?" I asked.

"Why not? You're the smartest girl I know." There was a genuine smile on his face and a gentle pleading in his eyes.

Mrs. Kavanaugh rang the bell, and everyone hustled to find a seat. Mrs. Kavanaugh started reading the daily Scripture verse, and my eyes were glued upon her. However, my mind was miles away in a town I'd never once visited—it was in Georgetown to be exact.

As I sat poking at my chicken and dumplings, my mind still reeled with thoughts of college. In a span of twelve hours, I'd gone from assuming it was out of the question to dreaming it would happen. But Momma had never mentioned even the remotest possibility of going to college or even normal school where teachers are trained. Perhaps, like me, she'd always thought of it as implausible, too unreal. Or, maybe she didn't want me to go. Maybe she needed me to help take in more sewing next year. Then again, with Poppa gone, she'd be all alone. I couldn't bear the thought of Momma being lonely, but I doubted she'd ever admit to it.

"Lilly Kate, stop picking at your food," Momma commanded in a tone that made it clear she was annoyed. "I fixed this supper because I knew you liked it, and now you've hardly eaten a thing."

"I'm sorry, Momma. I've just got a lot on my mind."

"Schoolwork giving you trouble? Are there some tests coming up?

"That's not it exactly."

"Well, then what is it that's got you in such a state you won't eat your mother's dumplings?"

"I was thinking about next year, after I graduate. I was thinking maybe I'd help you. I could take in more sewing, and we'd bring in more money."

Momma gave me a hard, serious look. "You may be my daughter, and it pains me to say this, but I think we'd both be better off if you stayed away from a needle and thread. It takes every bit of your sewing abilities just to get a button on straight. The last thing I need is to take time out of the day to correct your mistakes." Although her voice carried with it a slightly mocking tone, there was a great deal of truth in what she said. "I think you'd better make other plans, young lady."

Neither of us said anything for a little while, both lost in thought. It was Momma who finally broke the silence. "Have you thought about teaching? You're good with the children at church, and you seem to enjoy tutoring Beatrice. Maybe you should be a teacher."

I did enjoy the thought of running my own school like Fox Creek. My little stint tutoring Beatrice had helped me see how much I enjoyed teaching. I could probably take the teacher's exam and get appointed to a one-room rural school very quickly. I could board with a family and come back to town from time to time. It was a perfectly respectable position, as long as I was unmarried. Yes, it was an idea, one that had real merit. Yet, Huey's news that morning still nagged at me in such a way I knew I'd have to address it.

"Momma, I lied," I finally said.

"Whatever do you mean, child?" Momma's voice rose.

"I never actually ever thought I'd like to help you take in sewing," I admitted.

"Well, that's a relief!" Momma jibed.

"Actually, I had something else in mind—something Huey said today has got me thinking. I know it's a long shot, but I'd like to try. I'm not sure how you feel about it."

"Spit it out, Lilly Kate. You're talking like a magpie."

I breathed in deeply and shut my eyes for a moment. "I want to go to college," I blurted quickly so I wouldn't lose my nerve. When I opened my eyes Momma was still sitting in her chair looking at me as calmly as if I'd just told her it had stopped raining.

"Did you hear me?" I asked. "I said I think I'd like to go to college."

"Yes, daughter, I heard you," Momma said with a grin. "I may be getting older, but I'm not hard of hearing yet."

She sat for a moment with a smirk on her face as though she held the punch line to a joke or was privy to a juicy secret. Finally, she spoke again. "That's an awfully big step for a girl from Fox Creek. You're the first in the family to graduate from high school, let alone college."

My chin dropped to my chest. She was right. I may have been wishing for too much. A twinge of shame began to creep into my head. I was being vain and selfish to think a girl like me could go to college. It just wasn't done.

"I was wondering when you were going to bring this up," Momma finally spoke again with a hint of resignation in her voice.

My head popped up and my eyebrows furrowed as I tried to figure her out. This was certainly not the way I'd anticipated this conversation going. Momma rose to pour herself a cup of coffee. "Did you not realize I'm working on a dress for Huey's mother?"

I didn't.

"She came over for a fitting just this morning, and I heard all about Huey's news," Momma paused, allowing me to take it in. "She told me Huey was going to suggest you apply." I looked straight at her. Momma was smiling broadly. "I told her I thought you might like to give it a try."

"But what about you?" I asked. "What will you do?"

"Do you think I'm some helpless person who can't manage without you?"

"No," I stuttered. "I just didn't know what you thought. I mean, nobody in the family has ever…"

"Listen to me and hear me clearly," Momma interrupted. "I know I've lived in this county all my life. I know I've never been out of this state. But I can read the papers. I can see changes happening all around us. The day is coming when women will have more options. Someday,

I think we'll even have the right to vote. And when that day comes, I want my daughter to be ready, and schooling is the key."

"You mean you don't mind if I go?"

"Of course I mind! You're my baby. I'd have you stay here forever if I could, but I know that's not best. That's not who you are."

"So, it's okay if I apply?"

"Certainly. You've worked hard in school, and you've got the highest marks in your class. Why can't my daughter go to college? Of course, I can't afford to pay your way, but Mrs. Hughes says they sometimes give scholarships. If you can get one, I'd be proud to ... Lilly, where are you going?"

"I'll help with the dishes later!" I called over my shoulder on the way to the bedroom. "I've got to go write a letter!"

The first of December came and brought with it cold, gusty wind with the occasional snow flurry. The shops along Main Street had begun to decorate their windows with greenery and bows, and Ballard's had already put a variety of Christmas cards on display, eight choices no less. My heart warmed a little at the thought of the coming holidays, but my nose and cheeks stung from the cold air. On the way to the Riddles,' my mind rolled over all the possible gifts I could give Momma—a new tortoise-shell hair comb, a new hat, some needles and buttons, or powder and perfume. I knew she'd be pleased with any of those things, but I also knew she'd ask me for a short wish list of my own. She'd done so since Poppa died, stressing that there was no sense in purchasing something I didn't need or wouldn't use.

And this year's list was short, very short. However, Momma could do nothing about it. More than anything I'd decided I wanted to go to college. Other than a few teachers at school, I'd never actually met anyone who'd been. As far as I knew, I was the only girl in the class even interested. Most had plans to get married. I didn't really know much about college at all, but of what I did know, I liked. Thoughts of my own marriage or job options made my palms sweat. Something in me wanted more, much, much more. Continuing school somehow felt right. What I wanted for Christmas was an acceptance letter and a scholarship.

I was still feeling optimistic when I arrived at the Riddles' and began working with Beatrice on her lessons. By now she had officially reached the miserably uncomfortable stage and had grown a bit more pensive. I thought talk of Christmas might cheer her up.

"Hey, the stores downtown are beginning to decorate," I said with a little extra enthusiasm. "Hanks' Mercantile has already put sleigh bells on the door, and Ballard's has Christmas cards. One even shows a picture of St. Nicolas being stuck in a chimney."

"I'm not looking forward to Christmas," Beatrice said flatly. I sat perplexed and a little taken aback. "Why do you look so surprised?" Beatrice asked. "Surely you can see what I have to look forward to." She pointed at her protruding belly and then stared coldly out the window.

Yes, I'd been thoughtless, terribly thoughtless. The baby was due before Christmas, a baby I knew she wouldn't be keeping. From this year forward, Christmas would forever be a reminder of the child she bore but had to give away. The holiday would not only be a marker of the baby's birth, but her mantle would always be absent one little stocking. This year the wound to Beatrice's soul would be fresh, and while the passing of time might make future holidays easier, the scar would remain.

"Beatrice, I don't mean to be forward," I asked seriously, "but what's going to happen when the baby comes?"

Beatrice's eyes grew watery, and she took a deep breath. "Father has already contacted a doctor in Frankfort. I think his name is Dr. Pollard. As soon as the baby starts to come, Poppa's going to drive to get him, and Miz Tessie will take care of me until he arrives. After that, Dr. Pollard is going to take the baby to the state orphanage in Frankfort, and..." Beatrice voice broke, "and we're all suppose to act like this never happened."

I walked over to Beatrice, knelt next to her chair, and began stroking her back. "It's all so unfair. So, so unfair," I said. "You're the one suffering because of 'ole Tom Hanley. I promise, if I ever meet that guy I'll... I'll... I'll kick him right where the sun doesn't shine!"

My vehemence surprised even me. I'd not realized how protective I'd grown of Beatrice, but I felt partially responsible for her somehow. My candor must have caught Beatrice by surprise because she coughed out a laugh and turned her head toward me. "Do you mean that?" she asked.

"Of course I do!" I retorted. "Tom Hanley is a skunk. Don't you worry. He'll get what's coming to him someday," I added with a little more conviction than I felt.

"You'd have to beat Father to him," Beatrice said, smiling. "He's never been much of shot with a gun, but I have a feeling he'd like to use Tom for target practice." The two of us laughed at the mental image of J.T. Riddle chasing Tom Hanley down the road with a rifle.

"Lilly Kate," Beatrice said looking at me seriously. "I want you to be here when the baby's born."

A wave of surprise and reluctance swept over me, but I

knew I had to honor her request. "Certainly, Beatrice. I'll do whatever you want."

"You probably think I'm silly, but I just think it will be better if you're here."

"I'd be honored," I said.

"Well, don't feel too honored," Beatrice cautioned with a grin. "I haven't started yelling at anybody yet."

Chapter Fourteen

A week later I came home from school, happy to enter the warm glow of the house. I'd just received my marks for two tests and a report from the week before and was pleased with the results. Anxious to show Momma, I marched through the door expecting to see her working at the sewing machine. Instead, I found her pacing nervously back and forth in the parlor with Taft sitting at the hearth cleaning himself.

"What's wrong?" I begged.

"It's here," Momma said as she handed me an envelope. "It arrived earlier today, and it was everything I could do to wait until you got home."

There was no mistaking the return address. Georgetown, Kentucky. My hands began shaking as I took the envelope and quickly opened it. I gulped down a tremendous knot in my throat and began to read.

> December 10, 1911
> Dear Miss Overstreet:
> We appreciate your interest in Georgetown College. As you know, we are a school committed to excellence in both academics and Christian character. We would be happy to receive you as a student in the fall of 1912. However, at this time, we will not be able to grant you a scholarship. While your marks are exemplary, we have reserved the remaining funds for students who will be answering the call to the ministry. As this is the highest of all callings, we are certain you will understand.
> Please inform us of your future intentions.
>
> Respectfully yours,
> Dr. Clarence Wright

My heart broke. Without a scholarship, I knew I could never attend. Momma read the look on my face and knew immediately I wasn't pleased.

"Don't tell me you weren't accepted!" Momma said defensively. "You've got the best grades in your class!"

"No." I fought back the tears. "They said I was accepted. But there isn't any money for a scholarship."

Momma took the letter from my hands and quickly read it. I walked into the bedroom in an effort to maintain my composure. Everything about my going to college had seemed to be right. Deep down, I felt I would get a scholarship. Now the denial was a huge sting. It was as though I'd been walking down a well-lit path, only to come upon an insurmountable wall. I knew I couldn't handle any questions. Disappointment pulsated through my body along with a healthy dose of shame. Who was I to think I could go to college on a scholarship?

Mindlessly, I thumbed through my dictionary, the one that had been a gift upon graduation from Fox Creek. *The cream will rise to the top*, Miss Daphne had written. At the moment, I certainly didn't feel like cream, and if I ever was, I'd apparently curdled.

Sensing something was wrong, Taft jumped into my lap and started rubbing his head against my chest. Momma stepped in and leaned against the doorframe. "I'm sorry, honey. I wish there was something more I could do. If we had the money you know I'd send you in a heartbeat."

Hearing her guilt made me ache all over. "I know," I said choking. "It's okay. I'll just take the teacher examination after graduation." I was trying to convince both of us. "I'm sure I can find a teaching job."

Momma came and sat beside me on the bed and exhaled a long sigh. "You know how much I value the men in the ministry. The Lord only knows where I'd be without the church and the pastor." Momma mused, more to herself than to me. "But it seems to me a well-trained teacher is a type of minister too." She looked at me and placed my head on her shoulder. "Do you remember what your daddy used to say? He'd say, 'The young can bend.' Sometimes it wasn't just about the trees or crops. He was talking about people too."

"I know. It's just that this felt so right. I thought going to college was what I was supposed to do."

"There are other colleges."

"Yes, but … maybe this was God's way of telling me no. Maybe I just built it up in my own head when it wasn't his will at all."

"Perhaps. But maybe God's just shutting *this* door so you'll go through a door of his choosing."

Momma and I sat on the bed in silence as the sky grew darker, both of us lost in thought. Just as the sun was about to dip below the horizon, we heard a wagon swiftly approach our door. Momma and I exchanged worried looks as rushed to open it before a knock could even be heard.

"Mr. Dedman! Whatever is the matter?"

It was Miz Tessie's husband, Digger Dedman. He was as tall and lanky as she was rotund, but his loyalty to the Riddles was just as firm. "S'cuse me, Mrs. Overstreet, but Miss Beatrice sent me to fetch Miss Lilly Kate."

"I'm right here!" I called from the bedroom as I reached for my coat. "Momma, I might be gone a little while." I'd never told her about Beatrice's condition. I was afraid she would seriously question my leaving now.

"Lilly," Momma said, grabbing my arm. I was heading to the door, but she forced me to turn and look her in the eye. "I understand. Do you hear me? I understand." There was no mistaking her meaning. All I could do was nod and rush out to the waiting wagon.

The pounding of the horses' hooves seemed to match

the pounding in my heart. I'd helped Poppa with the delivery of dozens of farm animals, each making me nervous. Beatrice's impending delivery had me downright terrified. One thing was certain, I was never meant to be a midwife.

As we approached the house, the lights were on. To the casual observer, everything looked as natural as a family about to sit and eat supper together. I knew better, of course, and I noticed Mr. Riddle's car was not in the carriage house. Mr. Dedman pulled around back, and Mrs. Riddle met me at the door.

"Oh, thank goodness, you're here! Beatrice has been asking for you. This may help her to relax a bit. This baby seems to be coming quickly." Mrs. Riddle breathed with both relief and anxiety. By any stretch, I was not a nurse. I wasn't sure what they wanted me to do once I reached the room. I threw up a silent prayer for guidance and followed Mrs. Riddle upstairs.

When I walked in, I saw Miz Tessie organizing washcloths and linens. Beatrice was in her bed with an obvious look of discomfort on her face. She had beads of sweat already forming around her brow, even though the room seemed to have a slight chill. When she saw me, a forced smile spread across her face. "I guess this is it," she said with tone of resignation.

"Yes, it is."

"Lilly, I'm scared," she confessed as she reached for my hand.

"Me too," I honestly replied. "But Miz Tessie has delivered many babies. You're in good hands, and the doctor will be here soon." I was talking as much to comfort myself as Beatrice. "Can I get you anything? Do anything for you?"

"No, just stay with me. When I need something, I'll let you know."

For the next hour, Miz Tessie attended to Beatrice's

needs. My job was to sit with her and allow her to squeeze my hand when needed. My heart ached every time Beatrice groaned in pain, but Miz Tessie claimed everything was progressing as it should. Mrs. Riddle tried to be supportive, but her pacing and ceaseless chatter caused everyone else to be on edge.

"Mother," Beatrice commanded after an especially painful contraction. "I appreciate you being here, but why don't you go keep watch for Father?" It was a directive more than a question. In an odd reversal of roles, Mrs. Riddle was more than happy to oblige and went outside.

"Missus Othella always has been a little squeamish," Miz Tessie admitted with a little smile. "Even when she was a little girl she would try to run away from her own blood."

Tessie's admission made us both giggle a bit. It relieved some tension, but not for long. The baby was on its way, and Beatrice's pains were getting closer and stronger. *Oh, where is the doctor?* I wondered. The room was suddenly getting hotter. Droplets of sweat had begun to form on my own brow, and I fought the desire to panic.

"Here he comes!" Beatrice suddenly yelled as she clenched my hand with newfound strength. Miz Tessie and I locked eyes for a moment, and I choked down the knot in my throat. This child was not waiting for the doctor.

I lost all track of time. While one moment seemed to stand painfully still, others raced by as though the world was spinning faster. I tried to mirror Miz Tessie's calm demeanor, but I could only think of one other event when I had been so scared ... and the result had not been good. Beatrice clenched her teeth in pain and determination and bore down one last time while Miz Tessie barked words of encouragement. "Again!" Miz Tessie commanded. "Give Miz Tessie another good push!" I stayed by Beatrice, feeling out of place but honoring her wishes. The moment seemed too personal, too raw for me to witness. Yet I understood my role and wanted to make good on my promise.

In a second that was both glorious and frightening, Miz Tessie grasped the baby and held him up.

"It's a boy," she announced with a hint of sadness as the baby wailed for the first time.

Beatrice was gasping and staring at the ceiling. A faint smile came across her lips. "What did I tell you, Lilly Kate? I knew it would be a boy."

"You were right all along," I admitted.

Miz Tessie took the baby to the washstand to clean him up while I found a clean cloth and wiped the sweat off of Beatrice's face.

"Please, let me see him," she begged. "I want to at least hold him one time." Miz Tessie looked hard at Beatrice trying to determine what to do. "I think I've earned that much, don't you?"

Miz Tessie carried the baby, now wrapped and chewing his fist, and handed him to Beatrice. His little face was pink and puckered, but there was no mistaking his little blond wisps of hair that formed into a perfect widow's peak and the tiny heart-shaped chin that were traits of his mother.

"He must be hungry," Beatrice announced quickly. "I'll feed him."

"That may not be best, Miss Beatrice. No sense in you getting more attached than you already is. Let me takes him. I knows a wet nurse."

"No!" Beatrice yelled. "I will feed him." She looked down at the baby's little face, still chewing on his tiny fist. With tears streaming down her face, Beatrice began to expertly nurse the newborn as though she had done it often before. Had it not been for their imminent separation, the two would have made a perfect picture of mother and son, but we all knew that was not to be.

As the baby continued to nurse, we heard the motor-car pulling into the drive. "Better late than never, I suppose," Miz Tessie mumbled in protest. Within minutes, Mrs. Riddle escorted the doctor into the room. She cast a surprised look as she saw Beatrice nursing the baby, but she said nothing.

"It's a boy," Beatrice announced. "I always knew it would be a boy."

Tension filled the air as thick as smoke. For a passing moment, no one spoke or seemed to know what to do. No one dared even look at each other. I could hear the grand-father clock in the hallway strike midnight.

It was Dr. Pollard who finally broke the deafening silence. "Well, I'm truly sorry I missed the excitement," he quipped lightly toward Beatrice. "But at least let me examine you and the baby to make sure everyone is all right." Dr. Pollard gave both the baby and Beatrice an examination, asked Miz Tessie a few questions, and then announced all was well.

Meanwhile, Mrs. Riddle stood next to the wall, wring-ing her hands in discomfort. In no way could I compre-hend the complexities of her emotions at that moment. Yet, with a clarity that I do not normally possess, I sud-denly knew what I should do. I walked toward her and gently took her elbow. "Mrs. Riddle, why don't you come take a look at him?"

"Are you sure?" she asked, as though she was the child and I was the adult. I gently nodded and led her next to the bed.

"Oh, he's beautiful," Mrs. Riddle said with a gasp upon seeing the baby for the first time. "He's ... he's perfect."

The three of them shared an all too short but pre-cious moment together—their first and only. This was no ordinary birth, and it was Miz Tessie who stepped in to remind us of the gravity of the evening. "Mrs. Riddle, would you like me to travel with the baby to Frankfort?"

Mrs. Riddle opened her mouth to respond, but it was Beatrice who spoke up. "No, I want Lilly Kate to take him." With shock I turned and looked at Beatrice. "Please," she begged. "I told you I'd let you know when I needed you for something. I need you now! I can't hold him anymore, but will you hold him in my place? At least until you reach the orphanage?"

I wanted to run. Run to my own mother. Run from this heartbreaking situation. But there was only one appropriate reply. "Yes…yes, I'll go with him."

For the first time ever, I loaded myself into the back of an automobile. Miz Tessie handed me the baby, now a complete bundle of blankets. Mr. Riddle took his position in the driver's seat while Dr. Pollard sat beside him. Without a word spoken between us, Mr. Riddle started the car, drove down the driveway, and headed north to Frankfort.

A swell of grief filled my chest as I held the precious newborn in my arms. It was unfair what Tom Hanley had done to Beatrice, but it was just as unfair that an innocent baby had to be given away. Why should he suffer? Why should Beatrice suffer for that matter? Why could we as a caring community not surround her with love and understanding instead of judging her for something she did not do? It was all extremely unfair. *Why, Lord?* I asked. *Why?*

The baby wiggled and made a faint gurgle while I held him in my arms. I looked out the window at the cold, clear sky. The stars were twinkling, but one seemed more luminous than the rest. I was reminded of Mary and her baby boy who was born more than nineteen centuries ago. For the first time, I began to wonder what she had to endure as a mother. Did people talk about her and the baby? Did she pretend not to hear whispers? And how much did she understand about her baby's future, the pain and suffering they'd both endure? I mulled these things over and realized that even Mary, the mother of Jesus, had to give up her baby. No, not right away, but sooner than she'd like. The gospel of John says just before his death Jesus made provisions for the care of his mother. The realization brought me comfort, and I bowed my head in silent prayer, both for Beatrice and the baby in my arms.

When we arrived in downtown Frankfort, the city was asleep with the exception of the lighted dome of the newly constructed state capitol building. The irony that this child would be cared for in the shadows of the state's seat of government struck me hard. I wondered how many lawmakers would walk a few blocks and take a look at how some of their decisions were helping others. Justice is a mighty pithy topic until it has a name and face.

At the orphanage I saw no lights burning or a single sign that anyone was awake. "I sent a message before I left so that they would be ready. I told them we'd come in the back," Dr. Pollard explained.

"Good thinking, Marshall," Mr. Riddle responded, and it occurred to me those were the first words I'd heard him speak the entire evening.

With the efficiency of a well-planned attack, Mr. Riddle parked the car in the rear, opened the door, and escorted me inside. A large woman in her night coat and cap met us at the door. Once inside, all pleasantries were ignored as she led us into an interior office where the furnishings were clean but sparse, giving the impression of being cold and distant. I prayed once again for the baby to have a quick adoption so as to grow up in a place that was warm and inviting, regardless of its humble surroundings.

Mr. Riddle and Dr. Pollard followed the nurse to her desk and began to fill out some papers. When finished, Mr. Riddle handed what appeared to be a large sum of cash to the nurse and began to walk out the door, but he abruptly stopped and turned to me. With great effort he slowly walked to me and began to unfold the blankets in my arms just enough to see the newborn's sleeping face. Touching his tiny head, Mr. Riddle's chin began to quiver. Suddenly, he turned on his heel and walked out the door.

In truth, I wasn't sure I could stand much longer. The night had been long and emotional. I was beginning to feel my knees give way, but my arms remained firmly around the child. I knew the dreaded moment had arrived. The baby was now officially a ward of the state of Kentucky. Dr. Pollard must have sensed my hesitation, for when the nurse came to take the baby from my arms, he gently stopped her and walked to me instead.

"Miss, you've done more than your fair share. Why don't you allow me to take the baby?" I looked at the sweet child's face one last time, and a tear rolled down my cheek and settled on my chin. "I can assure you the boy will receive nothing but quality care here. There's a very good chance a healthy boy like this will find a good home soon."

Although intended to calm me, Dr. Pollard's words were empty and lifeless. Mechanically, I handed over the baby, knowing full well neither of us would ever be the same again.

Chapter Fifteen

The next morning when I awoke the sun was fully shining, and I could smell sausage. With a bolt, I jumped out of bed and ran to the clock.

"I'm late! Momma, I'm late for school!"

Momma came in from the kitchen completely dressed and wearing an apron. "Calm down, daughter. I sent word you wouldn't be there today. You've had quite a long night, and I thought you needed some rest."

My heart slowly began to return to rhythm as I tried to remember the events that brought me home. I remembered Dr. Pollard and the baby, as well as climbing into the car, but beyond that, everything was a bit fuzzy.

"Did Mr. Riddle drop me off?" I asked.

"Yes. I'm not surprised you don't remember. It took both of us to help you inside. You both looked like you'd had quite a night." Momma looked at me thoughtfully for a moment. My hair was a tangled mess, and my eyes were red and puffy. "We can talk about it later. Right now, you need to eat."

Almost on cue my stomach growled in agreement. I hadn't eaten since lunch the day before, and my insides felt as though they were turning inside out. Momma had made scrambled eggs, sausage links, and biscuits with portions reminiscent of our days on the farm. "I'm not sure I'll ever grow accustomed to cooking for two," she mused as she surveyed the loaded table.

"Don't worry," I chided. "This morning I truly think I can eat it all myself."

Momma gave an appreciative smile, and together we sat silently in our tiny, warm kitchen eating breakfast. I was content to serve myself seconds and thirds while Momma sipped her coffee and nibbled on a biscuit. It wasn't until my third helping that Momma finally broke the silence.

"Was the baby all right?" she asked.

I put down my biscuit and finished chewing. "Yes, it's a boy, but how did you know? I was so careful not to say anything!"

"It really doesn't matter how I found out. What matters is that you held up your end of the bargain." Momma paused and looked at me seriously, her eyes a little moist. "Lilly Kate, I'm very proud of you. You helped poor Beatrice during a very critical time. You've been a friend when she needed it most. I know it's been difficult for both of you. How's she doing now?"

"Oh, Momma. She was the bravest one of any of us! I'm not sure I could do what she did. I mean, it wasn't her fault! People would have gotten used to it."

"Perhaps. Then again, perhaps not. Sometimes people can be cruel. They'll often believe what they want to believe. I'm sure the Riddles felt the baby had a better chance of acceptance if he was adopted."

"But it's not fair!"

"No one ever said life was fair. I thought you learned that lesson long ago," Momma paused and gave me time to think. I dropped my head in shame. Memories of Poppa's accident came to mind. Then the college letter too. No, life wasn't always fair, but then again, with a little faith and some hard work, things did seem to have a way of working out—maybe just not the way we wished or hoped.

After breakfast, Momma cleaned up while I dressed. The events of the evening before had put me behind a bit in my schoolwork, so I decided to throw myself into the familiar act of studying. College might not be in the future, but there was still a good chance of being valedictorian. I was determined not give up on that goal.

But by midafternoon, I'd grown weary of history and geography. I was also trying to avoid algebra and, thus far, had been having great success at putting it off. I decided to take a lazy look at *The Anderson News*. I wanted to see some of the Christmas ads and maybe get some ideas for Momma. It was filled with the typical agriculture reports and tobacco prices. And there was Sheriff Johnson's announcement, telling people to get their taxes ready. The social page was still filled with its usual banter, listing illnesses and out-of-town visitors as well as upcoming parties. But my favorite of the week read, "J.C. Bradley, of Harrodsburg, was here Sunday to see a mighty attractive young lady." Poor Mr. Bradley. We all knew Mrs. Bond wrote the social page, and Eunice was the "mighty attractive young lady" in question. The man only wanted to make a visit, but instead made the news. Oh, the foibles of small-town living!

Yet, without question, the biggest story of the week was regarding Champ Clark's bid for the Democratic nomination for President. Beauchamp Clark was currently the Speaker of the House in Washington, D.C. Although he'd spent the vast majority of his life in Missouri, he was born in our tiny town of Lawrenceburg. Its current citizens felt that fact made him imminently more qualified than anyone else for the nation's highest office and were hoping he'd come back to give a stump speech sometime in the spring. Even Mrs. Kavanaugh was excited about Mr. Clark's bid for the presidency and used it frequently as a motivational point. "You see, you don't have to be from a great city or a great family to be a great person," she was fond of preaching and would punctuate her statement with a firm whack of her umbrella.

For me, Speaker Clark's candidacy was marred by the fact I wouldn't be able to vote, not because of my age, but because of my gender. Poppa had been fond of saying a woman with a good husband didn't need to vote. As much as it pained me to admit it, I was beginning to disagree with him. Not all women had good husbands, as I was learning. Some were mean, some were lazy, and some weren't worth their weight in salt. Other women didn't have a husband at all. I'd noticed women seemed to do more than their fair share of work, both on the farm and in town. Even Mr. Ballard admitted he couldn't run the store without his wife, and Miss Cunningham paid taxes like everyone else. Mr. and Mrs. Drury seemed to run their clothing store, The Fair, rather equally. It occurred to me that women should vote not only because they're citizens, but also because they'd earned it. I wasn't ready to grab a banner and start marching down the street, but I was beginning to warm to the idea.

With this in mind, I was reading the article about Champ Clark with a new interest. I was curious about his position on women's rights and was disappointed when the article failed to mention anything regarding women with the exception of the name of his mother. However, at the bottom of the page in the left corner, I spotted an inauspicious advertisement I'd never seen before.

State Normal—a Training School for Teachers
Courses—Preparatory, State Certificate, Life Diploma, County
Certificate, Review, Special
Tuition: Free to Appointees, Expenses very low. Ask about it.
J.G. Crabbe, president, Richmond, KY

I read the ad again. Then again. I glanced over at Momma working at her sewing machine. Just yesterday my hopes about college had been squelched, but this looked like an advertisement for a school begging for teachers. Tuition free to appointees? Expenses very low? True, it was a normal school, which was for two years, not four. Still, it seemed too good to be true. Rather than jump up and down with excitement or even get my hopes up, I simply copied the information and placed it in my coat pocket. *I'll ask Mrs. Rutherford about it tomorrow at school,* I mused to myself. *No sense getting excited over nothing.*

I didn't ask Mrs. Rutherford about State Normal the next day, or even the next. I preferred hanging onto the idea of it being a possibility to finding out it was a misleading ad to a second-rate school. Better to keep a lamp burning dim than to snuff it out completely, I reasoned.

Instead, I refocused my efforts on my studies and the school newspaper. Our Christmas edition was coming out with a special feature that allowed the juniors and seniors to write a letter to Santa. It had been a silly tradition since before I attended Kavanaugh and was typically our biggest selling edition of the year. Even people within the community would come and purchase copies, knowing full well the requests would be inventive and outrageous. This year's letters were no exception. Ruddy Saffle wished for an automobile and a trip to the moon, and Sadie Gash wrote in great detail about the sable coat and muff she hoped to find under the tree. One unsigned letter even begged for a more curvaceous figure, leaving me to wonder if it was a sincere request or not. Yet, the one that caught me off guard the most was Huey's. For reasons I couldn't quite understand, he'd asked Santa for a new suit.

"Huey, why did you write you wanted a new suit?" I asked when I caught up with him after school the next day. "Most people are putting the most outrageous items. Yours is so . . . so serious."

"It's true. More than anything I want a new suit. When I'm up there preaching, I want to look older, so people will take me seriously. I thought a new suit of clothes would help."

I gave a little laugh. "Well, if that's the case, you should've wished for some bigger muscles and a little facial hair!"

Immediately, I knew I'd gone too far. I'd just given my dear friend a sucker punch. Huey's eyes had the look of a wounded animal, and he began to turn away. "Huey, I'm so sorry! I didn't mean to . . . I don't know why I said it. Please, forgive me. I was just trying to make a joke and a poor one at that!"

Huey turned back around. "Is that how you really think of me? I'm just some little boy, your little pal? Is that how you really see me?" Huey's questions were pounding me like gunfire with no time to answer. His face had grown red, and his breathing was heavy, reminding me of a freight train at full speed. I'd never seen Huey so agitated, so hurt.

"Huey, I'm so sorry. Honestly, I was just teasing. Really. Please, forgive me."

"Ahh, geez, Lilly Kate. It's not just that." Huey shrugged and turned away for a moment. "I'm sorry for sounding off on you. I've just had so much on my mind, with college and all. I'm beginning to second-guess my call to the ministry. I just don't know if I can do it. Preachers are supposed to be serious and scholarly. I'm not like that. I've tried, but I'm just not."

"Says who?" I asked with conviction. Huey stepped back and gave me a look of surprise. "Tell me. Who says a minister must be serious all the time? I don't recall that being in Scripture anywhere. Seems to me a man of the cloth without a good sense of humor is only half a man at all."

Huey opened his mouth as if to speak but was cut off. "And furthermore, if memory serves me correctly, not one of the twelve disciples would have qualified as a scholar, not even close."

By now, Huey was smiling again, causing his freckles to meld together. "You know, you're right. I never thought of that." Huey began shaking his head up and down in agreement. "I guess I've just always seen preachers who were serious and dour. I don't suppose being a minister means I can't joke around a little, does it?"

"Of course not," I added in a mock confidential tone. "And between you and me, I don't really trust anybody who can't laugh at himself at least a little. I just don't think it would be natural."

Huey leaned back in laughter. "Lilly Kate, you beat all I ever saw. You know how to cheer a person up." Huey then grabbed me by the shoulders and gave me a big, fat, wet kiss on the cheek. "Thanks a million," he said, and then added as he started to walk away, "and change my Christmas wish to read 'a bottle of freckle remover lotion.' That really would be a Christmas miracle!"

I put my hand on my cheek, still feeling the kiss that was left, and only managed to nod in agreement.

As much as I enjoyed helping Huey sort out his troubles, not all problems were so easily rectified. Dink and Jimalee were spending more and more time together, which left me feeling slightly left out. And, of course, now that I wouldn't be going to college, there was the trouble with what to do with myself after graduation. Most girls my age were either already married or planning to be so soon.

My own mother and father were seriously courting by my age, but I hadn't had the first suitor. And, to be totally frank, the pickin's seemed rather slim.

Not that I had much time to think about it. School was keeping me busier than I'd have liked. Between tutoring Beatrice, keeping up with my own assignments, and managing the school paper, I sometimes felt like a sheet being squeezed through the wringer. I once told Momma not to be surprised if she found me in the bed flatter than a pancake and had to scrape me off with an egg turner. She calmly told me our home was not the opera house and to stop being so dramatic.

Still, I was determined not to allow the Christmas edition of the paper to be printed without my personal addition. Although not in line with protocol, I put my own pen to paper and printed my own letter to Santa. Since so many other students were taking the opportunity to dream lavishly, I decided to do the same. I wanted to go to college. I also wanted to be a teacher, but putting these things down on paper seemed much too personal, too much of a window to the soul.

Instead, I asked for a new typewriter and a leather-bound, gold embossed set of the complete works of the Brontë sisters. I'd seen their books for sale once in a magazine and thought they were absolutely beautiful. Since the public library had opened, I'd read every book written by a Brontë that was available, sometimes more than once. Yet, the price of the set was outrageous, far more than I or anyone else I knew would be willing to spend. Still, they were gorgeous and would look striking on any bookshelf.

The typewriter was equally as fanciful. Even the one at school needed constant attention with oiling, and the ink cylinder was forever leaking. I'd once even blackened my index finger with the letter *c* when I was working with the jammed keys. Jimalee claimed I had unconsciously but correctly labeled myself *c* for "clumsy." I was not as amused and wore gloves until the ink faded. A new typewriter of my own would allow me to do some writing from home.

The school paper was distributed on the last day of school before the Christmas break. There was already a festive feeling in the air, and everyone was in high spirits. The house boys were packed and ready to go home to see their families. The rest of us were passing out gifts and well wishes to all our friends. In the midst of all the activity, Huey took hold of my arm and led me to a quiet corner.

"Have you been avoiding me?" It was more of an accusation than a question, but not harsh.

"Of course not, Huey. I've just been a little overwhelmed, that's all."

Huey gave a quirky little laugh. "I suppose you have," he admitted. "Look, I got you something for Christmas."

My eyes grew wide, both with surprise and panic. "Oh, no, Huey! You shouldn't have. I didn't get anything for you."

"It's both a Christmas gift and a thank you, for setting me straight the other day." I opened the package to find a box of beautiful ivory stationary, the edges trimmed with the delicate outline of ivy. A smile immediately spread across my face. "No matter what happens, please promise you'll write me when I go to college next year," Huey begged. "I can't stand the thought of not hearing from you." His face held a tender expression I'd not often seen. "You're my best friend. My Lilly Kate."

I reached up to give Huey a hug. "I promise. I'll write sometime. No! I'll write often." No matter what else, Huey was my dear friend, and despite all that was going on around me and within me, I had no intentions of that ever changing.

As the day neared the end, noise within the school

grew to a low roar. Mrs. Kavanaugh was known for her discipline and order, but she was no ogre and let us have a bit of fun, at least for one afternoon. The year before she'd even passed out peppermint sticks and oranges to the entire student body. Shortly before dismissal, as we were all giving our last well wishes, someone let out a piercing squeal. All conversation immediately ceased, and our eyes flew to the front door. There standing in the doorway in her long winter coat and hat was Beatrice with Mrs. Riddle behind her. Beatrice was holding two tins of candy from Parker's Confectionary and looked more than a little apprehensive. No one had expected to see her until after the holidays, and most seemed a little taken aback by her appearance. Although nothing tangible, there was a definite, perceivable change about her. Her eyes were more serious and her cheeks no longer glowed a youthful pink. She certainly looked as though she was recovering from a rare malady, but I knew her true illness was a heavy heart.

"Hello," Beatrice said with uncharacteristic meekness. "I just wanted to bring some candy and wish everyone a Merry Christmas." With that, her old friends Ruby and Eunice flocked to her side and gave her a hug. Everyone else started peppering her with words of welcome and questions. The candy quickly made its way around, and everyone seemed joyous once more. Although there were certainly a number of questions being left unasked, people had the good sense to keep their mouths shut, at least for the moment. It was almost as though she'd never been gone.

For my part, I tried to give Beatrice her space. After the birth, I'd sent her a note expressing my prayers and support, but it had never been reciprocated. With her situation now changed, a part of me assumed Beatrice and I would once again only look at each other cautiously from across the room. *That might be better anyway*, I thought. *There may be fewer questions.*

But Beatrice would have none of that. Within a few minutes she came to me and gave me a hug. "I wanted to tell you thank you in person," she whispered. "My parents and I would like to invite you and your mother to a dinner at our house on New Year's Eve. Please tell me you'll come."

I glanced up and saw Ruby and Eunice giving me a curious look. A wave of relief passed through me as I realized Beatrice was not ashamed of our friendship and was making absolutely no efforts to hide it.

"Of course, we'll be there," I replied. "Can I bring anything?" I asked more out of habit than sincerity.

"Please, don't," Mrs. Riddle replied. She'd come up from behind and was now standing beside Beatrice. "Let this be our gift to you," she said graciously. I smiled and nodded as Beatrice and Mrs. Riddle went on to chat briefly with others in the room. I sighed a deep sigh of contentment, feeling very blessed indeed that I had received two gifts in one afternoon.

Chapter Sixteen

Christmas Eve arrived, and Momma and I bundled up to walk across the street to church for candlelight service. My coat had grown a little too snug and too short, but I tried to hide it by bending my knees and keeping my stomach sucked in. The effect was not good for my disposition, but I didn't dare complain for fear Momma would do without in order to buy me a new coat. For her part, Momma looked lovely in her winter hat, and her eyes sparkled with happiness. "This has got to be the most wonderful time of year! Don't you think?" Not trusting my voice to sound normal, I simply grinned and nodded in agreement.

It was snowing, but with no real accumulation; yet the wind was biting and cut through my coat. When we walked in the church, we were greeted by a warm wave of air and the sound of carols being played on the organ. I almost gasped when I finally saw the sanctuary. There had truly been a transformation. Boughs of holly had been strung across the balcony, cedar wreaths hung in every window, and red and white poinsettias sat in every sill. Dozens of candles filled the altar and surrounded the nativity scene in front, leaving me to feel as though I truly was standing on holy ground.

As we took our seats, Momma and I both remained in reverent silence. For some unknown reason, my mind flashed back to another Christmas Eve when I was about four years old. We were at Fox Creek Church, and I was still small enough to sit in Poppa's lap. Like most children,

I was excited about the arrival of Santa Claus and had trouble controlling myself. "Be still," Poppa said. "Be still or you might miss something." The tone of his voice was firm but full of love. I sat quietly in his large, warm lap and listened to the service. Everything had seemed very safe then, very certain. Poppa was holding me close, and Momma was near. It had never occurred to me life would be any different from what it was then.

But life was different. Change had come, and I felt completely unprepared for any of it. I bowed my head and began to pray. I prayed for Beatrice, her baby, and her family, as they dealt with the events of the last several months. I prayed for Momma, Jimalee, Huey, and the rest of the family. But most of all, I prayed for myself. I prayed for guidance. Much was changing in my life, and I wasn't at all sure what to do or even where to go. I prayed that God would show me the way to college if it was his will. I prayed that if it wasn't his will, he'd open other doors instead or at least take away the desire within me. Lastly, I prayed for peace, both in my heart and in the world.

When I opened my eyes and looked up, I had no revelation. No sudden voice came to me. I wish it were so, but I'd learned long ago God rarely uses megaphones. Instead, I just leaned closer to Momma and took hold of her hand. *Be still*, Poppa had said. *Be still.* And so I was.

On Christmas morning Momma and I allowed ourselves the luxury of sleeping late. Long gone were the days of waking at two or three in the morning and looking in my stocking. I'd reached the age where a long sleep in a warm bed was a gift in itself. Still, by eight-thirty we were both dressed and in the kitchen making cinnamon rolls. Momma had promised a few of the widows in the church that we'd visit them on Christmas Day, and the pastries were to be their gift.

We'd each eaten two when Momma announced it was

time to open gifts. When I'd been younger, forcing me to wait to open my presents had been like trying to break a wild horse. Every second had been pure agony. Momma and Poppa seemed to enjoy the suspense, and after me begging for the tenth or eleventh time, one would say, "Wait just a minute, let me finish my coffee," grinning behind the lid of the cup. One Christmas Momma had insisted that I wait to open my gifts until after Poppa brought in some firewood. I'd stomped my foot and pouted in protest, feeling the request was completely unreasonable. Internally, I fumed and thought the anticipation would surely kill me. When Poppa had finally come through the door, he was carrying a wooden rocking horse he'd made himself with a red bow on the seat.

Now, of course, times were different. For me, something of the mystery of Christmas had died with Poppa. Yet in its place I'd found a quiet contentment in the holiday. The gifts were no longer the highlight. Receiving them had become a secondary event. Even so, when Momma suggested we open our packages, I readily agreed, not so much for myself but for her.

"Are you ready?" she asked after I took a seat in the parlor.

"Of course, why do you ask?" I questioned as Momma quickly left the room, leaving me a little mystified by her actions.

"Ta-da!" Momma whipped around the corner holding a stunning long, black, wool coat with carved ivory buttons and a matching muff. I bolted from my chair to get a closer look.

"How did you … what did you … it's gorgeous!" I was tongue tied from surprise and excitement.

"Did you think I wouldn't notice your other coat left a great deal to be desired?" Momma teased.

"But, Momma, how could you?"

"Now listen. It's Christmas, and you're not supposed to ask about money, but if it will make you feel better, I'll tell you. I did some work for Mr. Drury down at The Fair. Instead of paying me, we did a little bartering. I just felt a young lady as classy as you needed a coat to match." Momma was smiling with pride as I tried it on. It was the most luxurious piece of clothing I'd ever owned. I twirled around in front of the mirror to get a look from every angle. The fit was perfect. It was truly gorgeous.

I still hadn't given Momma her gift. "Oh, I almost forgot!" I exclaimed. I went to what looked like her empty stocking on the mantel and pulled out a long, thin envelope.

"What's this?" Momma asked with a most uncertain voice.

I smiled with the pride of knowing. "You'll see."

Momma looked a bit uneasy as she began to open the envelope. The excitement from my new coat was matched by the joy of watching Momma. Since we'd moved to town, Momma had taken advantage of the library as much as me. Both of us enjoyed a good novel or biography, but I knew there was something she might like even better, something of her own.

Momma cautiously opened the envelope as if afraid something might jump out. She kept glancing at me with suspicious eyes, but as she began reading, I noticed the paper start to tremble and a smile sweep across her face.

"A subscription to *The Saturday Evening Post*! This is wonderful! How did you manage this?" It was a loaded question really. Momma knew a yearlong subscription wasn't cheap, but she also wasn't sure how I went about getting it.

"Didn't you just tell me you're not supposed to ask about money?" I teased. "Do you remember that terrible hat I purchased from Miss Cunningham's millinery a few year's back?" With time, I'd come to see the hat for the atrocity it was and knew it would get absolutely no use at all. Momma adamantly nodded her head, and I continued. "Well, I had a little talk with Miss Cunningham. She agreed to buy it back from me because, believe it or not, she was having requests for hats just like it. She said there was a picture in some magazine somewhere, and now ladies want those horrible ostrich feathers. It's all the rage. She even paid me exactly what I gave for it, saying she would get even more this time. Can you believe it?"

Momma and I sat in our parlor enjoying the spirit of the morning a few more moments before we decided it was time to go make our visits. We carefully packed some hot cinnamon rolls, I proudly bundled myself in my new coat, and we headed out the door to make our rounds. The sky was gray, and there continued to be some occasional flakes coming down, but nothing more. It wasn't so much a white Christmas as one that was gray and brown, but no matter. My heart was happy, and I gave a sigh of contentment. The weather held no control over my merry holiday.

As Momma and I walked down Main Street, we saw other townspeople out and about making their way to family gatherings and visits with friends. The mood was festive, and everyone called a Christmas greeting, even from across the street. There was a definite spring to everyone's step and a smile on each face.

Momma and I looked up when we heard the clip-clop of horses' hooves along with the jingle of bells. It was the Bond family coming through town. The entire family was dressed in holiday finery and proudly calling out greetings to neighbors. But it was the purple and red that caught my eye. As the carriage drew nearer, I could clearly make out the distinct form of ostrich feathers. They were sitting proudly atop the head of Eunice Bond. She made certain to nod and wave as she passed us, giving everyone a chance to see her new hat with its velvet crown and brim, the very one I'd returned to Miss Cunningham. A peacock could not have worn his feathers more proudly. Momma and I exchanged mystified glances then quickly began to snicker. "I guess birds of a feather do flock together!" I roared while we both held our sides from laughter.

Christmas night, Momma and I were both sitting in front of the fire relishing the last few moments of the holiday when a sudden knock came at the door. Momma put aside her quilt and quickly jumped up, each of us feeling a bit unnerved by the late call. When she opened the door, there stood Jimalee and Dink, holding each other and smiling so big you'd have thought their faces were frozen in that position. I immediately bolted from my chair and ran to greet them.

"We're getting married!" they both exclaimed before even the preliminary greetings could be made. Momma and I stood in the doorway, stupefied by the news for a split second before we regained our senses enough to invite them in. Congratulations and hugs were exchanged as coats were removed and hats were hung.

"Dink asked me this afternoon right after Christmas dinner," Jimalee reported. "He'd already asked my daddy." Jimalee's eyes were as bright and happy as I'd ever seen them. Both of them had pink faces from the cold and excitement, and I even looked down to make sure their feet were touching the floor.

"To tell the truth, askin' her daddy was the hard part," Dink admitted and gave Jimalee another squeeze. "He hemmed and hawed like he was stewin' over the price of his prize heifer." Once again, Dink's poetic prowess amazed me.

"When's the date?" Momma finally asked after several minutes of excited chatter. For me, just the idea of two of my dearest friends planning to get married was an event in itself. The very act of a wedding was a little more than I could grasp.

"Three months from today, March twenty-fifth!" Jimalee beamed. "Momma's gonna make me a new dress, Dink's gonna build us a new bed and dresser, and we've got to do some movin' around in the house 'cause we're gonna live with Momma and Daddy until we git a place of our own."

"Won't that be a bit crowded?" I blurted before I'd even thought the question through.

Dink was not deterred. He just continued to smile. "Considern' that passel of people I'm used to livin' with, I'm thinkin' it'll be nice 'n roomy!"

"Daddy is as pleased as punch Dink's gonna be around for spring plantin,' and we're hoping that when that new governor's mansion starts getting built over in Frankfort, Dink can get a job with that."

Two of my dearest friends were getting married, and as much as I wanted to share in their joy, my soul felt like a house divided against itself. One half was thrilled for them, simply pleased for their happiness. The other felt this sense of dread, this fear of unknown territory. There was the knowledge that things would never again be the same. Dink and Jimalee would now be a team of two. I'd always be welcome, and Jimalee and I would still have our chats. Dink would still tease and add his good humor. But they would belong to each other, and rightfully so. I just wasn't sure where that left me, and I hated myself for having such selfish thoughts.

Shortly after Jimalee and Dink left, Momma and I got changed and went to bed. The events of the day had left us both tired, but Momma's intuition must have sensed a change in my demeanor. "Anything you want to talk about?" she asked. I knew immediately she had

157

read through me. With my mother, I was completely transparent.

I fiddled with the buttons on my flannel gown and tried to articulate the way I felt.

"Why does everything have to change?" I finally asked. "Why does everything seem to happen at one time? First Beatrice, then Huey being a minister and going off to college, now Jimalee and Dink. And don't even get me started on what I'm doing after graduation! While everyone else seems to have plans neatly in place, I haven't the first clue. I almost feel as though I'm being left behind." The fear and trepidation of the future that had been simmering within me began to boil over as huge tears rolled down the side of my cheeks. "What do I do now? I thought God wanted me to go to college, but that doesn't seem possible now. Oh, why can't everything just stay the same? We're happy as we are, right?"

Momma came and sat beside me on the bed as she had so many times before. She put one arm around my shoulder and gave me a squeeze. "Lillian Katherine, have you ever stopped to think how sad it would be if everything remained the same?" I looked at her through my water-filled eyes. This was not the response I'd expected. "Look around you. There are now opportunities for young ladies to go to school that didn't exist twenty years ago. We've got automobiles and flying machines. People who are miles from each other can now talk together. Someday, you and I will probably even be able to vote." Momma paused a moment and stared forward, lost in thought. "Can you even begin to imagine the change that will take place in this country when women like you and I get to put in our two cents worth?" Momma gave me another nudge, and we both gave a gentle laugh.

"Change is always certain, honey. Always. Sometimes it's just more painful than others, like the one that brought us to town." I could hear Momma's voice crack a bit at the memory of Poppa and his accident, and the old ache in my chest flared up again.

The two of us sat together a couple of more moments, lost in our memories. Finally, Momma spoke up again. "Daughter, I'm not sure what the future holds, but I'm quite confident that it will be fantastic. Pray about it. Listen to that still small, voice, and you can't go wrong."

Chapter Seventeen

New Year's Eve arrived, and for the first time I could remember, Momma and I had a holiday dinner to attend. No one in Fox Creek held New Year's Eve parties, simply because the cows didn't know it was a holiday. The bovine ladies needed their early morning milking, regardless of the holiday, and woe be to the farmer who got his cows off schedule. Of course, we'd been off the farm for more than three years, but it was still our first New Year's Eve invitation. "I'm not sure what to expect, do you?" I asked Momma as we prepared to leave.

"Well, I'm no expert, but since they invited us to dinner, I'm assuming there'll be food," she replied with thick sarcasm.

I gave her a playful punch in the arm. "Let's go. I don't want to be the last ones there."

When we walked up the sidewalk, it was apparent we were not the last ones to arrive. In fact, it seemed quite the opposite. We saw no one else's carriages or horses. A little panic went through me as I began to question Beatrice's invitation. Had I understood correctly? Was the date correct?

Momma gave me a quizzical look but continued to walk toward the front door. After we rang the doorbell, I held my breath, half expecting to be told we'd been mistaken. But as soon as the door flung open, there stood Beatrice beaming with happiness at our arrival.

"Fantastic. You're here!" Beatrice tilted her head back over her shoulder. "Mother, they're here!"

Mrs. Riddle came quickly into the foyer. "Well, stop standing there with the door open and invite them in, for heaven's sake. You'd think I haven't tried to teach you any manners at all."

It was the first time Momma and I had been to the Riddle Mansion as guests. Quickly, we were whisked inside and had our coats taken for us while Mrs. Riddle politely inquired about our holiday festivities. She and Momma chatted for a moment while I looked around. The house was warm and bright with all the gas lamps and fireplaces burning. All the light made the crystal vases and chandeliers sparkle with a brilliance I'd not seen before in all my time visiting Beatrice. The effect was almost magical.

"I suppose we're a bit early," I said, feeling a bit awkward at our premature arrival.

"Of course not," Mrs. Riddle retorted. "You're right on time. Miz Tessie just told me the chicken was ready and the bread would be out any minute. She's even prepared some cushaw because she knows you like it so well."

With the very mention of sweetened cushaw, my mouth started watering. But before I had a chance to ask about the other guests, we were taken into the dining room. There, atop a massive mahogany table sat six place settings of fine porcelain china, leaded crystal, and silverware that I felt certain had been in the family since before the Civil War. I very nearly made a joke about hiding it from the Yankees before I thought better of it.

I leaned over to whisper into Beatrice's ear. "Why are there only six place settings? Aren't others coming?"

"No, silly! This is a dinner for you! You're the guest of honor. My parents wanted to thank you for being my tutor."

I immediately felt my cheeks begin to warm, my palms begin to sweat, and my right leg begin to twitch. And it wasn't because I was standing near the fire. I'd never dreamed the Riddles would have me as a special dinner guest, and to tell the truth, I wasn't sure I liked it. I'd planned on a more casual event where I could sit in a corner and chat one on one with someone else. The center of attention, no matter how small the circle, was not a comfortable place. Suddenly all the lighting and shining tableware were making me a bit dizzy, and I became incredibly self-conscious again.

Mrs. Riddle had left the room and come back with her husband and another young man whom I immediately recognized to be Beatrice's older brother Paul. I knew from the little conversation we'd had about him that Paul was a lawyer in Louisville, and by all accounts, doing very well, despite his father's desire for him to come and join the distillery business. He and Beatrice shared the same blond hair and bright eyes, but where Mr. Riddle was smallish and wiry, Paul was tall, athletically built, and as handsome as Beatrice was beautiful. Consequently, I noticed my left leg shaking in unison with my right. The night was not going at all as I had anticipated.

Now, I've never had the opportunity to dine with royalty, but I doubt eating with a queen would cause me to be any more uptight than I was eating dinner that night at the Riddles.' Thankfully, Momma had taken great pains to teach me table manners, so I was not completely lost. However, I'd never dined at a table so formal. I watched Mrs. Riddle and Beatrice the entire meal to see which utensil to pick up and how to use it. Knowing when in doubt, watch the hostess, I even tried to match my eating pace with that of Mrs. Riddle. However, after ten minutes had passed and she'd taken all of four bites, I decided starvation was a real possibility and forged ahead, pausing only long enough to make polite conversation. After all, I reasoned, food will only stay warm for so long.

Miz Tessie added a complete other dimension to my

discomfort. Throughout the years she'd become my friend and something of a mentor. It was Miz Tessie who'd taught me to put a little sugar in with my vegetables and be generous when using vanilla extract. Each time we met, she'd greet me with her big toothy smile and one of her infamous bear hugs. Occasionally, I'd dawdle in the kitchen to see her work her magic. To have her serve me now seemed somehow wrong. To the Riddles it was part of her job, but I felt a degree of shame about it through the entire meal.

When dinner was finally finished, I took my plate, ready to go to the kitchen and at least do my part to clean up. Miz Tessie suddenly took it from my hands. "Don't you worry about that tonight," she whispered hoarsely. "That be my job." My eyes widened as I tried to understand her sharpness. Sensing my discomfort, she reached out her brown, puffy hand and patted my shoulder. "Let this be my way of showin' you my appreciation." She smiled and turned to go into the kitchen.

With dessert finished, the adults went into the parlor for conversation while Beatrice and I headed to the basement. "I've got something to show you," she explained. "It won't take long. I promise."

Once downstairs, Beatrice grabbed the borrowed basketball and started dribbling. Even in her dress, she was agile and in control. She pretended to have a defender guarding her and put her back to the peach basket just like I'd taught her. With her imaginary man guarding her, Beatrice deftly switched dribbling between her left and right hands before turning and shooting the ball, only to have it bounce off the back wall and through the basket.

"Wow! You've been practicing!" I clapped my hands in admiration.

"I just don't want to be behind," Beatrice responded modestly.

"Oh, really? By the looks of that little show, you have a pretty dark competitive streak."

Beatrice grinned. "I do like this game. I'm anxious to try it with a full team." She walked over to the steps and took a seat next to me. Her hands rubbed back and forth across the top of the ball. "Playing helps me keep my mind off other things." There was a catch in her voice. We'd not really had a chance to talk since the night of the birth.

"How are you doing? Are you feeling well?" I didn't know what else to ask.

"My body feels fine, but it's almost like there is a hole in my chest. It feels so cold and empty." Tears started brimming in Beatrice's eyes. "Some moments I think I'm doing well, like everything is going to be fine. Other times, I find myself crying over the silliest things."

The two of us sat quietly on the steps. I placed my arm around her shoulders in an effort to show some bit of comfort. Beatrice continued. "I knew I couldn't keep that baby from the moment I found out I was expecting—even before I told mother and father. I tried, really tried not to care about him. I didn't hate him. I just tried not to care. But at night, when I'm alone in my room, all I can see is his tiny chin and blond hair. And I think, *How big is he now? Is he eating well? Is he being held enough?* I practically drive myself crazy with questions." Beatrice's cheeks were now wet with tears. "Oh, Lilly Kate, sometimes I feel as though I'm going to lose my mind!"

There are times in life when words are futile. I remembered when Poppa died, well-meaning neighbors would say things meant to comfort, but my heart wasn't yet ready to listen. At times it seemed their lips were moving but no sound was coming out. Only later, when the shock and dismay had dulled slightly, did their words bring any measure of peace. I suspected there was little I could say at that moment to lessen her sadness. So, I decided to just be still with my friend. Be still.

Beatrice and I sat in silence for only a few moments before Mrs. Riddle opened the door and called down. "Lilly Kate, will you come up to Mr. Riddle's study for a moment? He has something he'd like to discuss with you." I glanced questioningly at Beatrice. She'd stopped crying, but her eyes were still moist and a few tear stains streaked her cheeks. But her lips held slight curve that said she knew this meeting would happen.

Beatrice's knowing glance brought me only a tiny modicum of comfort. Mr. Riddle and I had never exchanged more than a dozen words, and at least half of those were words of greeting. Even on the way home from Frankfort the night of the baby's birth, we'd ridden in utter silence, both lost in thought and fatigue. To be summoned to his study was just another event of the evening well out of my normal routine.

"Come in, Lilly Kate," Mr. Riddle said heartily as Mrs. Riddle showed me to the door. "Please, have a seat."

My eyes flashed around the study. Each time I'd passed before the double pocket doors they had been pulled closed, so I was getting a full picture for the first time. Like everything else in the home, it was ornate, each detail meticulously executed. The crown molding, trim, and bookshelves all seemed to be made of the same rich, deep-colored wood that glistened in the lamplight. Mr. Riddle sat behind his impressive desk, which was larger than most kitchen tables I'd seen. He eyed me thoughtfully as he lit his pipe and shook out the match. The comforting smell of the sweet cured tobacco reached my nose, and for a second it was almost as though Poppa was in the room with us.

Mr. Riddle leaned back in his chair and puffed his pipe. "Young lady, I don't think I've ever thanked you properly for all the help you've been to our Beatrice during these last few months."

"You're quite welcome. Tutoring Beatrice was really quite easy. She's an excellent student."

Mr. Riddle smiled and leaned forward, placing his elbows on his desk. "I don't just mean the tutoring. Of course, education is important, and she wanted to keep up with her studies, but you became more. You became our daughter's friend at a time when she needed a friend the most." He cleared his throat, rose from his chair, and began walking around the room, looking at the shelves as though trying to find a book. "This has been a very difficult time for all of us, as I'm sure you understand. It's difficult for a father to stand back and watch his daughter in a time of need and be so helpless." Mr. Riddle stopped in front of an old portrait, one I assumed to be a Riddle ancestor. He pulled out a handkerchief from his pocket and wiped his eyes before continuing.

"Sending the child to the state home was not an easy decision for any of us. We just felt that under the circumstances, he could find a home in a place where he'd be more readily accepted." Mr. Riddle seemed to be speaking more to himself than to me.

"I've been praying the child would find a loving family," I replied rather meekly.

Mr. Riddle sat back in his chair and looked at me seriously. "Yes, I'm sure you have. You know, I hadn't been much of a religious man prior to all this, but during the last eight months or so, I seem to have found a good deal of comfort in prayer." Mr. Riddle and I exchanged smiles before he continued.

"Mrs. Riddle and I would like to show you how grateful we are for your services." Mr. Riddle reached into his desk and pulled out a large, leather-bound book. When he opened it, I could see it was filled with blank checks.

Reaching for his pen, he began to write. "I'd like for you to take this money for the services you've given to Beatrice and the rest of the family. I'm sure an industrious young lady such as you will find a good use for it."

Mr. Riddle handed me the check from across the table. Cautiously, I took it and glanced at the amount. It was the most money I'd ever held in my hand at one time. There were certainly a hundred uses for it, but only one came to mind—college. For a moment, my heart began to patter with the thought that this might be the answer to my prayers; this was God's way of providing. Surely the money was meant to be used for school.

But just as quickly as I thought of college, there popped into my head a memory of the day I'd agreed to help Beatrice. It had been the first day of school, holding with it all the promises that only a first day can. When Mrs. Kavanaugh had asked me to help, I'd been more than a little reluctant. In fact, I'd been a bit angry. I'd thought helping Beatrice would be a massive inconvenience, an intrusion on my plans. There were multiple reasons to turn down the job. Yet, on the walk home, I'd remembered the sermon Reverend Searcy had preached about loving your neighbor and giving a cup of cold water in Jesus's name. I hadn't wanted to help, but I did it because helping is what I was called to do.

Then I thought of Beatrice, still in mourning for her little boy. Through it all we'd become friends, bonded friends, the kind of friends who share a deep experience that binds them for life. That alone was a reward I'd never expected. To take money for it would seem to trivialize everything. As much as I wanted the money, as much as I needed it, taking money for friendship would only taint it. My head desperately wanted to fold the check and place it carefully in my pocket; yet, the still, small voice in my heart said differently.

"I hope you find it generous," Mr. Riddle offered when he saw the check shaking in my hand.

"Yes, sir. More than generous." I licked my lips and placed my hand on my leg to stop the twitching. "It's very kind of you. It really is, but I don't think I can accept it."

"Can't accept it? Of course you can! You've done this family a tremendous service!" Mr. Riddle seemed shocked, almost indignant at my reply. It occurred to me no one might have ever turned down one of his checks.

"I don't mean to sound ungrateful, Mr. Riddle. In fact, it's quite the opposite. I didn't become Beatrice's tutor for the money. I did it because it's what I felt I was supposed to do. Then, quite to my surprise, we became friends. That in itself was more than I ever expected. I'm not saying I couldn't use the money. Certainly I could, but if I took it, then it would be like paying me for my friendship, and that's not for sale. It's free."

Mr. Riddle had once again started to puff on his pipe. He was looking at me thoughtfully, although I wasn't sure of his expression. A part of me expected him to argue with me to try to convince me to take the money, and frankly I wasn't sure I could withstand the argument. But, much to my surprise, he simply sat in his chair, lost in thought. "Well!" he finally exclaimed as he slapped both hands atop his desk. "Miss Overstreet, you certainly are a peculiar young lady. Still, I respect your choice." Mr. Riddle rose from his chair, walked around his desk and motioned for me to get out of my seat. "Can I at least give you a hug?" He smiled as he stretched out his arms. I nodded as Mr. Riddle, the richest man in town, wrapped his fatherly arms around me in a hug of gratitude.

Chapter Eighteen

By the time school started back, the weather had taken a bitter turn. It felt as though someone had left the door to the Arctic open, and it was blowing right onto our town. Momma and I had started warming bricks on the stove, wrapping them in towels, and taking them to bed with us. Even Taft was allowed in our bed, not so much because Momma felt sorry for him on the floor, but because he added another degree or two of warmth.

At school the students all remained in their coats for the majority of the day. The grandeur of the house that made it spacious enough for a school was the very quality that made it difficult to heat. Mrs. K had put the house boys in charge of keeping wood cut for the fireplaces, but the heat seemed to escape up the chimney. Desks or chairs next to a fireplace became so coveted that some students began getting to school an hour early just to secure a spot. Even so, Huey was back to his jovial self and tried to make light of the situation. "Just think," he blurted at lunch one day as we all huddled over our lunches, "when it warms up in here, we can kill some hogs." The comic relief was lost on all the townies who didn't understand that meat should be butchered in the cold so as to avoid spoiling, but we were well below hog-killing temps. Consequently, I found myself guffawing solo and attracting numerous stares of bewilderment.

It was during this time that I seriously began to question my decision not to accept Mr. Riddle's check. Each time I heard Huey mention Georgetown or some of the house boys discuss the military academy, a wave of regret would engulf me. The small voice that had seemed so clear on New Year's Eve in Mr. Riddle's study was gone now, and left in its place was the haunting feeling that perhaps I'd misunderstood. Maybe there had been no small voice at all. I began to wonder if the missionaries in China ever questioned their calling and wished to stow away on a boat back to America. Or better yet, did Reverend Searcy ever wish to board a train and leave the congregation with all its problems—especially after a deacons' meeting?

There were, however, some bright spots in the bleak winter weeks. Beatrice was back at school, but not exactly as her old self of years past. If anything, she had matured. She still wore her expensive clothes and finery, but she didn't seem to have the need to show them off. No longer did she have her crass nature or give disdainful looks. Instead, she was more patient, more thoughtful. She had a sensitivity to her that had not been present before, one that seemed to have its source in the well of pain she'd been thrust into. Nor did Beatrice ignore those people who were not previously in her inner circle. While Eunice and Ruby were still her pals, she spoke kindly to everyone, including me.

The first day back when Beatrice asked me to eat lunch with her, I noticed Eunice and Ruby exchange looks of surprise. Beatrice must have noticed it too and said quite pointedly, "I'm sure you both know how much of a friend Lilly Kate was to me during my illness." Ruby and Eunice said no more, and the four of us had a pleasant lunch together. Even so, at times when she thought no one was looking, I'd spot Beatrice staring listlessly out the window. It was at those times I saw a sadness in her eyes and knew her heart to be deeply bruised.

For Mrs. Rutherford, the frozen ground of winter was a blessed thing. Each day, if the ground wasn't covered in ice or the sky wasn't pouring snow, Mrs. Rutherford would have all the girls layer on their clothing and go out back to the bare patch of dirt and practice basketball. She claimed the exercise was good for our lungs, but when mine started burning like a fire had been started within them, I had some serious doubts. Nonetheless, she insisted. By this time, everyone had become so taken with the game that the school had two real goals set up on a makeshift court instead of an old basket nailed to the side of the school. Each day for a week, Mrs. Rutherford would cajole the junior and senior girls outside and force us into some physical activity. I'd overheard some of the other girls say their mothers were afraid we'd catch pneumonia, but after a few weeks of playing on the tundra, as we called it, the ladies were sniffling less than the boys.

Within a few weeks of Mrs. Rutherford starting this ritual, I began to realize I was actually looking forward to playing basketball each day. I liked the way my muscles stretched and had begun to take on a tautness I hadn't realized I'd lost since we had moved to town. My arms felt stronger, and the pounding in my heart felt like raw energy pushing through my entire body. The air outside was still icy and crisp, but once we began playing, I could feel my insides begin to warm.

Only once did I hear anyone complain. Eunice Bond claimed it wasn't in her nature to be so physical and to sweat. "It's just so…so crude! And it's so cold!" she lamented. Before I could even think of a response, Beatrice told her in no uncertain terms, "Stop behaving like you are some china doll. We are not being asked to haul timber. Get out there and hustle!" Eunice did as she was told, and based on the swiftness with which the other girls were putting on their outdoor clothes and the smiles on their faces, I suspected they were secretly applauding Beatrice's remarks.

Mrs. Rutherford had me playing forward, mostly because I was not especially adept at dribbling. My job, as I understood it, was to stay near the basket and catch the ball as it was thrown to me. Then, if open, I was to take a shot. Mrs. Rutherford was careful to teach us the proper technique for a more feminine, one-armed jump shot, stating that some people felt the two-armed shot that flattened the chest was unladylike. In theory this sounded easy, but as we progressed, everyone's defense became more aggressive, and I found myself having to wiggle my way for an open shot or else pass the ball. As luck would have it, Eunice was our center because of her height. After Beatrice's sharp reprimand, she came down off her high horse and settled into a pretty good player, her three-inch height advantage making it easier to take a shot. However, she hadn't yet mastered the art of handling the ball and was prone to losing it. The other forward was Ruby Likens. Another senior girl, Sara Birdwhistell, played the second guard position.

But the star by everyone's admission was Beatrice. Those hours she'd wiled away in her basement were paying off. She had the most control when she dribbled, and she was the best shot of anyone. Boys and girls alike were taken aback to see her play with such ferocity and skill. When Beatrice confessed that I'd taught her about the game during her recuperation, everyone accepted her explanation, but I knew she'd spent hours in her basement perfecting her game in an effort to keep her mind from drifting elsewhere.

Five other girls, all juniors, made up our only competition, but even the boys were becoming intrigued. Despite the fence that hid us from view of the school, we'd sometimes see a few fellows watching through the holes or simply be brave and sit atop the fencerow. At first, some of them wanted to heckle a bit and poke fun at a group of girls playing a sport. But after one afternoon when Beatrice sunk three shots in a row, the jibing turned to cheers, and the boys became our biggest supporters. Every once in a while, Mrs. K herself came and watched us a bit, and I noticed a distinct grin on her face every time. I think deep down there was a little piece of her that wanted to play too.

Basketball became the great winter distraction. It gave everyone something to which they could look forward. As the season wore on, we played every day that we could. On those days when the weather wouldn't cooperate or the ground was just too soggy, Mrs. Rutherford would announce there could be no basketball that day. The result was an audible groan from both boys and girls alike.

As the winter thawed and spring began to come on, we were able to shed some of our outer layers as we played. It was at this time we truly began to notice what a hindrance skirts could be. As our ball handling skills improved, our skirts became more and more cumbersome, causing more than their fair share of mistakes and the real threat of a nasty fall.

"Blast these skirts!" Eunice yelled one day after the ball had bounced off the hem of her dress. "I've half a mind to play in my bloomers!" To her credit, Eunice's sense of propriety had been severely altered as her interest in the game heightened. Her enthusiasm for the game came in second only to Beatrice's.

"Why can't we, Mrs. Rutherford?" Ruby asked. "We could do so much better if we played in our bloomers, just so long as the boys aren't watching."

"You'll do no such thing!" Mrs. Rutherford exclaimed. "I've taken enough criticism for teaching you girls a sport. I won't have people in the community claiming I've allowed you to scurry around indecent. They'd run me out of town. For now, you'll just have to make do."

And make do is exactly what we did. As necessity is the mother of invention, so is discomfort. We tried several fixes to our problems with our skirts. Our first effort included pinning up the hem to just below our knees. The few minutes our legs had of this freedom brought untold joy. Never have ten young ladies experienced such happiness from the ability to run freely. But when Mrs. Kavanaugh spotted us playing with our ankles and legs visible for all to see, we received a severe tongue-lashing, and the hems came down. Our freedom was short lived.

A few days later, Sara tried taking pins and placing them up the middle of her skirt, holding the front and back together. The result was, in effect, a split skirt such as those used for horseback riding. The plan may have worked, but midway through the game she let out a hair-raising scream that caused everyone to stop dead in their tracks and start staring. We all turned to see Sara yanking a pin out of her mid-thigh. Most of us watched in disbelief, and a few of the boys turned green as a stream of blood made it to the surface of the material. Mrs. Rutherford rushed her inside, and the rest of us decided to call off the game for the rest of the day. Mrs. Kavanaugh seriously considered forbidding us to play thereafter, claiming she could not support an activity that brought with it such unladylike results. But when Sara came back to school the next day, she begged Mrs. K not to punish everyone else for her failed experiment. "You can't blame the team for my foolishness," she begged Mrs. Kavanaugh. "We'll play in our skirts from now on with no complaints. We promise."

And play we did, although the complaining didn't really diminish; it was only kept out of earshot from Mrs. Kavanaugh.

Chapter Nineteen

"Beware the Ides of March," Shakespeare had written. Although it was in reference to the murder of Julius Caesar, the middle of March 1912 brought with it its own heartbreak for me. Since their Christmas announcement, I'd dreaded the wedding of Jimalee and Dink. Not that I didn't think they made a terrific couple. Quite the contrary, they were a perfect fit. Dink's easy-going personality was an elixir for Jimalee's brusque ways. Both had similar values and work ethic, and neither one cared one iota what other people thought. "I don't know why you're so sensitive," Jimalee scolded me one day. "You're skin is so thin, it's a wonder you ain't covered in bruises."

To which I added, "And yours is so tough you ought to be a human pin cushion."

Since the engagement, Jimalee had ceased coming over in the middle of the week for a visit. I still saw her on the weekends, but only briefly since she and Dink were busy making plans. Most of the time I was able to put the hurt in the back of my mind. School, the paper, and basketball were keeping me plenty busy, but at night when my homework was done, I missed my friend fiercely. No amount of activities could take the place of a good friend.

"Aw, shucks, Lilly Kate, you're thinking about this too much," Huey said, trying to console me when I confessed my feelings. "You know as well as I do that Jimalee Jenkins is not going to change. You two will be friends for the rest of your lives."

"I know that! Jimalee won't change, but the situation will!"

"Of course, it will! Times always change. It's a good thing. Life would be sad if nothing ever changed."

"You sound like my mother."

"Well, it's true."

"Maybe for you! You've got college to look forward to. Jimalee and Dink have marriage and their life together. Sometimes I feel like I'm just going to stay here and grow old."

"With that attitude you will probably be very successful at it," Huey retorted. It was not the sympathy I was expecting or craving. "Yes, you heard me! You're just feeling sorry for yourself, and let me tell you something: it's not pretty. Ever since I've known you, you've been encouraging me, giving me a boost when I needed it. More than any other person you've challenged me and forced me to work harder. Well, now I'm giving you a taste of your own medicine." Huey's eyes were blazing, and his breathing was heavy. "Yes, one of your best friends is getting married, and another will be going to college, but I'm not going to apologize for that. Those are happy and joyous things. I wish Georgetown had worked out for you. I honestly do. But it didn't, and now you've got to get your head out of that shell you've been hiding in and stop feeling sorry for yourself."

I stared blankly at Huey. My mouth was dry and a hard lump appeared in my throat. I knew I was going to cry. The hot, stinging tears were welling up in my eyes, and I had to clench my teeth to keep my chin from quivering. Slowly, with books pressed to my chest, I began to walk away. Huey touched my shoulder and turned me around. His eyes had grown softer, and he spoke with more gentleness in his voice. "I'm sorry, Lilly Kate. The last thing I want is to hurt you, and the first thing I want is to see you happy. Honest. But I can't do that for you. You have to do that for yourself."

Oh, the truth spoken by a friend can hurt. Friends can make the deepest cuts in a soul. At that moment I'd had a mirror held up in front of me, and I didn't like what I saw. Self-pity is never attractive.

All the way home I wanted nothing more than to smack Huey broadly across the face. *I'll even take off a few freckles in the process,* I thought. How dare he talk to me as though I were a child? By the time I arrived on Posey Street, my nose was dripping, my eyes were still stinging, and if I'd stopped by a mirror to look, there might have even been a bit of steam coming out of my ears. I began to wonder what kind of right hook I had and if Huey would mind being a test case.

I huffed into the house, half expecting Momma to chastise me for slamming the door, only to find Jimalee sitting down in one of the wicker chairs and Momma sitting next to her. Jimalee's cheeks were tearstained, and she was fiddling with what looked like a well-used handkerchief. Momma popped up from her seat and quickly gathered her things to go. "Lilly Kate, Jimalee has something she'd like to discuss with you," she said. "I've got to go to the post office, and I'll leave you two alone."

The anger I'd felt over Huey's reprimand quickly disappeared. In its place, I began to worry over my friend. In all the time we'd known each other, I'd never seen Jimalee look so distraught, so shaken. My immediate thought was that there had been an accident or someone had died. Maybe someone was sick. I hastily threw down my books and ran to her side. "Oh, Jimalee, what's happened?"

Jimalee put her head on my shoulder and began to sob. "Oh, Lilly Kate, me and Dink had the most terrible, terrible fight. It was awful, just awful!"

What slight relief I felt from the news no one was

physically hurt was immediately replaced by concern for my friend. Strands of her hair were stuck to her moist cheeks, and her breathing was labored between cries. I put my arms around her and began to rub her back, much like Momma had done for me so many times in the past. "Surely it's not so bad," I tried to console. "Talk to me about it. I'm sure this can be all worked out."

Jimalee pulled away from me and began to choke out the story. "Well, we was takin' a walk and talkin' about all our plans. Dink was tellin' me about all the nice furniture he'd been building and how careful he'd been to select just the right wood. Then all of the sudden, he started talkin' about buildin' baby furniture. I told him I sure wouldn't mind a baby or two, but I didn't care for a baker's dozen like the family he's come from." Jimalee paused to blow her nose, and I could almost tell where this story was going. "Then Dink said to me, 'What's wrong with a big family like mine?' and I said, 'There's nothin' wrong with it, but you're the baby and haven't had to do a fraction of the work that comes from feeding all those mouths, changing all those diapers, or washin' all those clothes.' I then told him I'd spent most of my life helping to raise my wily brothers, thank you very much, and I didn't have any intention of birthin' a baby every year for the next ten to fifteen years!'"

Jimalee stopped and let out a few more wails of anguish before continuing. "When Dink insisted a big family was something to be proud of and I should be happy to work so hard for all the children, I told him he didn't want me to be his wife. He wanted me to be his slave! After that, Dink called me a hard-headed mule and stormed off. I haven't seen him since."

We sat there together in silence for a moment. Jimalee's tears had begun to lessen. Although I tried with all my might to keep a face of concern, I was inwardly laughing.

I could feel the muscles in my abdomen tighten as I tried to suppress a giggle. Jimalee's sharp tongue had finally landed her in a barrel of brine—one that she'd helped to create, no less. And now she needed some help to find her way out.

"Jims," I began with all the compassion I could muster, "I know you've worked hard helping to raise Matthew, Mark, Luke, and John. But those are your brothers. Do you think it's possible you might feel differently if they were your own children?"

"*No!*" Jimalee screamed. "I'll never enjoy hanging out the wash or scrubbing floors!"

"I didn't say you'd enjoy it. I said you might feel differently. Besides, you don't even know what's going to happen. After a few children, either one of you might change your minds. You're borrowing trouble by worrying about things that haven't even happened yet. You might decide motherhood is the greatest gift ever. Or maybe, Dink will decide a small family is wonderful too."

Jimalee sniffed. "I suppose you've got a point."

"You bet I do." I felt like a preacher at the pulpit. My pulse rate began to rise. "And besides that, I'm sure no matter how many children you have, Dink Pruitt will be a good father and a loving husband. That boy doesn't even know the meaning of the words selfish, lazy, or highstrung." If I'd had a podium, I would've pounded it with my fist. I felt almost touched by the spirit. No wonder so many preachers broke out in a sweat. "But most importantly, Dink loves you with all his heart. I can see it in his eyes every time he looks at you. I'm certain he'd never purposely do anything that he knew would make you unhappy."

Jimalee stood up from her chair for the first time since I'd walked in. "Yes, I suppose you're right," she said as she stared at the wall thoughtfully. "But what about all those terrible things I said to him? What do I do?"

"Go and apologize. I'm sure Dink will understand."

"I've never been very good at apologies," Jimalee admitted.

Immediately, I understood this gap in her abilities came from lack of practice. "No, I don't reckon you have, but if you want Dink to meet you at the altar next Sunday afternoon, I think you'd better give it a try."

"You're right. You're absolutely right." Jimalee reached for her shawl. "I'm going to go right now and straighten all this out." Jimalee reached for the door and abruptly stopped and turned around. She looked at me and began to speak, her voice softened a bit. "Thanks, Lilly Kate. Thank you for listening...and for being such a good friend." Jimalee wrapped her arms around me and gave me another tight hug, this one filled with hope instead of sadness. I watched as she walked away and felt a spring of contentment well up inside me. For the first time since they'd made their announcement, I was looking forward to their wedding.

The week leading up to Dink and Jimalee's big day was considered by the old-timers in town to be the Great Thaw. It was as though the earth's axis had suddenly tilted, giving everyone a taste of spring. Yellow daffodils began to bloom in flowerbeds, fencerows, and the sides of the roads. The single yellow flower gave everyone an extra lift in his or her step. When Sunday morning finally arrived, I walked to church without my coat for the first time since Christmas morning. The wind still had a chill, but I felt free to be out of so many layers. The goose bumps were worth it.

Jimalee and Dink had chosen to get married on Sunday for one simple reason—everyone would already be dressed up. "No need in anybody takin' two baths in one week on account of us," Dink humbly mused. That morning Momma allowed me to go to the Jenkins' right after Sunday school so that I could be of some help. When I arrived and walked onto the front porch, I noticed everything was eerily quiet. Never had I been to the Jenkins' home without being greeted by the screams of young boys, whether playing or arguing.

Jimalee flung open the door, wearing a massive smile and wiggling so much I thought she might jump out of her skin. "Guess what?" she hollered. "I'm getting married!"

Jimalee continued to laugh at her own joke, so I finally let myself in and gave her a hug. "Glad to see you're doing well, but where are the boys?"

"Oh, they were makin' such a ruckus that Momma sent them hunting for anything green or bloomin,'" Jimalee said over her shoulder as we went upstairs to her room.

"Knowing your brothers, do you think that's safe?"

"Knowing my brothers, do you think I care?"

At thirty minutes before the wedding, the Jenkins' lawn was already covered with wagons and carriages, and a steady line was still coming down the road, most from the direction of Fox Creek. "Those Pruitts stick together like burrs on a dog," Jimalee observed. "If Dink ever decides he wants to run for office, I believe he'd win."

I smiled and watched my friend as she looked out the window. The giddiness she had felt earlier had dissipated, and in its place was something akin to serenity. Now she was dressed and awaiting her wedding. Jimalee's mother had made good on her promise to make a new dress, and by any standard she had done an excellent job. Cream-colored lace was prevalent on the entire dress, from the bodice and neck all the way to the cuffs of her sleeves.

The floor-length pattern had a fitted waist that was high-lighted by a peach-colored satin sash. I couldn't help but notice it seemed to match the color of her cheeks.

"You look truly beautiful, Jimalee," I complimented.

Jimalee turned from the window and gave a sigh of relief. "Do you really think so? I was afraid I looked like an overgrown snowflake."

I swallowed a laugh. "No," I replied. "You look more beautiful than any bride I've ever seen."

Just then, a knock came at the door, and Jimalee's mother walked in. "Girls, it's almost time. Lilly Kate, why don't you go and take your place? I'd like a couple of moments with my daughter."

I quickly gave Jimalee one last hug. As we embraced, it occurred to me that the next hug I gave her she would be Mrs. Hezekiah Pruitt. That tiny fact seemed somehow profound, as though it marked a definitive end to child-hood and an absolute beginning to adulthood. Seldom does someone see a turning point in life before it actually happens, but I could feel the winds of change blowing through the room at that moment. Yet, instead of feeling something close to sorrow and grief as I had held in recent months, I was able to feel the joy of the moment and the happiness that comes from new beginnings. "I'm truly happy for you," I whispered to Jimalee. And this time, I meant it with all my heart.

After the ceremony and the proverbial feast from the "fruit of the swine" that followed, Dink and Jimalee loaded up a borrowed carriage and headed toward Frankfort, where they would be staying with Dink's great aunt for a few days. I had so wanted to give her a hug and tell them both good-bye, but I never could get their attention to do so.

It seemed every guest wanted a moment of their time. I'd resigned myself to being one of the crowd waving them off. Then, surprisingly, I felt a light tap from behind on my shoulder. I turned to see Jimalee and Dink standing together dressed in their travel clothes.

"We wanted to give you this," Jimalee said as she held out a small, colorful box. I reached for it with a bewildered expression on my face.

"It's because you're the reason we met in the first place," Dink offered. His good eye was beaming from happiness, and the other was twitching from all the excitement. "We just wanted you to know how much you mean to us."

"Don't open it now. Wait until later," Jimalee interjected. "I don't think I can take one more sentimental moment today," she added in an unusual display of emotional candor.

My mouth tried to form words for gratitude, but none came out. Instead, I threw my arms around both of them and began to cry for the first time that day. "I love you both. You know that, don't you?" Tears began to flow, and Jimalee nodded her head in agreement.

"Now, now!" Dink interrupted, wiping his nose with his sleeve. "Let's not all get weepy like collard greens. This here's a happy time. Come on, Jimalee, we've got to get goin' if we're going to make it by nightfall."

Jimalee nodded and squeezed my hand as Dink guided his new bride away to their daffodil-covered carriage. It was apparent the Jenkins' boys had been successful in their hunt for flowers and had chosen to string them through every available crevice in the carriage. Even the team of horses had a few looped through their harnesses. The effect was more of a large, gangly dandelion than a princess's chariot, but it somehow seemed to suit them both.

Once Momma and I walked back home, I went to the bedroom while she went out back to check her garden bed. I was thrilled to open the gift in private. The cube-shaped box had been fully wrapped in bright blue paper and tied with twine. Quietly, I pulled the string, peeled back the paper, and lifted the lid. Inside was a note that read:

> "Thought every teacher needed one like this. Thank you, Jims and Dink."

Buried deep beneath some tissue paper was a shell-carved cameo brooch. It wasn't as ornate or as detailed as some I'd seen before, but the effect was certainly lovely. In the middle was a Victorian-looking lady turned to her left shoulder. It was surrounded by a wreath-like frame made of leaves. My mind immediately flashed back to Miss Daphne. Every day for the eight years that she stood in front of the classroom teaching, she'd worn one similar. It became such a part of her attire, I'd completely forgotten about it. Apparently, Dink had not and somehow felt it was a necessary accessory for being a teacher, like paper and chalk.

All the emotions I'd carried throughout the day surfaced, and I began to laugh and cry at the same time.

"Whatever is the matter in here?" Momma came in with a start.

"Look!" I handed her the gift and note.

"Well, that's just about the most thoughtful thing I've ever seen," Momma announced. Coming from her, that was no small compliment.

"It's even more than thoughtful," I confessed. "It's almost prophetic."

"Whatever do you mean?" Momma gave me a look that said I'd better have a good response. She thought I might be bordering on blasphemy.

"Well, I don't recall ever talking to Jimalee or Dink about taking the teacher's exam," I confessed.

Momma's eyes softened as she took the brooch out of the box to look at it more closely. "You know, some things are just obvious."

"You mean that, Momma?"

"Yes, daughter, I really do." She stood and looked out the back window. "Some things are as obvious as who took my daffodils and left a big hole in my flower bed!"

Chapter Twenty

During the course of the next month, everything became greener, and the world seemed to wake up from a deep sleep. The air was still chilly in the mornings, but by noon, the weather was simply too nice to stay indoors. After a winter of being huddled up around the fireplaces, the students of Kavanaugh took to eating their lunches on the front porch or even the lawn. When we'd come back in, the teachers would sometimes have to work extra hard at regaining our attention. Consequently, they accused us of having spring fever. But I spotted more than one instructor staring wistfully out the window. Spring fever is apparently contagious and does not discriminate against age.

Mrs. Kavanaugh, however, was oblivious to the weather or any other element that might distract from our education. If anything, the fact that military school entrance exams and graduation were both drawing near seemed to galvanize her resolve to fill us with as much education as possible. Her determination could be calculated by the number of hard whacks she gave her black umbrella. "As you can see (*thwack!*), this geometric proof is incorrect (*thwack!*). Try it again (*thwack!*)!" Just as seats near the fireplace became valued commodities in the winter, so did seats in the back of the room when Mrs. Kavanaugh began using her umbrella. When I asked one of the house boys how things were going after the regular school hours, he gave me a glassy look and told me he simply couldn't discuss it.

To take a break from all our studies, the junior and

senior girls would finish lunch early and go out back for a quick game of basketball. Mrs. Rutherford had long gone on to teaching something else, but basketball seemed to have gotten into everyone's blood. It was a terrific release from having been cooped up, and now that everyone understood the game, it had become even more enjoyable.

One Monday in April, a few of the guys had been watching us and began to tease us when we played, yelling little jabs or making animal noises. We ignored it for a while, but Frankie Crawford went too far and ended up with more than he could handle.

"Aww! You girls are just trying to act like boys out there playing a sport!" he teased from behind the goal. "What's next? Are you going to wear a suit and tie and try to run for governor?" I couldn't help but wonder if he was echoing something he'd heard at home from his father, Duce, and this troubled me. I chose to ignore it, but Eunice Bond was in no mood to listen to Frankie or any other boy tease her. I don't know if she'd had a poor night's sleep or had been simmering for weeks, but when Frankie started teasing, she tensed up and whipped her body around with tornado-like force. With the basketball in hand she marched right over and stood in front of Frankie.

"We are *not* trying to be boys. If that was the case, we'd be yelling insults and snorting and spitting! Can't a young lady enjoy some physical exercise? What's more, if you'd like to play with us, you're more than welcome, but you'll need to put on a skirt in order to make it fair!" She then threw Frankie the ball, which he failed to catch, consequently popping him in the nose.

The other boys were now whooping and hollering, letting Frankie know he'd been bested. His face became red from both the pain of injury and the pain of insult. He mumbled something under his breath and stormed his way inside. The thought crossed my mind to give Eunice a big kiss on the cheek for work well done, but Mrs. Rutherford came outside and signaled everyone to come on in. Lunch break was over.

Immediately, everyone began passing questioning looks. We had at least ten more minutes. Something was amiss. Frankie was certainly being a jerk, but he was no tattletale.

As we walked in, we could see the classroom doors were all open, just as they had been on opening day. No chairs were put out, but we were instructed to stand and wait for Mrs. Kavanaugh to speak with us. She had an announcement.

Frankie was already standing in a corner, sulking. His nose didn't look like it was any worse for the wear with the exception of a little redness, but I couldn't help but wonder if the injuries didn't go well below the surface.

"What do you think is going on?" Beatrice whispered. Somehow she had the sense this was a serious issue.

"I don't know. It seems a little odd. We've never been called in from lunch this early."

Within one minute Mrs. K descended from upstairs and stood on the first landing in order for everyone to see and hear. Her eyes looked even more serious than usual, and she wasn't carrying her black umbrella. In its place was a starch-white handkerchief. Without a single word spoken, we all knew something was frightfully wrong.

"Students," she began, "I have a most unfortunate announcement to make. As you are aware, the largest ocean liner ever built, *Titanic*, set sail last Wednesday."

Yes, we were all aware. The teachers at school had been fascinated by the story of the monstrous ship and had mentioned it to us from time to time. "You'll want to tell your grandchildren that you remember the maiden voyage of this ship," a few had declared. "Perhaps someday you'll get to sail on it yourself." Such declarations had been met with more than a few pairs of rolling, uninterested eyes.

Personally, the idea of a ship that was actually larger than Main Street Lawrenceburg seemed foreign to me. I'd read about its tonnage, unbelievable horsepower, and plush accommodations, but try as I might, it wasn't a real interest. I'd grown up surrounded by hills and had never seen the ocean. While the idea of a floating, unsinkable city had a certain fairy tale quality to it, my limited experiences wouldn't allow me to comprehend its magnitude. However, several adults in the community had followed the story of the *Titanic* quite closely, Mrs. K being one of them.

Beatrice was also completely enthralled. Her trip to Europe the summer before had made her our resident expert on all things maritime, if only with regard to descriptions of dining halls and sleeping quarters. "I thought our ship was like a floating palace," she'd admitted. "But compared to the descriptions of the *Titanic*, we were practically riding on a row boat."

"I've just read the paper," Mrs. Kavanaugh continued. "It seems there's been a terrible accident." She paused and blotted her eyes with her handkerchief. It was the first time I'd ever seen her moved in such a way, and it frightened me. Prior to that moment I'd always considered her unshakable. "The *Titanic* sunk in the early hours of yesterday morning." An audible gasp could be heard throughout the room. Everyone looked at each other with a stunned expression. "There are some survivors, but there are many more who didn't make it. Estimates are that well over a thousand lost their lives, some of them children."

Heads throughout the room dropped as the magnitude of the news began to register. More than a thousand people? We couldn't grasp it. I didn't even know a thousand people. It would be like erasing our entire town, perhaps our whole county. And the children. There were children who hadn't even had a chance to start out in life who were now gone. What about the children who did survive? Did they lose a parent or perhaps both? The senselessness of it all seemed to grow with every second.

The room was eerily still. Only the ticking of the clock and a few sniffles could be heard for a full minute. Finally someone broke the silence, and questions began flying throughout the room?

"How did it happen?"

"Where was the ship?"

"I thought it was unsinkable. Was it sabotage?"

"Weren't there a lot of wealthy people on the ship? What happened to them?"

"Quiet, please," Mrs. Kavanaugh called. She was missing her umbrella so she slapped the banister with her hand, making a loud popping noise. "I know you all have questions, but I don't have the answers. No one does. At least not yet. I will let you read the paper, but beyond that, I cannot help you. Suffice it to say, this is an international tragedy." She used her handkerchief again and cleared her throat. "For now, I thought it best to tell you and take this opportunity to join in prayer."

Bowing our heads, Mrs. Kavanaugh led us in prayer. No matter how far removed any of us were from what had happened, there was a great sense of loss. None of us had lived through a national tragedy of this magnitude. Most of us had grown up listening to tales of the War Between the States or even the Spanish-American War. Grandpas and great uncles seemed to have a flare for relaying stories of battle, suffering, and heroism. But when told in the comfort of a parlor or in the relaxed atmosphere of a church picnic, such stories were simply that. Stories. They were memories recalled of a bygone era, similar to those found in a book at the library. Now, the *Titanic* disaster was a tragedy in our own time. We each felt the weight of it in our chests and knew beyond the shadow of a doubt that this moment would be etched in our memories for the rest of our lives.

The rest of the day was rather subdued. Rather than reprimand us and proclaim we all had spring fever, the teachers were a bit more understanding. Everyone was wrestling with a variety of emotions that held a good deal of shock mixed with equal parts of curiosity and grief. Yet, it was Beatrice who seemed the most disturbed of all. For the rest of the afternoon, she remained quiet. I noticed creases in her forehead and lines around her mouth that reminded me of the night her baby had been born. When school was finally dismissed, she silently gathered her things and hastily left without a word of good-bye to anyone. The others either didn't seem to notice or gave her extra levity due to the day's events, but I had the sense that a still-fresh wound had been opened again.

I went to the Riddles' house later that afternoon to check on Beatrice. Miz Tessie met me at the back door with a rib-squeezing hug and a plate of fresh cookies. "I made these for Miss Beatrice, but she acted like she was feelin' poorly and wouldn't eat one," she said with a little hurt in her voice.

"That's why I came by," I explained. "I wanted to check on her. Do you mind if I go upstairs and see how she's doing?"

"Chil,' you know you're welcome in this house. Go on up. And here, take these cookies with you. Maybe she'll feel like eatin' some now."

I went upstairs and knocked on Beatrice's door. "Momma, I told you I was fine. I just need to be left alone for a little while."

"Beatrice, it's not your mother. It's me, Lilly Kate. I wanted to check on you."

I could hear the bed creak as Beatrice got up, and the squeak of the wooden floor grow louder as she made her way to the door. "Come on in," she said without conviction.

I followed Beatrice as she walked back to her bed in silence. Beatrice laid down on her back and stared at her canopy while I sat awkwardly on the edge of the bed, unsure of what to do.

"Do you want to talk about it?" I asked after a couple of silent moments.

"I'm not sure I can." Beatrice wiped away a tear that was making its way down her cheek onto her pillow. "It's just that when Mrs. K announced about the *Titanic* and how some of the victims were children…I…I thought about my own baby. He's getting close to four months old now, you know. And, well, I don't know how to explain it, but hearing about all that loss and grief brought back my own pain."

"I could tell at school something was wrong." I crawled up into Beatrice's bed and sat at Beatrice's feet. "If I could take it away for you, I would."

Beatrice sat up and plopped a pillow into her lap. She twisted her index finger around a lock of her golden hair for a moment before continuing. "Thanks, but it's more than just a sadness, though. I also have great sense of shame. Oh, I know you're going to tell me that the baby wasn't my fault, and my family did what they all thought was best, but I just have this terrible feeling God is angry with me for what I did. There's this heavy blanket of shame on top of me."

This conversation was going well beyond my normal repertoire, and I suddenly became nervous and offered up a silent prayer asking for guidance or, better yet, someone with pastoral experience to come walking through the door. Both of us continued to sit on the bed while the grandfather clock in the hall made four strikes. Still, no one came to the door, nor was I struck with an epiphany or sudden revelation.

Beatrice was the first to speak again. "I just feel dirty," she said with conviction. "Dirty all over."

Slowly, an old memory began to creep to the front of my thoughts. It was an episode that I had long since buried but was seemingly rising again like Lazarus. There came upon me this overwhelming sense that I should tell it to Beatrice. "Did I ever tell you I was once a thief?"

"You?" Beatrice was smiling. "I don't believe it."

"It's true. I've never told anybody, not even my mother."

"When did this happen?"

"Back when I was in first grade at Fox Creek, I was having a bit of trouble with my penmanship. My handwriting was fair, but I wanted to make my letters pretty like I'd seen some of the older kids do. I noticed my teacher, Miss Daphne, had a shiny, new black fountain pen. I thought it was beautiful. For a few weeks, I watched her write with it and see the sun dance off its brass nib. When I would see the paper she was writing on, it had the most beautiful script I'd ever seen. I thought that pen was like a magic wand that would suddenly turn my pitiful chicken scratch into something grand.

"So, one sunny day when everyone was enjoying recess outside, I asked Miss Daphne if I could go back in. I don't even remember why I asked, I just did. She, of course, obliged. When I went in, there, sitting in its usual spot, was her fountain pen. To this day, I can still see it lying neatly atop a stack of freshly graded papers. Without so much as a second thought, I slipped it into my petticoat and went back outside to finish recess.

"When everyone came back inside, Miss Daphne spent a good five minutes looking for her pen, but of course, she did not find it. She had to have known it was me, but said nothing.

"For the next week or so, I'd find any excuse I could to go down to our barn. While I was there, I'd climb into the hayloft with the pen and some paper tucked beneath my dress and then whip them out and try to practice my letters. But no matter how hard I tried, my writing did not look nearly so nice as Miss Daphne's. To make matters worse, I was getting black spots all over my hands and quickly ran out of ink.

"Eventually, the excitement of using the new pen died away and a guilty conscience crept in. To try and make it right, I snuck back in the school at lunch and returned the pen to Miss Daphne's desk, thinking my guilt would go away. Mind you, Miss Daphne had never said a word about the incident.

"However, the guilt remained. I began losing sleep and my appetite. Even Momma and Poppa noticed I wasn't myself and had begun to think I was coming down with the fever.

"Finally, about three weeks after I took the pen, the weight of the shame became too great. I gathered up the nerve to go and apologize to Miss Daphne. Although my stomach was churning and my head was pounding, I somehow knew I personally had to ask for her forgiveness. So, one day after school when everyone else had already gone home, I swallowed the knot in my throat and admitted everything to Miss Daphne. I had decided that whatever punishment she gave me would be better than living with the guilt. And do you know what she said?"

"She was angry, wasn't she?"

"Not at all. In fact, she seemed rather serene. At the time I thought it was the strangest thing, but now I think I understand. She said, 'Lillian Katherine, I knew you'd taken my pen all along. I was ready to forgive you right away. All you needed to do was ask.' Then she gave me a hug, said she loved me, and told me to go home and do my homework."

"That was all?"

"That was it. To this day, I can still remember the wave of relief I felt after I talked with her."

"But you said you'd never told anybody. Why not?"

"Well, just because I felt released from the guilt didn't mean I was proud of it. Even now I'm still embarrassed that I stole something from my teacher."

Beatrice cuddled one of her pillows, raking her fingers over the gold fringe. "So you think I was wrong and need to ask God for forgiveness?"

"Apparently, *you* feel you were wrong. So, ask God for forgiveness. I'm sure he's willing to give it to you."

"You make it sound so easy."

"I've always thought God's forgiveness is easy. The hard part is forgiving yourself. Maybe that's why I never told anybody about the pen until now."

Three light taps were made on the door followed by a loud creaking noise. "Oh, hello, Lilly Kate." It was Mrs. Riddle. "I didn't realize you were here. I was just checking on Beatrice. Sweetheart, are you okay? You seemed a little upset when you came home from school."

Beatrice looked at me and grinned slightly, then looked at her mother. "I think I'll be okay," she said with more strength than I would have expected. "Something was bothering me, but I have a better idea on how to handle it now."

Mrs. Riddle's eyes jumped back and forth between us as though trying to decipher a code, then sighed as though resigned to not understanding. "All right. If you're sure."

The door closed, and we could hear her steps fade away. Beatrice looked at me like she had just discovered a secret. An impish look came across her face that made me a little nervous. "What?" I finally asked in exasperation.

"I just never would have guessed it."

"What are you talking about?"

"You, Little Miss Perfect, had sticky fingers!" Beatrice rolled back on the bed and let out a shriek filled with mischief.

"Well, I'm not sure I would phrase it that way," I weakly defended.

"Too late," Beatrice chided. "From now on, I'm going to start calling you Jesse James!" Squeals of delight filled the room.

Exasperated, I gathered my things. "I'd better get home," I said. "Momma might worry."

"Sure thing, Jesse!" Beatrice teased as I walked out the door. "But try to resist the urge to rob a bank on the way home!"

Chapter Twenty-one

During the course of the next week, details of the *Titanic* tragedy made their way down to us. One of Mrs. K's former house boys, now at West Point, sent a newspaper from New York. From it we learned more than fifteen hundred were killed, some of them needlessly because not all life boats had been filled. Among the dead were some of the biggest names in commerce: Aster, Guggenheim, and Straus. John Jacob Aster's expectant wife also died with him. Others weren't so well known but were equally valued, like the priest who was headed to New York to officiate his younger brother's wedding. Still, what troubled me most were those not mentioned—the third-class passengers. If I had been on the boat, that's surely where I would have been. Those were the people to whom I could relate, yet they were the ones least discussed.

The tragedy forced everyone to face a certain amount of pause, but quickly following was a sense of helplessness. There was a real desire within the school to lend some sort of aid, but what could a group of kids in a small town in the middle of Kentucky do about an accident so far away? It was a question everyone entertained, but most people dismissed it quickly. Not until Beatrice forced us to change our focus did anyone think twice about organizing some sort of effort.

"Why don't we do something for all the people in need around here?" Beatrice asked one day before the bell rang. Everyone within earshot of the question quickly stopped all other discussion and glared at Beatrice in disbelief. No one knew that Beatrice Riddle was even aware there *were* people in the world who didn't regularly eat off china.

"Well, why not?" she asked the group, pretending to be oblivious to their looks of surprise. "Surely there are people around here who need help just as much as anybody in New York. Don't we have some widows, or maybe there are some orphans?"

No sooner had the words come out of Beatrice's mouth than I knew what she was thinking. Helping those in need might be something of a salve for her wounded heart. Elora Hicks and her siblings also came to my mind, along with the others I'd visited with Momma .

"Beatrice is right," I said, thinking back to the dirt floor and dilapidated home of Elora and her siblings. "There are plenty of people right here in our community who could use some help. Instead of wringing our hands and complaining about how we're too young or too far away to help people in New York, we could do something for our neighbors right here."

"Fine, then," Ruby conceded. "But what do you propose we do?"

"Maybe we could have a bake sale!" Huey offered with an overabundance of enthusiasm. "I'll even bake some gingerbread," he joked.

The crowd groaned, and Eunice spoke for the group. "Huey, the only time we want you to bake anything is when we need bricks for a new school! Until then, don't bother."

Everyone grew quiet when a tiny idea began to form in my mind. I almost didn't mention it because it was so unusual, maybe even a bit risky, but as the moments passed, the idea seemed more and more plausible.

"Maybe we should have a basketball game," I offered.

"Not now!" Beatrice scoffed. "We can do that at lunch."

"I'm not talking about right now! I'm talking about having a basketball game as a fundraiser. Think about it.

Everybody at school likes to watch us play, and people all over town have heard about it. Maybe they'd pay a small fee for admission."

"But where would you play?" someone asked. "You can't very well charge people to watch you girls play on the muddy patch out back."

Beatrice stepped in. "You know. I think Lilly Kate's got a terrific idea. We could play inside the opera house. It already has seats, and I think the floor is big enough for us to have a game. They'd just need to push back some of the chairs."

"Oh, come on!" Frankie Crawford sneered. "Do you really think anybody is going to pay their hard-earned money to watch ten girls run up and down a floor?" His tone enraged me, and I had to resist the urge not to slug him. It was followed by a rather annoyed chuckle and an exchange of knowing glances among a group of boys. I had no intention of letting such a remark go by without a proper rebuttal.

"Indeed, I think it's a splendid idea!" boomed a voice from across the porch just as I had opened my mouth to speak. Mrs. Kavanaugh was standing there with the bell firmly in her right hand. She charged toward the group. Frankie shuffled behind one of the bigger house boys. "I'm thrilled to see my students being so civic minded. You'll have to work out some details and assignments, of course, but I think you might have struck on a goldmine of an idea." She then turned and looked directly at Frankie. "I wish you all the best of luck. Let me know how I can be of assistance. Now, get inside, everyone. It's time to begin class."

Within three days, plans for the junior-senior girls' basketball game were well underway. We'd play two weeks from Saturday at eight p.m. at the Lawrenceburg Opera House. Although the manager, Mr. Kessler, was initially uncertain, Beatrice and I convinced him the event was strictly for philanthropic purposes. "And think of all the people who will come to the game and see the schedule of your upcoming shows," we added. "It might increase your future ticket sales." That, coupled with my promise to deliver him two pecan pies free of charge, helped to seal the deal. Two of the house boys would serve as referees under the careful guidance of Mrs. Rutherford. Those girls not playing in the game were instructed to bring in items that could be sold at a refreshment stand, while the other students were in charge of advertising and ticket sales.

There was, however, still the issue of what we were to wear. Mrs. Kavanaugh admitted we shouldn't play in our skirts, but pinning them up didn't seem appropriate either.

"What about us all wearing a white middy blouse and the same kind of split skirt?" Beatrice asked. "Then it would look a little more like wearing a uniform."

"But where are we going to get enough skirts for all ten of us?" Ruby asked. "The game is supposed to be in two weeks."

"We'll make them!" I offered. All heads turned to me with gleeful expressions of hope. "Well, not exactly all of them," I corrected. "Everyone can be responsible for buying her own fabric. The juniors will get one color, the seniors another. I'm sure my mother and I could make a few, and surely the rest of you could either make your own or know someone who could."

"Neither Mother nor I are very good at sewing, Lilly Kate. That's why we always hire your mom."

"Yeah," Eunice agreed. "You might as well be asking me to fly."

"Oh, buck up!" I teased. "Momma or I will help you

cut the pattern, and then surely you can sew a straight line. Even I can do that. They won't be fancy. Besides, we'll only be wearing them this one time."

"All right, but do you think people will approve of us showing that much leg?" Eunice asked with genuine concern. Admittedly, it was an issue.

"Well, it's for a good cause, and it's not like we'll be running around just in our bloomers," Beatrice pointed out. "We'll still have our stockings. Surely no one will mind." Surely.

Eight days before the big game, all was progressing nicely. Advertisements were posted in most every store window in town. Knowing a needle and thread were not my strong suit, Momma had helped me with my split skirt. A group of us had gone together and picked out the fabric everyone would purchase. For a while, I was lobbying for a hideous pink, green, and rose-colored fabric. "Come on!" I teased. "This will make us look the most feminine. And, if we run fast enough, we'll make the court look like a flower garden." In the end, we all decided on a plain navy material, both because it was conservative and the least expensive. The result was a simple piece of material that still came to the mid-calf or below, but it allowed us to run without fear of tripping. The juniors chose the same type of fabric but in a muted shade of golendrod.

As part of the event, a special edition of *Tiger Beat* was to come out the next Tuesday. In it, we were posting the rules of the game as well as plenty of advertisements both for the game and its cause. A few of the more artistic staff members had even offered to draw some illustrations that would show various aspects of the game. Because it was considered a special edition, we were even planning on printing extra copies to be sold in the community.

I was working late after school on the issue, wrestling once again with the ornery typewriter, when I heard the front door open and heavy steps come into the front foyer. When the footsteps stopped, I turned and met the concentrated gaze of Duce Crawford. A knot immediately began to form in my stomach. Something told me he wasn't there to discuss Frankie's academic progress.

"Good afternoon, Miss Overstreet," he said with gruff politeness. My mouth suddenly felt filled with cotton, so I tried to politely nod my head. "Could you please point me to Mrs. Kavanaugh's office?"

Before I could respond, the door to Mrs. K's office opened. "Hello, Mr. Crawford. I heard you come in. I'm sorry, did we have an appointment?"

Duce cleared his throat and shuffled his feet a bit before straightening his shoulders. Apparently, Mrs. Kavanaugh had the same intimidating effect on everyone, regardless of age. "No, I'm sorry," he started. "I didn't make an appointment, but I was hoping I could take just a moment of your time and speak with you."

"Certainly. Right this way."

I watched the two of them walk into her office and listened to the door shut. A part of me wanted to be a fly on the other side of that door and find out what was happening. Another part wasn't sure I ever wanted to know. Either way, I definitely smelled the makings of a bona fide stink.

The next day Mrs. Kavanaugh called all the basketball players into the front classroom for a brief meeting. Instinctively I knew the hammer was about to come down. The night before I'd told Momma about my suspicions, but she'd chastised me for reading too much into a simple meeting.

"You have no idea why Mr. Crawford met with Mrs. Kavanaugh. It may have been something completely unrelated to that game entirely."

"Maybe, but I have my doubts. I just have this feeling that he went in there to stir up trouble."

"Young lady, it is not your place to question that man's motives, and I refuse to hear another word about it. You understand?"

Momma's word had been final, and I didn't speak another syllable about the incident the rest of the night. But that didn't keep me from letting it stew in my brain until the wee hours of the morning. When I finally did get to sleep, it seemed only a couple of moments had passed before it was time to get up. I went through the morning routine feeling groggy and all the more miffed.

"Ladies," Mrs. Kavanaugh began. "We need to have a serious discussion about this basketball game." The girls' backs stiffened throughout the room as though bracing themselves for bad news. "It has come to my attention that there are those in our community who have some real concerns about young women such as yourselves playing a basketball game publicly."

Immediately chatter filled the room, and everyone started asking questions and defending our right to play. "Now, now!" Mrs. K commanded, raising both hands in the air. "No one said we were canceling the game. That was a strong suggestion, but I think you all realize how much I appreciate good, clean physical exercise and competition. So, I flatly refused." Everyone's backs began to relax, and I could feel myself breathe again for what felt like the first time since the previous afternoon. "However, to ease anxieties, I did make a few allowances. First, there is to be absolutely no diving after any balls. There are those who feel seeing a lady exerting herself in such a way is inappropriate if not somewhat scandalous. Secondly, for the same reasons, there is to be no screaming, grunting, or any other barbaric noises coming from you as you play."

Mrs. Kavanaugh paused and looked each girl in the eye to make sure we all understood. "I realize this may seem a bit unfair to some of you, but let me assure you I am trying to protect your best interests. With that in mind, please return to your classes."

Silently, we all walked out and did as we were told. Yet, inwardly, I felt as though my temperature was rising. Certainly there was a sense of relief that the game was still to be held. A part of me had been afraid it would be canceled. Nonetheless, I didn't appreciate such restrictions being placed on us, especially not when I considered the source and knew full well such demands would not have been made on the boys.

Through the rest of the day, I heard very little of what any teacher said. In my mind I was making a list of all the reasons such requests were unfair. And it wasn't just basketball either. Months of pent-up frustration came to mind as I thought about the lack of educational opportunities available to women, Beatrice's baby that was given away, and now the simple request to play a game—one that was being done for charity no less—being met with opposition. By the time everyone else was ready to go home, every muscle in my body felt ready to pounce, like a lioness ready to defend her cubs. Rather than spew my frustrations all over some unsuspecting soul, I decided to use the school's typewriter to help me articulate my feelings.

For at least an hour after school, I poked, clanked, and jabbed out words from the machine. I didn't even hear the four o'clock train roll by on the nearby tracks. A form of energy bordering on hostility poured through my fingertips. With each perfectly chosen word or phrase, there came upon me a sense of accomplishment. Never before had I written something so passionate, so personal. It was as though for the first time, I was having my say. As I reached the last paragraph, the frustration I'd felt earlier had morphed into excitement, maybe even exhilaration.

By the time I was finished, Mrs. Kavanaugh had come in to check on me. "You're making such a racket in here I thought you were building something," she teased, a rarity for her even after school hours.

I turned to Mrs. Kavanaugh and unconsciously covered up my work. "I'm sorry," I muttered. "I was just trying to write something. It's nothing really. Just something to make me feel better."

"I could tell you were frustrated by my announcement today. I can assure you I did not make those adjustments lightly, nor did I do it to stifle the game."

"Oh, we all understand that!" I quickly defended. "It's not just that, it's..." My words began to falter. It was almost as if I'd used up every decent noun and verb combination in my writing and now couldn't articulate a coherent sentence. Meekly, I handed my work to Mrs. K, wanting her to realize my frustration did not reside with her personally. She took it and read.

> It has come to my attention that there are those in this community who are uncomfortable with a group of young ladies publicly playing an organized sport. It seems that physical exertion is "inappropriate," that perspiration is "unladylike," and such exertion is nearly "scandalous." It has even been suggested that we young women are trying to "be like the boys."
> While I cannot speak for an entire half of our country's population, nor can I speak for all school-aged females, I can speak for myself and in doing so represent the ladies of this school.
> First, let me say that I have never wished to be a male. The thought has never once crossed my mind. Despite the social and legal distinctions that are

often made between the two genders, I have never once wanted to be nor tried to be masculine. In fact, I have rather enjoyed being a lady and the roles of hospitality, congeniality, and even propriety that it has allowed me to fill. As I mature, I'm quite sure I'll grow to enjoy my role as a woman even more as I become a wife and mother, neither of which can be filled by a male.

Secondly, the argument that a sport forces women to exert themselves in ways that may be deemed improper reeks of inconsistency. If physical exertion to the point of perspiration and exhaustion should be avoided by women, then countless hordes of females would have died throughout the ages. It is through the sweat of female brows that food has been planted, cultivated, harvested, and preserved. It is through this same sweat that wood has been chopped, meals have been fixed, clothes have been laundered, and, yes, at times, fields have been plowed. Through the ages as men have gone off to explore, hunt, work, or fight wars, it has been the woman who has exerted herself in both body and spirit to keep the homestead intact, mouths fed, and bodies clothed.

Now, however, with advances in technology and intellectual enlightenment, there are those who feel the woman need not exert herself anymore, most especially when the activity is deemed frivolous or unnecessary. However, I would argue the basketball game next Friday is not simply a game for entertainment purposes. As Jesus himself said, "The poor you will always have." Our event is a modern attempt to help feed and clothe those who may be considered "the least of these." If feeding the hungry and clothing those who are cold requires a little bit of feminine exertion and even a bit of sweat, I don't see it as at all scandalous, even if it is wrapped up as a game. Instead, I see it as a clean, fun way of helping my neighbor, just as we all, male and female, have been called to do.

My leg started twitching as Mrs. Kavanaugh scanned the paper. I watched her face and saw her eyebrows go up and down as she read various parts, but her thoughts were not easily deciphered. She began pacing slowly across the room, placing her hand against her chin as though lost in deep thought. I believed what I'd written to be true, but just how Mrs. Kavanaugh would feel about it was a mystery. Finally, she handed the paper back to me.

"You've got some pretty strong opinions there, Miss Overstreet," she confided. I nodded in agreement, unsure if she was giving me a compliment or simple statement of fact. "And you've grown into a good writer. In many ways, I agree with you," she finally admitted.

Mrs. Kavanaugh walked across the room and started straightening desks. In doing so, she continued her conversation. "I don't completely blame you for your frustration. I'm sure my requests today seemed a bit old-fashioned to most of you."

Desperately not wanting her to misunderstand my motives, I jumped in and cut her off. "Oh, no, Mrs. Kavanaugh. I'm not angry at you. I'm just frustrated because so often things seem unfair."

"You're quite right about that, Miss Overstreet. Life is often unfair. Young people frequently seemed surprised when they realize it. But no one ever said life was fair. Quite the contrary. It's often very unfair. Yet, sometimes it's unfair in our favor."

My eyes followed Mrs. Kavanaugh as she walked toward me and stood with her arms folded across her chest.

"I'm sorry," I said. "I don't quite understand what you mean."

Mrs. K straightened her glasses. "Did you ever stop to think how ridiculously unfair it is that we live in a big country full of freedoms while people in other parts of the world suffer from dictatorships or ineffective monarchies?" I shook my head. Indeed, I hadn't. "Or, have you ever thought about how unfair it is that even right here in our own community, a girl like you has a loving mother, a warm bed, and plenty to eat while other children, through no fault of their own, don't have these things?"

My head dropped in shame. All day long I'd been focusing on the unfairness in the world as it related to me instead of unfairness as it related to others. Once again, my mind shifted to that gray shack near the river and the poor children living in it. We were supposed to be playing the game for them in the first place, and I had turned it into something personal. Mrs. Kavanaugh saw my remorse and seemed to relax slightly. "I'm not trying to fuss at you," she mused. "I just want you to see the bigger picture. Fighting for justice and fairness is what we should be doing, but this is not the little skirmish you want to fight. There are many more injustices with much bigger implications than this one. Keep your passion. Don't lose your idealism. Just pick your battles so your energy will be used most wisely. I have the greatest confidence that you'll do great things in this world."

I lifted my head and looked at Mrs. Kavanaugh. For the first time I began to wonder what she had been like when she was my age. Had she been quiet or talkative? Was she sensitive or strong willed? Did she ever lose sleep over what she would become? Would I ever possess her same steely resolve or focus?

"Thank you," I replied. It was all I knew to say.

"Oh, you're quite welcome. And don't worry about this basketball game. Whether you realize it or not, you ladies are going to be blazing a trail. It'll be the first time people will be paying money to see a basketball game in this town, boys' or girls.'"

"I hadn't thought of that."

"It's true. What's more, I've grown rather fond of the game myself. It's good exercise and teaches teamwork, both of which are heavily emphasized at the military academies. I'm thinking we'll start some boys' teams next year. Who knows, this simple round ball game might become rather popular someday."

Chapter Twenty-two

When game day finally arrived, Momma thought she was going to have to hog tie me to the bed in order to get me to calm down. "Daughter, you are running around this house with so much energy I'm afraid you're going to hurt something, maybe even me! Calm down. Save some of that energy for tonight. Now get over here, and eat your eggs."

"I can't, Momma. My stomach is so tight they could use *it* for the game ball."

"Relax. You'll do fine."

I forced myself into the chair and began poking at my food with disinterest. "I just hope I don't make a fool of myself."

"Think of it this way. Most of us who'll be watching don't even know how the game is supposed to be played. If you make a mistake, we'll probably never even notice."

"Maybe. But if I fall on my face and bust my nose, chances are somebody's going to catch on to that one."

As the day wore on, my adrenaline went back to a normal level, and I was able to settle down a bit. Game or no game, Momma was not going to let a Saturday go by without cleaning. I sometimes wondered why she insisted on being so regimented about our housework. After all, our home was tiny, and with only two of us living in it, there never seemed to be much of a mess. Nonetheless, Momma usually had me dusting and mopping every Saturday. And today, she had me cleaning out the dresser drawers so that everything could be aired. In doing so,

I ran across one of Poppa's old tobacco pipes that was tucked back in the bottom drawer and wrapped carefully in one of his old shirts. Momma had put it there after he'd died.

I carefully unwrapped his shirt and examined the pipe. It was a standard English pipe made of two different woods, walnut for the bowl and hickory for the stem and bit. Poppa's teeth marks could be seen on the mouthpiece. He always did have a habit of chewing too hard on his pipe. "It's all part of the experience," he claimed when Momma or I would tease him about it. Now, I was glad he had. Somehow seeing visible evidence of his existence made me feel comforted and saddened all at the same time. I put my nose inside the bowl, almost touching the bottom, and inhaled deeply. The sweet smell of tobacco was faint, but it was still there nonetheless. Oh, how I missed him.

"Is it still there?" Momma was standing in the doorway. I hadn't seen her come in.

"A little." I handed the pipe to Momma and let her have a sniff.

She pressed the pipe firmly to her nose and breathed in deeply. "Oh, this smells just like home." Momma's eyes started to well up. "It brings back many, many memories."

"Sometimes," I confessed, "it's a little hard to see Poppa in my mind. But when I smell pipe smoke, I see him clearly, as if he was standing right here."

"Memories are like that—fuzzy at times, then clear as a stream at others. I always think of him when I eat mashed potatoes."

"Mashed potatoes? You never make mashed potatoes." I looked at Momma, thinking I'd surely misunderstood.

"Yes." Momma began to chuckle. "Mashed potatoes. I never seemed to be able to get them just the way he liked them. They were either too salty or too runny or there was not enough cream. When we first got married, if he tasted another woman's mashed potatoes that he thought were particularly good, he would tell me to go and ask her how she did it. I wanted to wring his neck every time he said that. After a while I gave up on mashing potatoes and just started frying them."

"I never knew that."

"Well, as I said, 'fuzzy at times, then clear as a stream.'"

We sat silent for a moment, both lost in thought with me rubbing my thumb along the length of the pipe.

"You know what," I said, finally breaking the silence. "I think Poppa would be proud of us, Momma—of how hard you've worked in your business and at church and now of me getting ready to graduate. I really think he'd be happy for us."

Bittersweet tears fell down Momma's cheeks, one drop getting caught in the corner of her mouth. She nodded her head. "I know he would."

Momma placed the pipe back in the shirt and began to fold carefully. "I know something else," she continued. "He'd be proud you're playing in that basketball game tonight."

"Really? I never thought of Poppa as a sports fan."

"Back when we were in school together, your daddy was known around Fox Creek to be a mighty good pitcher."

"You never told me that!" I felt like I was seeing a part of my daddy for the first time, a glimpse into his past that had never been revealed. "I suppose you spent your recess time watching the game and cheering him on?" I teased Momma.

Momma was already walking out of the room as if trying to leave a conversation she'd unintentionally started. "I wouldn't exactly put it that way. Who do you think was the catcher for the other team?"

At ten minutes till eight the night of the game, the opera house had only a couple dozen seats left. I couldn't determine if people were coming as a sign of support to the school or if they were coming out of curiosity. Our little band of players discussed this on the sidelines as we waited, and we decided there might be yet another reason for the large turnout: it was Saturday night, and there was no other show in town.

Whatever the reason, people were flocking to the game like flies to sorghum, as Poppa would say. The refreshment line was no less than five people deep. The ticket line looked to be steady, and the dessert auction table was full of cakes and pies. Someone had come up with the idea to auction desserts during the mid-game break and raise a few extra dollars. Mrs. Kavanaugh had readily agreed, knowing full well most of the people in the room would enjoy a sweet treat after a Sunday dinner.

Momma had suggested that I make a pound cake since it would keep so well and be easy to carry home. However, I decided to try my hand at angel food cake. Mrs. Hoskins from church had brought one to a social a few weeks prior, and I'd thought it was like eating a sweet piece of a cloud. She gave me her recipe and allowed me to borrow her pan that was two regular cake layers deep and had a hole in the middle. "You must use this, dear," she explained. "Angel food cake doesn't cook like other cakes."

I followed Mrs. Hoskins's recipe and directions carefully but was to the point of kicking myself when I was trying to beat air into all the egg whites. I whipped so long and so hard I thought my arm would fall off onto the counter. Momma even took over for a few minutes as I massaged my muscles. "This is almost as strenuous as the game itself," I whined. But when the finished product came out of the oven, the work had been worth it. Even the smell was light and fairy-like. Once it cooled, I drizzled a little sugar glaze on top and knew immediately I'd found my new favorite cake.

Now the angel food sat amid the other desserts on the table awaiting auction as more spectators meandered by. Mrs. Kavanaugh had taken her seat in the middle of the front row and looked as stately as any European monarch. In a sense, it was her kingdom. She even had her umbrella on hand despite the clear skies outside. One had to wonder if she planned to use it on any unruly patrons or poorly behaved players. It didn't really matter. Mrs. K and her umbrella did not discriminate.

Momma was also in attendance, sitting discreetly next to Huey's mother and father. Our eyes met, and she faintly nodded as if to say, "Yes, I see you. Now behave yourself." Three rows back and a little to Momma's left I spotted two smiling faces who were both waving their hands in an effort to get my attention. It was Jimalee and Dink. They looked as happy as they had when they'd ridden off together after their wedding. Our times together had been brief since then, but I understood and did not feel slighted. Also prominently seated in the fourth row was none other than Duce Crawford. When I saw him sitting there laughing with a neighbor as though this glorious event was his own idea, a part of me wanted to take off my shoe and throw it at him. The thought crossed my mind that if we all pointed our toes as we ran and jumped, Duce might think he was watching a ballet.

Mrs. Rutherford signaled us that the game was about to begin, and the two teams took their places along the sidelines. Reverend Searcy walked to the middle of the floor and quieted the crowd. He bowed his head for a pre-game prayer, and then everyone dutifully followed. I'd never heard of him having any disapproval for the event, but when I heard his petition to the Lord simultaneously remind everyone in the room that "this game is a charitable event, and all participants should conduct themselves in a manner pleasing to the saints in heaven," I began to wonder.

Ralph Sayers and Garvis Vaughn were our referees. They'd been trained by Mrs. Rutherford and had been participating in our practice sessions since we'd scheduled the game. None of the players were thrilled that we'd be officiated by two people who'd never played the game, but all agreed that Mrs. Rutherford, a married woman, should not be running up and down the court. We were pushing the boundaries of small-town civility enough as it was. Even so, she was seated next to Mrs. Kavanaugh on the front row so as to see every move.

The teams were called to the court, and the centers for each team were signaled to come together for tipoff. Sara and I stood behind Eunice, so as to defend our goal if the juniors got the ball. Beatrice and Ruby were on the other side hoping to catch the tip. Garvis blew the whistle and threw the ball into the air. The first basketball game in our town had begun.

For the first six-minute quarter, the majority of the crowd was trying to figure out the point of the game and the role of each player. The fact that we weren't all that good didn't help matters any. We didn't run any set plays or have any defensive strategy. We wouldn't have even known what those were if you'd asked us. Instead, we just ran (in as feminine a way as possible) up and down the court and tried to keep the other team from throwing the ball into the basket. Soon, the crowd figured out the girl with the ball couldn't run without bouncing it and to touch someone was considered a foul. There must have been a moment of clarity come across Duce Crawford when he realized this dramatic difference from football. I saw him smile and nod his head after the whistle was blown on Ruby for fouling another player. It occurred to me that he may have had a misconception of the game, perhaps thinking the sport was rougher and more dangerous than it was. For the first time, I began to see things from his vantage point and understand his objections a little better. I still didn't like it, mind you. I'd already choked back at least ten grunts or screams just because he was in the stands.

By the beginning of the second quarter, the crowd had enough understanding to grow excited and watch each possession with interest. They cheered every time somebody new touched the ball, regardless of the team. The newness of the game must have kept the crowd interested because our scoring prowess was nothing short of pathetic. The ball seemed determined not to go through the basket, and as such, we ended the half 5–3 in favor of the juniors. We were terrible, but thankfully no one really knew the difference.

Halftime couldn't come fast enough for any of us. We were used to playing games at lunch and maybe after school, but the crowd seemed to require us to use more energy. By the time both teams reached the bench, we were all huffing like trains but trying desperately to look cool and collected so as not to appear "overexerted."

Some of the boys carefully brought out the dessert table to the middle of the floor in preparation for the auction and were actually to play the role of auctioneers. However, in a decision that I thought contained a hint of brilliance, Mrs. Kavanaugh was going to stand with them and oversee the sale. I knew if she didn't think an item was bringing enough money, she'd cast a single glance at some unsuspecting soul that would scare him so much he might start bidding against himself. She stood in the middle of the floor as straight as a lightning rod, holding her umbrella primly in front of her.

"Thank you all for coming," Mrs. Kavanaugh began. "I'm sure you are all aware that tonight's proceeds will go to assist those in need right here in our own community. With that in mind, I have every confidence that each of you will be noble neighbors and as such, quite generous."

Indeed.

I waited anxiously for people to start bidding on my cake, but I had to sit through three pies, four batches of cookies, and two loaves of salt-risen bread before it was held up. There's an understanding among folks that she whose desserts bring a high price has reason to be extra proud. It's a form of being publicly acknowledged for your kitchen skills. While I knew I wasn't a good seamstress or a fantastic basketball player, I did place high value on my cooking and was most anxious to see the results.

"Now," the auctioneer began, "we have an angel food cake with a thin sugar glaze made by Lilly Kate Overstreet. Let's start the bidding at fifty cents."

My eyes darted through the crowd, hoping desperately that someone would be willing to pay fifty cents for my cake. That was about the same as two cans of sliced peaches, and surely and angel food cake was worth that. I felt the cake deserved fifty cents just for whipping up those egg whites. A few hands shot up, and I was relieved to know the price would at least not need to be lowered.

After the initial bid, the price went up in nickel increments. As the price reached the one-dollar mark, I relaxed enough to allow myself a modest grin. Surely a dollar for a cake would put it near the top sellers, and that was fine with me. Yet, the price continued upward. Those not bidding began straining their necks to watch the action, and the price began to steadily rise ... $1.25 ... $1.40 ... $1.50. It had exceeded my modest expectations and did not show signs of stopping ... $2.00 ... $2.50 ... $2.75!

Finally, from the fourth row there came a deep, robust voice. "I'm willing to pay $5.00 for that cake!" All heads turned to follow the sound of the voice. Duce Crawford stood up and repeated himself. "Mrs. Kavanaugh, I'm offering $5.00. If anyone wants to pay more, let him speak now."

A mumble could be heard throughout the room, but no other bids were made. "Very well," Mrs. Kavanaugh said. "Sold to Duce Crawford for $5.00!" Then she punctuated the sale by whacking her umbrella against the hard oak floors.

A round of applause could be heard as Mr. Crawford stepped forward to claim his prize. Some of the girls on the bench turned to see my reaction. A few gave me a jovial pat on the back. I said nothing. I was too stunned to speak, for as much as I wanted to dislike the man, it was now impossible to do so. He'd just paid me a very public compliment.

By the time the second half began, a quick mental calculation told me we'd made $18.50 from the auction. Not bad at all. Only later did we learn the event had raised a little more than $45. That would be several pounds of flour, dozens of eggs, and numerous canned goods for several families. The look of pleasure on the other girls' faces said they were thinking about it too. No wonder Andrew Carnegie seemed to enjoy spreading out his money.

The auction and break reinvigorated all of us, so when the whistle blew signaling the beginning of the third quarter, we were all ready. Unfortunately, our enthusiasm did not translate into better offense. It was beyond dismal. Every time I threw up a shot, it either bounced off the backboard with a horrendous thud, or worse, it never touched the basket at all. Beatrice and Eunice were the only ones giving us any points. Eunice had an advantage because she was taller, and Beatrice's private practice in her family's basement seemed to be paying off.

The only upside to having a low-scoring game is that when either team does finally get a ball to fall through, the crowd goes wild with relief. I even got to the point I was happy to see the juniors score just to know it was possible.

As the fourth and final quarter began, everyone was a bit winded and consequently making even more mistakes. It was only through the grace of foul shots that the seniors were able to get within one point and make the score 9–8. As the seconds slowly ticked off, it looked as though we were out of steam. Then, suddenly, Beatrice called a time-out. When we got into the huddle, Beatrice gave us an unexpected tongue lashing.

"We can do better than this!" she hissed. "What's happening?"

"We're all exhausted, Bea," Ruby complained.

"I am too, and so are they!" she retorted. Her eyes were boring holes in the rest of us as she spoke. "They may have another chance to play this game, but we won't. We need to win."

"She's right," Sara chimed in. "This is our one and only chance."

"All right," I asked. "What do you want us to do?"

Beatrice turned and looked at the other team. All of them had their hands on their hips and were gasping for breath as well. "I think we need to guard them more closely. I know we've practiced standing back a bit, but that's because we were wearing fuller skirts. We can get closer now. Then, whenever we have the ball, either throw it to me or to Eunice."

"Why do you and Eunice get the ball?" Ruby whined.

"Eunice is the tallest, and Beatrice has the best shot," I defended. "It's a good plan, or at least the only plan we've got. I'm ready." Everyone nodded in agreement just as the whistle was blown.

Our team walked to the floor and assumed the defensive position. "Closer!" Beatrice yelled, apparently not concerned about appearing ladylike with the game on the line. We did as we were instructed, guarding the other girls at a closer range and with renewed ferocity.

"What are you doing?" my opponent, Maggie, complained. "You're too close."

Their possession seemed to last for minutes, but in reality, only twenty seconds had passed. I could hear the cheers of the crowd increase as they recognized our new strategy, only fueling our vigor.

"I feel like a hunted animal, Lilly Kate," Maggie complained again. She kept running from side to side, desperately trying to get around me. It was like herding the hens in the chicken coop, trying to keep them all in. Both jobs had some striking similarities.

Then, through a turn of events that shocked everyone but most especially herself, Eunice managed to steal the ball from their center. Everyone was momentarily shocked and stood staring at her as though we'd just witnessed a divine miracle. Eunice's eyes darted from player to player, as if pleading with us to tell her what to do with her newfound object. "Over here!" Beatrice called, waving her arms in the air. The seniors tried to snap back into offense and started running toward the other end of the court as Eunice passed Beatrice the ball. My eyes followed the ball as I turned to our basket, breaking out in a run. In doing so, I collided with the Maggie, leaving us both in a huddled mass on the floor. Maggie hopped up quickly and started running again. I tried to do the same but quickly sat back down on the floor. It felt like a red hot poker had been thrust into my ankle. I swallowed a guttural scream and waved at Garvis for help. He immediately blew the whistle to halt the game, causing the other nine players more than a little frustration.

Beatrice was the first to run up to me. "What happened?"

"I got tangled and fell on my ankle."

"Can you get up? Can you still play?"

The other players were huddled around, looking with both concern and curiosity. Mrs. Rutherford made her way through the pack. "Lilly Kate, are you all right?" She was breathing heavily as though she'd run across the floor.

"It's my ankle. I think I twisted it."

"If you're hurt, we can stop the game," Mrs. Rutherford announced. I looked up and saw the other girls pleading with their eyes. If I couldn't play, the game would be called, and the juniors would win. A part of me also instinctively understood that if I didn't get up, basketball might be deemed too dangerous for young ladies.

When I was five years old, Poppa put a nasty slice in his hand while butchering meat. Momma had wrapped it up and put ointment on it as best she could, but the cut continued to be aggravated by all the other work Poppa had to do on the farm, particularly chopping wood. Night after night, Momma would sit by the fire and try to doctor his hand, but healing was slow. She'd reprimand Poppa and tell him he needed to take it a bit easy so the wound would heal, otherwise he'd be left with a nasty scar. "Ruth," he said seriously. "I can live with a scar. I can even live with the pain of chopping wood and doin' the other chores, but I can't live with the thought of not providing for my family. I got people countin' on me, and that's just the way it's goin' to be."

Now I had people counting on me, and the thought of disappointing them was even more painful than my ankle. "I can play," I announced. "Just help me up." Sighs of relief were made, and somebody reached out a hand to help me to my feet.

The crowd gave a polite applause. I scanned the room and found Momma, looking at me curiously. I gave a little nod and started walking to the other side of the court where the ball would be inbounded. The pain was intense, but I tried to keep my face firm, knowing full well neither Mrs. Rutherford nor Mrs. Kavanaugh would think twice about stopping the game.

Sara inbounded the ball to Ruby, who then dribbled around, looking to pass it to Beatrice. Unfortunately, the juniors had taken a note from us and were now guarding us closely as well. Beatrice was unable to get open. In desperation Ruby threw the ball to me, which I was able to catch easily, but I knew full well that dribbling around with the ball would be out of the question. I could barely walk as it was, let alone dribble and try to shake off a defender.

Thankfully, through what I like to think was a bit of heavenly intervention, Beatrice was able to break away from her defender and get open. I quickly passed her the ball using a chest pass as we'd been taught. Beatrice caught the ball and, with confidence in her eyes, threw up a shot. She looked as natural and relaxed as she had those countless times she'd practiced in her basement, as though no other soul was even on the court. Everyone held their breath and tilted their heads as the ball arched through the air toward the basket. The ball hit the backboard with a smacking sound and then bounced through the basket without even touching the rim. Two points! The crowd came to its feet with cheers of admiration, and the rest of the seniors jumped up and down with excitement. For the first time the entire game, we were ahead 10–9.

But the game wasn't over.

Even though Beatrice had instructed us to guard more

closely, I quickly discovered I'd move my feet considerably less if I stood back a bit.

The ball was inbounded and brought down the court. Only thirty-one seconds remained on the clock, but the juniors still had time to score. Everyone remained standing. The excitement was intense, almost palatable. Momma later admitted her heart hadn't beat so fast in years. I didn't realize it then, but we had come upon a pivotal moment in school history.

Someone threw Maggie the ball. My pulse started quickening. I knew I couldn't chase her all over the floor. She looked at me knowingly and dribbled to get clear. I shuffled my feet to catch up with her, but she was a good two steps ahead of me. Seven…six…five.…Maggie found herself open and took a shot. I reached her after the ball had been released but before the ball went overhead. Using my good ankle, I jumped up to try to deflect the ball. I could feel my body stretch out like an accordion, muscles rippling throughout. There was no way for me to get a good hand on it but maybe, just maybe…

Reaching the top of my jump as the ball came over my head, I stretched to try and eek out another fraction of an inch. I felt my middle finger make contact with the cool, smooth surface of the ball. It wasn't much but enough to slow down its speed and change its direction. When I landed, a pain shot through my body that very nearly took my breath away. I turned in time to see the ball fall far short of the basket and be caught by Eunice. At that very moment, Ralph and Garvis blew their whistles. Game over. The seniors had won!

The crowd was more than appreciative for such an exciting ending. Some stood in their spots and cheered while others came down to the court to congratulate everyone on a game well played. First in that line was Mrs. Kavanaugh, who looked as pleased as I'd ever seen her. "Well, done, ladies. Well, done," she kept repeating. It was a compliment of the highest order.

Dink and Jimalee ran up to me, giddy with excitement. Jimalee hugged me enthusiastically and hollered over the din of the crowd. "That was so excitin'! How's your foot? Do you think you can teach me this game? Who would have ever guessed you'd be such a good player?" On and on she went, not really wanting an answer. Dink just stood back, grinning and looking at me approvingly with his good eye. He hadn't seen my competitive side for a while, and I think he was proud to see it resurface.

Momma quickly made her way through the crowd and gave me a hug like Miz Tessie. "Oh, I'm so proud of you all!" she said, eyes beaming. "How's your foot?"

"It's my ankle, and I think I'm going to be paying for this tomorrow. But right now, the rest of me feels so good, it'll be worth it." Momma gave me a motherly look of concern and then smiled knowingly.

Behind her, waiting patiently, stood Huey. "Looks like you ladies have started something," he said with a hint of pride.

"That may be so," I conceded.

Huey took my hand and wrapped it inside the crook of his elbow. "Lean on me," he instructed. "And no arguments," he added before I could protest. "I know you're hurt worse that you're letting on."

With Huey's help, I hobbled over to Beatrice to congratulate her on the game and her winning shot. She was surrounded by a mob of people doing the same. Among them was Duce Crawford, who, while waiting his turn, was talking to anyone who would listen. "I'll admit I had my doubts about this whole event," he confessed to the crowd as he wiped his brow. "But this turned out to be some good, clean fun—a fine way for young people to learn to work together. Yes indeed, most enjoyable."

When I finally got my turn to congratulate Beatrice, she was flanked by her parents and was still flush with excitement. "Looks like all that practice paid off," I teased as I gave her a friendly jab.

"Thanks for teaching me the game," Beatrice said, smiling. "It's been good for me." Beatrice and I exchanged knowing looks and parted ways. *Good for all of us*, I thought. *Good for all of us.*

Chapter Twenty-three

The next morning my ankle was swollen and had turned a very unique shade of purple. Dink and Jimalee had thankfully given us a ride home, and Momma had immediately started wrapping it with cold cloths, but the damage had been done.

"That's a beauty all right," Momma said after inspecting it. "It'll probably be sore for the next week or so." Momma gently put my foot back on the floor and started walking toward the kitchen. "I'll wrap it up," she said. "Then, we've got to get a move on if we're going to make it to church on time."

"Church?" I questioned. "I can hardly walk!"

"Young lady, you don't need to walk in order to listen to Scripture or feel the Holy Spirit. Now get busy."

That was that. I hobbled around and got dressed. I leaned on Momma as we made our way down Posey Street, across Main, and up the church steps. Once inside, I could already feel perspiration beading up on my forehead and was a little perturbed at being forced to come to church with such an injury. I shouldn't have been surprised, though. One Easter back at Fox Creek I'd complained of a stomachache the entire time we got ready for church. When we arrived at the church and I hopped down out of the wagon, I let the proof of my illness splatter all over a nearby cluster of rocks. I looked up at Momma, sure she'd have some sympathy. "Now, I'm sure you feel much better," she proclaimed. "Let's go inside."

Today, however, I was glad she'd forced me to come.

The game was still all the talk, and I was treated like a hero come home from war. I had to weave my way to Sunday school through a wave of back slaps and handshakes, some from people I'd never met. Suddenly, my ankle didn't feel so bad. By the time I made it into the classroom, Ruby and Eunice were already seated, and by the looks on their faces, they'd experienced the same triumphal entry. "Well, ladies," began our teacher Mrs. Dowling, "I think you may have started something in this town." Ruby, Eunice, and I flashed each other knowing glances. We didn't think we'd started something; we were certain of it.

After returning to school the following Monday, we were quickly pulled back into a regular routine. Final exams were coming up, and the Annapolis and West Point applicants were just days away from entrance exams. Mrs. Kavanaugh had even pulled them out of their regular classes to tutor them herself, only coming out of their back room for lunch. When they did see the light of day, their eyes were red and blurry and faces drawn like whipped dogs. I heard more than one complain that none of the sergeants at the academy could be as hard as Mrs. Kavanaugh. While I didn't envy their current situation, a part of me did still wish I could be going to college.

I busied myself with my own final exams and graduation preparations. All the girls were asked to wear white, long-sleeve dresses, so Momma set to making me a new one with great enthusiasm. She was initially nervous, claiming she'd never made a dress for such an important occasion before, but she quickly got plenty of practice as she was also hired to make dresses for Eunice and Ruby. I tried to convince Momma that she could make mine plainer and simpler so as to focus on the others. "Don't be silly," she chided. "What kind of mother would I be if I dressed other people's children with more care than my own? Besides, this means as much to me as it does to you. You're the first in our family to get a high school diploma!"

I didn't completely mirror Momma's enthusiasm. While I was certainly proud of obtaining a diploma, it was the end of an era. I wouldn't miss the mounds of homework or the late nights reading textbooks by the lamp, or even the confounded school typewriter. However, I would miss the people. Even though most people in the class were staying in town, either to get married or take on jobs, I knew it would never be the same. The class of 1912 had forged together to create a unique unit, and we would always be linked by the time we spent at Kavanaugh. But time has a way of marching on, and just as life had changed for me when I started high school, I knew it would change when I left.

One afternoon I was feeling especially reminiscent when Mrs. Kavanaugh called me into her office once again. My heart didn't race with quite the rapidity it did the first time I was asked to speak with her privately, but I did notice my palms began to sweat, and I had the sudden desire for a cold cup of water.

When I entered, the room was exactly as it had been several months earlier with the exception of few pieces of paper and some files on Mrs. Kavanaugh's desk. Even the smell was the same, a combination of leather, liniment, and tea. I stood by the same chair and tried to take a deep breath, only to discover my ribcage was already contracted as much as humanly possible. I must have stopped breathing when I walked through the office door.

"Please have a seat, Miss Overstreet." I quickly did as I was told and for good measure looked around the room to see where the black umbrella was placed. "I never had the chance to properly thank you for the time you spent with Beatrice Riddle last semester. Based on her work thus far, it would appear you did an outstanding job of keeping her up on her studies."

"Thank you, Mrs. Kavanaugh. I must admit, Beatrice was a quick read. She took care of most things herself."

"Fair enough, but your discretion during this time has been very commendable. I'm sure I'm not out of line when I say that we are all grateful for your work." Mrs. Kavanaugh folded her hands neatly atop the desk and looked at me seriously. For the first time all day I noticed she had a spot of unblended powder on the bottom of her right cheek. I had the sudden urge to leap across the desk and blend it in for her.

"Lilly Kate, are you listening to me?"

My eyes shot back into focus. "Oh, yes, ma'am. I'm sorry."

"Yes, well, we're all very grateful. And, I wanted to take this opportunity to ask you about your plans for next year."

There it was again. Plans. Everyone seemed to have some but me. I toyed with the idea of asking Mrs. K if I could go and order some plans from a Sears-Roebuck catalogue because I wasn't having much luck finding any around Lawrenceburg, but then thought better of it. Mrs. Kavanaugh wasn't a huge fan of sarcasm. Instead, I responded sincerely, which was no fun at all. "I had thought I might take the teacher's exam upon graduation. Maybe I'll get appointed to a county school."

"That is an option, but a young woman of your talents has several others, you know."

No, I didn't know. That was part of my dilemma. "I tried applying to Georgetown and they did accept me, but they had no money for a scholarship. At least not for a girl planning on being a teacher."

"Georgetown College is a fine school. I'm proud when

any of our students attend there. However, there are other options. Have you given no thought to anyplace else?"

"I'm not familiar with colleges. I did see an ad for someplace in the paper a while back, but I'd never heard of it before."

"Precisely!" Mrs. Kavanaugh opened her desk and pulled out a familiar slip of paper. It had my handwriting and the information regarding the State Normal School in Richmond. "Your mother found this in an old coat and wanted to know a bit about it. I told her I'd love to speak with you myself. You haven't applied, have you?"

"No, ma'am. I suppose I was so disappointed about Georgetown that I was afraid to apply." My chin dropped slightly, and I began to smooth out my skirt.

Mrs. Kavanaugh rose from her chair and started pacing around the room. "Miss Overstreet, you do realize you're very likely going to be our class valedictorian, don't you?"

"Yes, I knew I was close."

"I don't think you fully understand or appreciate what an achievement that will be. Ever since I started this school, I expected nothing but the absolute best from every one of my students, boys and girls alike. But when I started prepping young men for Annapolis and West Point, the curriculum became even more rigorous. To this day, I have never had a young man fail his military school entrance exam, and I plan to do everything within my power to keep it that way. I'm sure you realize there are young men in your class right now who are headed to these schools."

"Yes, ma'am. I've known the house boys were planning on attending one of those two schools ever since I started. But forgive my confusion. What do those boys have to do with me? I can't attend Annapolis or West Point."

Mrs. Kavanaugh moved back to her desk and sat on the front edge, facing me. She placed her hand on my shoulder and looked me fiercely in the eye. "What that means, young lady, is that as class valedictorian, you have outpaced the best of the best. Regardless of your background or your gender, you have proven to me and to everyone else even remotely associated with this school that you have an incredible mind. This school in Richmond, it's rather new. It was started with the sole purpose of training teachers for our state. It's not a four-year institution, only two. However, given your desire to teach, I think it would be a perfect fit."

Mrs. Kavanaugh rose from her desk and walked to a file cabinet, giving time for the weight of her words to sink in. She opened the drawer and pulled out a long, off-white envelope, then walked back and handed it to me. "This contains a copy of your grades and a letter of recommendation from me. Tonight, you have an assignment. I want you to go home and write a letter to President Crabbe at the State Normal School expressing your deep desire and interest to further your education."

I took the envelope from Mrs. Kavanaugh with shaky hands. My eyes were wide with both the surprise and joy that came from heartfelt words of praise. My mouth began to form words of gratitude, but no sound was coming out. Mrs. Kavanaugh laughed and began to escort me out of the room. "Now, Miss Overstreet, if you do not complete this assignment, I'm afraid you leave me no choice but to put you over my knees and give you a good whopping from my umbrella. I'm certain you wouldn't want that," she added with a smile.

I stopped and turned at the door. "Oh, Mrs. Kavanaugh, thank you for…for everything. I just hope it's not too late."

"Child, if they don't accept you, then they've got no business opening that school in the first place."

Chapter Twenty-four

Three weeks later I sat in my new dress on the front lawn of the school, listening to Mrs. Kavanaugh speak. In the crowd sat Momma, beaming with pride. Next to her sat Miss Daphne, who said she'd have crawled on her knees to be there if necessary. My uncles Pete and Chester were also in attendance, although I think they were lured by the thought of the free meal Momma was hosting in my honor. And, just behind Momma sat Jimalee and Dink, straining their necks to see every move.

Huey sat in front of me, fidgeting as always, but looking rather dapper in his new suit he'd gotten for Christmas after all. He was a good thirty pounds heavier than he was when we'd first met, but his infectious grin was the same, as was his sense of humor. We'd been friends since our first day at Kavanagh, and I had no intentions of that changing. He once called me *his* Lilly Kate. Likewise, I'd always think of him as *my* Huey.

Beatrice was three seats down, looking serene and thoughtful. Certainly our relationship had changed, but so had each of us personally. Both of us had grown and matured in ways we'd never dreamed possible. In the end, we'd become great friends. I knew more than anyone else that she still struggled, still mourned for her baby. She probably always would, but she was also more compassionate and patient from the experience. Beatrice said she wasn't sure what she wanted to do after graduation, but her parents agreed to let her go to Louisville for the summer and stay with her brother Paul.

Eunice and Ruby sat in the row behind me. Momma had done a beautiful job on their dresses, and they had told me so more than once. But Momma had kept her word and did special work on mine. The fine details coupled with all the lace made it exquisite; it was so nice, in fact, that I refused to walk in it to school. Instead, I had carried it over my arm and changed shortly before the ceremony began. Yet, despite all of Momma's hard work, my fingers rubbed the one detail that made it all the more special, my cameo brooch.

Dink and Jimalee had given me the brooch under the assumption that I would become a teacher, and in their minds, all teachers wore brooches. Now, it looked as though they were correct, although not in the manner any of us had guessed. Mrs. Kavanaugh's suggestion that I apply to the State Normal School in Richmond had been correct. Within two weeks I not only had received an acceptance letter, but also a separate letter asking me if I would be interested in working for my tuition, room, and board by taking a job in the school's cafeteria. When the letter arrived, I initially wept over my good fortune and couldn't stop babbling about my luck. Momma quickly corrected me. "Daughter, luck had nothing to do with this. What we have here is an answer to prayer." Once again, she was right, of course.

"Lillian Katherine Overstreet," Mrs. Kavanaugh announced. I stood and went forward to accept my diploma. I walked to the platform, feeling both proud and a bit intimidated by all the eyes that were following me. As I started to reach for my diploma, Mrs. Kavanaugh motioned for me to stop, and she turned to address the guests once again. "Miss Overstreet came to us from one of our county's fine rural schools and has done exemplary work. I'm proud to say she is the valedictorian for the class of 1912, and she will be attending the State Normal School

in Richmond come fall. I'm sure she'll make an outstanding teacher. If we're lucky, maybe she'll even come back to
Lawrenceburg and teach at her alma mater."

My cheeks grew red from both embarrassment and
pride. The crowd applauded heartily, but I could distinctly
make out the undignified cheers of Dink and Jimalee.
Momma and Miss Daphne looked as though they both
might bust their buttons, and I didn't feel my feet touch
the ground for the rest of the afternoon.

After the ceremony and all the congratulations were
made, Momma happily led our troupe of guests to our
tiny home for a celebration dinner. The house was far too
small to hold so many people, but Momma and I had set
up tables in our backyard. Throughout the years Momma
had nursed the scraggly patch of land with seedlings and
cuttings she'd found elsewhere. Now the space was a garden brimming with color from climbing morning glories,
hearty peonies, and a large assortment of other perennials.

Since Momma had done so much for the Women's
Aid Society during the last four years, a few of them had
volunteered to help Momma with the dinner while she
attended graduation. While we were at the ceremony, they
had graciously made the final touches on certain recipes
and had kept food warm or cool, depending on the dish.
For this I was abundantly grateful, not just because it was
in my honor, but because their help allowed Momma to
enjoy the day and spend more time with our guests.

As we approached the house, Momma led everyone
around back to be seated. I took the opportunity to change
my dress, knowing full well I stood a very good chance of
spilling something on the gown and ruining it forever.

Upon entering, I saw two large crates and one small

package sitting in the middle of our parlor. I stopped in the middle of the doorway, gaping at the surprise. "What's this?" I was finally able to mutter to one of the church ladies.

Mrs. Davenport, who had insisted on helping, came into the parlor wiping her hands on a towel. "I don't know what it is. We thought you might know something about it. They were delivered about an hour ago."

I walked to the boxes and found a note wedged between the top crate and the smaller package. The envelope had my name clearly printed on the outside. With shaking hands, I opened the note and read.

> Dear Lilly Kate,
> You wouldn't let us pay you for your help earlier this year. However, you're kindness will never be forgotten. Please accept these gifts, not as payment for your friendship, but as tokens of our respect and admiration. We will be forever indebted. Thank you again, and best wishes on your future plans.
> With deepest sincerity,
> Mrs. and Mrs. J.T. Riddle and Beatrice

I opened the smallest package first and began laughing hysterically as soon as I realized what it was. Inside a brown leather case was a beautiful, black, onyx fountain pen with a brass colored nib.

Mrs. Davenport came in with a couple of large kitchen knives, and we began opening the other two crates. I couldn't fathom what they might be, but my heart was beating like a six-year-old on her birthday. Although we could have used a crowbar, Mrs. Johnson, Mrs. Davenport, and I finally pried open the first crate. Slowly, I pulled away the packing straw only to find another box. This one, however, was clearly labeled from the Remington Company, Ilion, New York. I squealed with delight.

"For heaven's sake, child, what is it?" Mrs. Davenport's voice carried both concern and curiosity.

For a moment, I could do nothing but point. I'd been surprised mute, no small task indeed, but I was eventually able to spit out a few jumbled words. "It's a new type-writer! I can't believe it. They must have … oh, my good-ness … this is … oh, my goodness!"

I grabbed the knife again and started trying to pry open the next box. I knew exactly what was in there, but I had to see them for myself. With Mrs. Davenport's help, I was able to jar loose the top lid and peer inside. In a flurry, I threw out the straw packing and finally felt the leather in my hand. As if holding a priceless treasure, I pulled out a leather bound, gold-embossed copy of *Jane Eyre* by Charlotte Brontë. I allowed my fingers gently to rub the book's spine, taking in every detail. Then, opening the book, I put my nose to the pages and inhaled its deep, rich aroma. Still inside the crate were other books written by the Brontë sisters.

"Lilly Kate!" Momma called as she came through the back door. "What's taking you so long? The guests are …" Her voice trailed as she walked into the parlor and saw the crates and packing strung throughout the room. "What's all this?" she demanded.

"They're graduation gifts from the Riddles," I replied, still holding the book close to my chest. Momma walked through the mess and looked in each crate. For a moment, her face held no expression, but as she picked up the note and read it, she covered her mouth with her hand in sur-prise and then turned to me. "I can keep them, can't I?" I asked hopefully.

Momma quickly looked over the items once again, dropped her hand and smiled. "Of course you can!" she said as she walked across the room and gave me a hug.

"Seems to me it would be rude to return them. Besides, I know I'm a little biased, but I think you've earned them."

"I agree!" boomed Mrs. Davenport. She hadn't spoken since Momma had come in and had thus far kept her opinion to herself. "I also think this food is going to spoil if we don't hurry up and get it eaten, so you two dry up your happy tears and go out there and be with your guests. We've got work to do. Now, get along!"

Momma and I both wiped our eyes, and she headed out the back door while I ran to the bedroom to change. "Lilly Kate!" Momma called from the back door.

"Yes, what is it?" I came from the bedroom, still fumbling with my buttons.

"I don't think I've told you enough how very proud I am of you. It's not just high school, and it's not just going to college, it's the person you've become on the inside that makes me most proud."

I dropped my head, unaccustomed to such compliments from Momma.

"I'm sure your father would be so pleased at the lady you've become. It's just that … well, despite all the obstacles, you've turned into someone I think is mighty special."

My chin began to quiver. Momma, sensing I was uncomfortable, stopped, turned, and started out the door. "There's just one more thing," she called.

"What is it?" I asked, hoping to get my emotions under control.

"I don't ever recall you asking for a fountain pen. Whatever made the Riddles think of that?"

I stood still for a couple of seconds, frantically searching for the right words. "Let's just say," I began, "that it's from a lesson learned in time."

And indeed it was.

Author's Note

Kavanaugh High School was a very real place, and the colorful Mrs. Kavanaugh was a very real person. My grandparents met at the school in the late 1940s. By that time, the school already had a solid reputation as a boys' basketball powerhouse, in addition to prepping young men for military academies.

Growing up, I heard stories about "Mrs. K" and was continually fascinated by her and the idea of school taking place in her Georgian-style home. When I got to college, I chose Kavanaugh High as the subject of a research paper. While pilfering through old clippings in my hometown library, I came upon an article that contained two pictures from 1912, both with five girls and a basketball prominently displayed. The article went on to explain how these junior and senior girls introduced the town to the game of basketball as a means of raising money for the school's library. That clipping became the inspiration for *With Purpose and Promise*.

Today, Kavanaugh High School is a bed and breakfast. Guests are treated to rich southern food and hospitality. There are no lectures held or tests given, but visitors can see evidence of the building's past in the pictures that grace the walls and in the stories swapped between some of the patrons.